Where is my Father?

A journal by Gelany Lantern

L. J. OSBORNE

L. J. Osborne .

Island of Tansay

Dedicated to my husband Chris, and our three children, who have patiently read my first novel and offered useful suggestions and encouragement.

CONTENTS

1

My Life

Wednesday, 8th June, 1921

It seems the older you get the more unwelcome your birthdays become. They just bring more responsibility, or in Mother's case - another grey hair. It was my sixteenth birthday three days ago. Now I can get married, but I don't know anyone I want to marry, or I can leave home, but I've got nowhere else to go. The only good thing is that I don't need my mother's permission to do anything anymore, so I've made up my mind - I'm going to look for my father.

My mother wouldn't agree to me doing that. She doesn't even want to talk about Daddy. It seems like she's been cross ever since he didn't come home eight years ago, which is a long time.

Daddy would have made my sixteenth birthday special. When I was young, he used to make me surprise presents out of wood. Before my birthday, I would hear his hammer tapping away in the shed at the bottom of our garden. He wouldn't let me in, so I knew he was making something for me. One time it was a doll with arms and legs that moved, then a farmyard with animals, later a dolls' house with furniture, and he made all the furniture in my bedroom.

My mother gave me a green hooded top for my birthday this year, as my blue one is getting too small. Everyone wears these, as they are the only hooded tops the Clothes Factory, on the island, makes. I suppose I do need a new one, but it would have been nice to have something more exciting for my special birthday. She said I should have my hair cut short now I'm sixteen, but I don't think I will, I like tying it back in a ponytail. She also said that I should wear a dress sometimes instead of trousers, but I'm not too keen on that idea either.

We were invited for a birthday meal at my Uncle Ray's house, which was nice. He's my mother's brother and is married to Aunt Pearl. They have three children, my cousins, Rayson 18, Jimmy 13, and Ruby 7. They live on a farm, about 10 minutes' walk away, on the road to town, and are like a second family to me. I used to go to their place after school, until my mother fetched me on her way home from work. Their present was this writing book, and Rayson painted the picture that is stuck on the front cover. It is of me and my dog sitting on the cliffs looking out to sea. The sky is cloudy, but rays of sunlight are shining through, making a patch of golden sea. I'm going to write about me and my life in this book.

My name is Gelany Lantern. My first name was made up by my Father. My surname is because somewhere in my ancestry was a man who held a lantern, for the fishing boats to see the shore at night. So I have been told.

I live with my mother and my dog Ruffles, who is 2

years old. I love my dog, she is the best thing that's happened in my life. The worst part about my life is that my father disappeared when I was 8 years old. I heard my parents arguing the night before it happened. I couldn't hear what they were saying, but I could hear their raised voices as I lay in bed. The next day, I waited at the gate to greet Daddy, when it was time for him to come home from work. I always looked forward to him coming home. I loved him so much, and he loved me, I am sure of that. But when I had waited and waited, and I couldn't see him coming down the road, I asked my mother where he was. She said she didn't know. When he still didn't come home days later, she told me he didn't love us anymore. I found that hard to believe. I was sure he loved me, even if he didn't love her anymore. I had spent lots of time with Daddy. I always went with him to the allotment, where he grew fruit and vegetables. He showed me how to grow things and let me help. He talked with me and answered my questions. He carried me when I was small, held my hand when we walked, and often gave me hugs. I loved him so much. I am still waiting for Daddy to come home.

We live in a little cottage all on ground level. It has a fireplace in the middle, which helps to keep all the rooms round it warm, when the fire is lit. There are two bedrooms, a kitchen, and a sitting room (with the fireplace). There is another useful little room, a large glass-covered porch, on the back, where we keep our boots, do washing, store wood, and wash the dog. The house is surrounded by a small garden, where flowers and shrubs grow, and I try to keep it nice. But it's not as nice as it was, when Daddy looked after it.

Thursday, 9th June

The island I live on is called Tansay, and I think it is about 20 miles long and 15 miles wide. Of course this is average, as the coast goes in and out. You cannot get down to the beach anywhere except at the eastern end, where the main town of Easten is. This is because the cliffs are tall and straight all along the coast, around the Island. It is annoying because I can see some lovely sandy beaches near us, with waves crashing onto the sand, and I cannot get down to them. I live at the western end, so far away from the beach at Easten. There is a huge lake in the middle of the Island, and a river flows down from this to Easten, and then into the sea. Inland, by the river, is a settlement of huge houses, surrounded by a high wall. This is where the rulers live.

The rulers of this Island are a family named Tansa, and they are horrible. (I must find somewhere to hide this journal, as we are not allowed to speak against them). Their ancestors were nicer. Evidently, a hundred years ago the Island was in a bad way, as there wasn't enough food to feed the people, and many were ill. Reginald Tansa came to the rescue and organised the people, and changed things for the better.

One thing he did was that he got people to build the Electra, which is a circular track that goes right round the island. It moves along at about ten miles an hour, and is powered by electricity, made from wave power. It has four stations, that are exactly the same distance apart, and at each station, carriages are fixed onto the track. When the track moves one lot of carriages to the next station, all the other three lots of carriages have moved on to the next stations too. You can put things directly onto the track anywhere, when it has stopped, and even climb on yourself, but it is more comfortable to sit in a carriage. It is useful for transporting things around the Island, like food and goods, as well as people. I think it is very clever, but it often breaks down now, as it is getting rather old.

Anyway, generations later, the Tansa family aren't so nice, they are getting greedy and scary. They have a large army of police to control us, to make us obey their laws.

Friday, 10th June

My life follows the same pattern every week. Five mornings a week, I work at the Information Centre in Wells. The town of Wells is another ten minutes' walk past Uncle Ray's farm. In the afternoons I work on our allotment. Any surplus food that I grow, I take to the Market Barn near Wells, where Mr Mars buys it off me. He then sells it on his stall. In the winter, when there is not much to do on the allotment, I can make baskets in the Craft Barn for Mrs Strawler, who sells them on her stall. In the evenings I walk with Ruffles along the cliffs. It only takes me a few minutes to get to the coast.

I think I will start going to the youth club in Wells, on Saturday evenings, soon. My mother said I had to wait until I was sixteen, although I think you can go when you are younger than that, with your parents' permission. My favourite times are walking with my dog or working on the allotment, I like being outside.

This evening, I sat down on the cliffs and stared out at the blue, wavy sea, stretching endlessly into the distance. It was comforting to put my arm round

Ruffles, who sat close beside me. I often do this, and think of Daddy and wonder where he is. I sometimes wonder if he has gone off in a boat across the sea, and I look for him to see if he is coming back. I wonder why he doesn't come. If he is still on the Island, I'm sure he would come to see me. Sometimes I wonder if he's dead and no one will tell me. It seems like he's dead.

Sunday, 12th June

This morning I went to the farm to visit my Uncle's family, and stayed to lunch with them. I often go to see them on Sundays. Ruby is always pleased to see me, and thinks of me as her older sister. As soon as I got there, she took me to the barn to show me the newly born kittens. They are really cute, and their eyes are still shut.

It was my Uncle who let me have Ruffles. She was the runt of a litter of collie puppies, born on the farm, and not really expected to live. I loved her straight away, and called in every day after work, to cuddle her and make sure she was getting enough to eat. He didn't think she would be a good working dog, so he said I could have her. He had to persuade my mother, as she wasn't keen on having a dog. 'An extra mouth to feed,' she said. But my Uncle said it would be good for me to have a dog, what with me being an only child. So she reluctantly agreed, and I was so happy. I named her Ruffles because the black fur on her back is very wavy. She has black patches around her eyes, like a mask, a pure white chest, and four white paws.

I thought I would ask my Uncle and Aunt about my father again. Surely I am old enough to know the truth now. It is really bothering me lately that I don't know what happened to him. Perhaps when I was younger I just had to accept it, but now I want to find out. So as we sat round the table at lunch time, and Aunt Pearl asked me how things were with me, it seemed like a good opening.

'I keep wondering what happened to Daddy lately, and how I could find out.'

I saw Aunt Pearl and Uncle Ray exchange worried glances, and my cousins all looked up, their minds taken off their plates of food.

'Well, we don't know the answer to that, do we,' replied Aunt Pearl.

Uncle Ray smiled sympathetically and said 'It was a long time ago Gelany, I don't see how you could find out now.'

'I'm glad you haven't disappeared Daddy,' said Ruby. I remembered that she is almost the same age as I was when it happened, so there is still a chance it could happen to her. But I hope it doesn't, because I like Uncle Ray and I'd miss him too.

'People don't just disappear, do they?' asked Jimmy.

'Well he did, I remember it happening. It was just before my tenth birthday.' said Rayson.

'He must be somewhere,' persisted Jimmy.

'But how do I find out?' I was beginning to feel tearful and wished I hadn't brought the subject up. No one seemed to have any answers.

'I think you must ask your mother. We don't know. I'm sorry,' replied Uncle Ray.

Well that was the end of that. I know I won't get anywhere with Mother. It just makes her cross if I bring the subject up.

Monday, 13th June

The Information Centre, where I work in Wells, is in a red building in the middle of the town. There is an Information Centre in each of the four towns on the island. The largest town is Easten, and the others are Normarket on the north side, and Soumarket, on the south side. My main job is to get any news together and put it in a folder. Most of the news comes from Easten Information Centre. I make a new folder for each month, and people come in to read it. I also put posters on a noticeboard outside, with important announcements on. Mrs Newsby is in charge, and she's alright, so long as you do what you are told, and do a good job. She handles all the laws and stuff that come from the Tansa family. I wouldn't like that job, it would make me annoyed all the time. Sascha looks after records, mainly about people on the Island. She is 17, and works there in the mornings like me. Sascha was my best friend at school, I'm so glad she works there too.

Today I got some news that a huge statue of Ferdinand Tansa is being built by the beach, in Easten. He is going to be called King Ferdinand now, and taking over from his father, who is getting quite old. We usually go to Easten about twice a year, and I'm not sure I want to go anymore. I think the statue will spoil the beach.

I'm a bit fed up with the rain. It seems like it has been raining for weeks, and was so dark when I walked home from work. There was a big black cloud hanging over me. But after lunch, it cleared and I went down to the allotment. I've got most of the plants in now, so I suppose the rain will help them to grow. Ruffles got rather muddy. She saw a rabbit over the other side, and ran across all the allotments to chase it. I went and caught her and tied her up, I don't think people like her running across their patch. Old Mr Ditchling frowned at me, I think she bent some of his cabbage plants. His allotment is next to mine, and he is never friendly towards me, I don't know why.

I had a lovely beef stew ready when Mother got in from work, and I thought she would be pleased. But she just seemed preoccupied and tired. She works at the hospital in Wells, as a nurse. She said they hadn't got enough staff today, as some of them were off sick. I decided it wasn't a good time to ask her about Daddy.

I'm writing this sitting at a small table in my room, by my window. Ruffles is curled up in her basket. I like this time of year, when we don't need fires or oil lamps, and I can spend lots of time outdoors. The sun is setting and the sky is purple and pink, with big dark clouds scurrying across it. I must go out and see it.

Tuesday, 14th June

My Daddy was a carpenter. He worked at a shop called Woodalls in Wells, where they make all sorts of things out of wood. They get timber from Maplehurst Forest, which is quite near here. All the furniture in our house was made by Daddy. He painted the furniture in my bedroom pale pink or pale blue. In the rest of the house the furniture is just natural wood.

On my wall I have a picture that Rayson painted, and gave me for my birthday last year. It is of geese flying across a pond. I like it very much.

Daddy was going to build a veranda on the front of

our cottage, after we saw one on a house near Wells. It had a rocking chair on it, and roses growing up the sides. I liked it so much, Daddy said he would build me one. Mother liked the idea too. He carried a few slats of wood home from work sometimes, and laid them down by the back porch. They are still lying there, because he disappeared before he started it.

I don't have any grandparents anymore, at least I don't think I have. My mother's parents died. They used to live in Wells, so we saw them quite often. I stopped seeing Daddy's parents after he disappeared. I didn't see them much before that because they lived near Easten. My mother went to see them about a week after Daddy didn't come home and left me with Uncle Ray's family. I couldn't wait for her to come back, because I thought she would bring Daddy home with her. But she didn't. She said they didn't know where he was. We never went to see them again, and I don't know whether they are still alive or not.

Wednesday, 15th June

I started going to school in Wells, every weekday morning, when I was six years old. I left when I was thirteen, and started to work at the Information Centre. At school we learnt to read and write, and about numbers mainly. We did singing and dancing, which was fun. We learnt a song called 'The Carta', which is a worship song for the Tansa family. We had to sing it every morning, before lessons started, and also when the inspector came. I didn't like singing that.

As we got older, we were taught skills that are needed for jobs around the Island. We also did countryside studies, where we learnt to identify wild plants, and which ones are good to eat.

We also learnt about how things came into existence, by Developmentation. Evidently at first, there were only fish and plants living in the water. When a fish had a strong desire to walk on the land, it gave birth to a land animal. When an animal had a strong desire to fly, it gave birth to a creature with wings, that was a bird. Animals gave birth to people, when they wanted to walk on two legs. It was the same with plants, sometimes their seeds would start something new, different to themselves. It all happened a long time ago. I wonder if anything else is going to develop.

We were taught at school that the Tansa family are great, and we have to be grateful to them. We were told about how Reginald Tansa came to the rescue of the Island 100 years ago. He thought the problem of lack of food, was that each individual family was trying to provide for itself, and there was a surplus of food in some areas, whilst others didn't have enough. He employed people to mine metal and coal, and create electric power from the waves. Then they built the Electra track, which meant things could be moved around the Island.

The Tansa family made a printing press and printed money to pay the workers, and the money became a means of exchange for goods and services as it circulated. They also built four schools, four hospitals and four Information Centres, in each of the towns. Things became better on the Island.

Each generation of the Tansa family has only ever had sons. Now, a few generations later, the rulers are

Ferdinand (the new King), Oswald (in charge of taxes), Charles (I don't know what he does), and Reginald (head of the police).

At school, the teacher didn't talk about how people are paid low wages, and then most of the money they are given is taken back, when they have to pay taxes on any land they use. This has kept the people poor and made the Tansa family rich.

I quite liked school, but a morning was enough for me, then I longed to be outside. There was always work to be done on the allotment, except for a few months in winter, and there was wild food to look for too.

Thursday, 16th June

I have found somewhere to hide this journal. I managed to lever up a wooden floorboard, under my rug, using a screwdriver out of Daddy's toolbox. The floor looks quite normal when I put the floorboard back, so I think it is quite safe there. Now I can say what I like in this journal, because I don't think anyone will find it.

Today a news item arrived, at work, that said Charles Tansa is looking for a wife. The Tansas choose wives from young girls on the Island, and they sometimes have more than one wife each. Women, who are chosen, have to go and live on their estate. Someone at school heard about a girl being taken off the streets in Easten once, and told us about it. Oswald got the police to capture her, and put her in a horse-drawn carriage. She was crying and calling out to her mother, but she couldn't do anything about it. I would hate to go and live with them, so I am going to keep out of his way.

After work, I bought some fish in the Market Barn.

It is caught in Tansay Bay, off the beach in Easten, and then delivered by someone on the Electra. When we go to Easten, my favourite place is the beach. I like sitting on the sand, and watching the fishing boats come in. Then seeing the fishermen sort the fish out. I much prefer the beach to the town and shopping. Mother likes to go in all the shops, whether she is going to buy something or not. She just likes looking at stuff.

When I was at the allotment this afternoon, Sarah came over and gave me some sweetcorn plants. She said she noticed I had some space, and she had some plants left over. She is a big, jolly lady, with a toothy smile. I like her, but she is usually too busy to talk, always in a rush. Mr Ditchling looked over and frowned, but didn't say anything. I don't know why he is so unfriendly. He is getting old and it looks like he finds the allotment hard work. I think he used to work at Woodalls.

Saturday, 18th June

My mother commented that I had cleaned the kitchen nicely today. So I thought it seemed a good time to bring up the subject of Daddy, although I still found it difficult. Just say anything I told myself.

'Mum, I keep thinking about Daddy lately, and wondering where he is. Do you know how I could find out?'

'Gelany, don't you think I've tried?'

I didn't seem to be getting anywhere. A new approach was needed.

'Do you have any idea of why he left us?'

'No, but it must have been his decision.'

Now to dig deeper.

'I heard you arguing, the night before he didn't come home. What was it about?'

'I don't know, it was so long ago. Anyway couples have disagreements, they get over them. It doesn't mean they have to leave.'

She was getting a bit cross, but I had started so I may as well have it all out.

'But he must be somewhere on the Island, how do I find out? I want to see him.'

'Gelany, I don't know where he is, and why he hasn't come home. He can't love us. I know it hurts. We have to wait for him to want to come back.'

So that was that. No progress really. I can't keep waiting, I've done that for eight years, and it doesn't work. After that, I had an idea, and I don't know why I haven't thought of it before. Sascha, at work, looks after the records on people. Maybe she can find out where Daddy is. I'll ask her tonight, at the Youth Club.

Sunday, 19th June

My mother was a bit cool towards me this morning, she's not talking to me. I expect she is cross with me for bringing the subject of Daddy up. After he didn't come home, she had to go and work at the hospital, as she said we needed the money. Although we own the cottage, we have to pay a lot of taxes to the Tansa family, as they say they own all of the land on the island. I don't think they did 100 years ago. But they didn't teach us about that at school, what it was like before the Tansa family took over. I would like to know about that. Anyway, if she didn't want to have to go to work at the hospital, she shouldn't have argued with Daddy.

Yesterday, I went to the Youth Club for the first time. They meet in the Wells Central Hall, which is used for all sorts of meetings and gatherings. I was glad to find Sascha there and I sat with her on some chairs around a table. Mr and Mrs Bunny run the Youth Club and they seem quite nice. Mrs Bunny was in the kitchen, selling drinks and snacks through a hatch. Sascha told me that sometimes a country dance is organised, with musicians, and in the Summer they go to a field and play games like rounders. I saw my cousins Rayson and Jimmy there.

Sascha and I played table tennis together, which I liked, and found I was quite good at it. We also had a go at skittles and darts, but I wasn't any good at those. Sascha's brother Peter came over and asked me to play table tennis with him. He's quite nice. He played very well and won easily.

Afterwards, when he was sitting with Sascha and I, at a table, he told us he went to Easten yesterday, and he heard the guns firing. That is always scary, as it means the guards have seen something in the sea that may threaten the safety of the Island. Sometimes cannons are fired off the cliffs. If I heard them when I was small, it used to make me jump and I'd to cling to Daddy. He told me they were firing at aliens. I wondered what aliens looked like. Do they look like us, or did they develop differently, and are green with three eyes, or something. I wonder if it means there are other islands like ours, where aliens live. I'm glad we have guns and cannons to protect our Island from them. They cannot land anywhere except on the beach at Easten, because all the beaches at the foot of the cliffs get covered by the sea when the tide is in, and they can't climb up the cliffs. There are also a lot of rocks in the sea around the island, even the fishing boats don't go there. This makes me feel safer to live at the other end of the island, but I don't like hearing the guns.

I asked Sascha if she could look in the records at work, to see if she could find Daddy's name, which is Timothy Lantern. She said she would, but she told me that the records she has are only for people who live at the western end of the island.

Monday, 20th June

I had two news reports at work today, sent on the Electra from Easten. One was that a boat had been spotted in the sea, and it wasn't from this Island. That explains why Peter heard the guns firing. I wonder what was in the boat. It could have been aliens or it might have been Daddy trying to get back to see me. They are not sure if they hit it or if it went away. The other piece of news is that the river Ease has overflowed its banks, as it hasn't been able to cope with all the rain we have been having lately. Evidently the Tansa family's land has been flooded, although their houses are alright. They shouldn't live so close to the river.

I kept glancing over to Sascha, trying to see if she had found out anything about Daddy. I couldn't concentrate on my work. In the end I went over to ask her. She said she hadn't found anything yet. Mrs Newsby came over and told me to stop talking and get on with my work. So I had to wait until lunchtime to ask again. Sascha said she was sorry but she couldn't find his name in the records. She told me that the Information

Centres, in the other three towns, have records of people who live in their areas, and to try those. I don't know how I could get to them at the moment, and keep it a secret from Mother. I feel so unhappy, I just have this longing for Daddy and his love. I want to cry, but can't do that with Mother around, she'd ask me why, and I can't cope with her being cross about it. Ruffles seems to understand, she has her head on my knees, as I write this at my desk.

Your sixteenth birthday is supposed to be special, but mine didn't feel special. If Daddy had been here I'm sure he would have made a big fuss about my birthday. It just made me miss him more than ever. Oh Daddy, why didn't you come, you must have remembered it was my birthday and that I am sixteen now.

2

Where is my Father?

Tuesday, 21st June

This evening, when I took Ruffles on the cliffs for a walk, she chased some birds and ran towards the edge. Then I heard a loud cracking sound and a rumble, and suddenly, a large part of the cliff fell down, with Ruffles on it. She just disappeared before my eyes. I ran shouting 'Ruffles, oh Ruffles', and started crying desperately. I thought I had lost her, I thought she would probably be dead or injured. If she was still alive, I wondered how on earth I would get her up again. My insides felt painful as I ran. I was so distraught, and there was no one around to help me.

Kneeling down at the edge of the cliff, I peered cautiously over, to see if I could see her. I couldn't, but I heard a dog barking. It was a weird echoing bark. The tide was partially out, exposing a wet, sandy beach. Then I noticed that the rocks and earth had fallen in such a way, that they made a nearly perfect staircase. It looked as though I could climb down, but I was a bit worried that there might be another cliff fall, and then I wouldn't be able to get back up. As there was no one else around to help and the tide might be coming in, I decided to go down. I found myself saying aloud 'Please don't let the cliffs fall again,' and then wondered who I was speaking to. We were told at school that there is no God, but at that moment I wished there was one.

On the way down, I used my hands as well as my feet, as there were some big drops between the rocks. The sound of the waves crashing onto the shore got louder as I descended. It was a relief, when with one last jump, my feet were walking on the wet, golden sandy beach. As I looked around, I couldn't see Ruffles anywhere. Then I heard a muffled bark coming from the cliff, and I turned round and saw a cave. As I went inside, the barks got louder. I called Ruffles, and she came running up to greet me. I was so relieved, and amazed, to see that she was unharmed. I bent down, cuddled her, and found myself saying 'Thank you', then I wondered who I was thanking. Ruffles pulled away from me and ran towards the back of the cave again. I followed her, and saw a large crab trying to hide under a rock. Ruffles barked, and pawed at the bit of the crab that was still sticking out.

I have never been in a cave before, and I looked around at the jagged rocks in the walls and the layers of rock that made shelves around it. It looked as though it would make a nice house, if the sea didn't come inside. A glimpse of red caught my eye at the back of one of the shelves. On closer inspection, I saw that it looked like a box. Climbing up on a rock and reaching out with my hand, I managed to touch it. Wiggling it with my fingers, it gradually moved towards the front of the shelf and then fell down on to the sand. I picked it up and saw that it was an oblong, metal box with a lid. I took it out of the cave, into the light to examine it. It was quite rusty and the lid wouldn't move. I wondered how it could have got into the cave and what was inside, and decided to take it home with me.

The sea was coming in, so we couldn't stay and enjoy the beach any longer, but I thought we could go back again tomorrow, now we had a stairway to climb down. I put the metal box into my hood which was hanging down my back, so that my hands were free, to help me get up the rocks again. Then I called Ruffles, and we started to climb back up. We went past a huge, thick, piece of grassy turf, that had stayed intact when it fell. I think that was probably what Ruffles was standing on, and it must have saved her life.

Ruffles climbed ahead of me, and sometimes I helped her up the steep bits, by pushing her from behind. It was quite hard, so I was very relieved when we got back up on the top. We collapsed down on the grass, well away from the cliff edge, to recover and get our breath back. I put my arm round Ruffles and pulled her close to me. It was lovely to have her back, safe and sound.

I told my mother what had happened when I got in. She looked a bit worried, and said I shouldn't go so close to the edge of the cliffs with the dog. I didn't tell her about the box I had found. I still can't get the lid off, even though I tried levering it up with a screwdriver. So I have hidden it under the floorboard for now, until I can think of a way to get the rusted lid open. I wonder what's inside, maybe it is some sort of treasure.

Wednesday, 22nd June

I went back to where the cliff had fallen this evening. I was longing to be back down on that sandy beach, and with the tide being an hour later today, it would be further out. I put Ruffles on her lead, went to the edge of the cliff, and peered down. The rocky staircase has gone! There must have been another cliff fall after that one, and now the cliffs are sheer straight drops again. I had worried, as I lay in bed last night, that the aliens might be able to climb up onto the Island now. So although I was sad I couldn't get down, I was also relieved that they can't get up either.

I sat on the cliffs, and started thinking about how I had promised myself that as soon as I was sixteen, I would start looking for Daddy. Then a plan hatched in my mind. At dinnertime, Mother had told me that she has to work all day on Saturday, as they are still short of staff. I wonder if I could ride on the Electra on Saturday, round the Island, and visit Soumarket, Easten and Normarket Information Centres, and be back in time to cook dinner. Then she won't know I've gone. I will look at the Electra timetable tomorrow, at work, and see if it is possible.

Thursday, 23rd June

I think I can do that journey on Saturday. The carriages take one hour to move from one station to the next, where they stop for 15 minutes. By my calculations, the whole journey should take eight and a half hours, giving me one and a half hours in each of the towns. The track starts moving at 8am, so I should get home by 5pm. I will have to leave before Mother goes to work, but I will tell her I am walking the dog. In a way it is true, because I am going to take Ruffles with me. I should be working on the allotment, but that will have to wait.

Sascha told me that Peter wants to play table tennis with me again on Saturday. So I hope I can go to the Youth Club that evening too.

Sunday, 26th June

I have been so busy, I haven't had time to write in my journal until today, so have some catching up to do. It felt quite an adventure yesterday, going on the Electra to Easten. It was the first time I had gone by myself. I kept Ruffles on the lead the whole time, and she was a good companion.

The Electra is free to go on, paid for out of our taxes, so I suppose not completely free. But they can't stop people jumping on anywhere when the track has stopped moving, so I it would be hard to collect all the fares.

I got a seat in a carriage at Wells and quite enjoyed the journey, looking at the countryside as we travelled to Soumarket. Most of the fields had crops growing in them, but some had cows, sheep or pigs. I found the Information Centre quite easily, as it was a red building just like the one where I work. The lady working there was quite helpful. She found quite a lot of people with the surname Lantern, but no one called Timothy. She told me that an old lady named Isabella Lantern lived near the station, and it might be worth asking her if she had heard of a Timothy Lantern, as Isabella knew all the Lanterns and all that was going on with them. She told me exactly where the house was and that it had a green door.

I went back through the town, found the house, and knocked on the door. After a short wait, the door was opened by an old lady, bent over with age, and with long grey hair.

'Hello, are you Isabella Lantern?'

'Yes, and who might you be?'

'I'm Gelany Lantern. I'm looking for my father, Timothy Lantern. The lady at the Information Centre said it might be worth asking if you have seen him, as you know all the Lanterns around here.'

'She's right. I do. But I've not heard of a Timothy Lantern. How did you come to lose your father?'

'I didn't lose him, he disappeared. He didn't come home eight years ago.'

'Well, I'm sorry, but he hasn't been here. Do you know who he's related to? Who are his parents?'

' I don't know. They lived near Easten, and I only knew them as Grandma and Grandpa.'

'Easten, eh? Well, some of the Lanterns around here came from Easten, so I expect you are related. Would you like to come in for a drink?'

I looked at my watch and saw that I only had 10 minutes to go before the carriages would leave the station.

'No, sorry, I don't have time today, I have to get back to the Electra, as I'm going to Easten.'

'Well, I hope you have better luck, finding him there. Where do you come from?'

'Near Wells.'

'Come and see me again, when you have more time. I don't think I can help you with your father, but it would be nice to have a chat.'

'Yes, goodbye.'

I ran to the station and managed to get in a carriage, just before the Electra started moving.

I was quite hopeful of finding Daddy's name in Easten, which was the next stop. The red Information Centre was easy to find, as it was on the road between the station and the beach. But the lady there only found three Lanterns, and none of them was called Timothy. I did wonder if it could possibly be Grandma and Grandpa, but she said they were all females and they lived in Easten town. I knew my grandparents had lived outside the town. I was getting hungry, so I walked to the beach, to eat the lunch that I had packed in my bag. I passed the site where they are building a statue of Ferdinand Tansa. It was fenced off and two men were inside working on a huge stump of something, that I assumed would be his legs. Why did they have to put it by the beach and spoil it, I wondered crossly.

I sat down on the sand, next to some boats, where three fishermen were sorting out their catch. Ruffles had her dog biscuits, and I ate my lunch, looking at the waves turning over and crashing down on the sand.

Suddenly I heard one of the fisherman say 'Look out, Charles is about!'

I turned round, and saw a tall man dressed in a colourful cloak with a huge hood down his back. He was inspecting the statue. My immediate reaction was to get up and climb into the boat next to me, pulling Ruffles in too. As I crouched down, hiding from the wife-seeking Charles Tansa, I heard a laugh above me. I looked up and saw a handsome face, surrounded by short dark curls, looking back down at me. It belonged to one of the fishermen.

'What's up with you?' he asked smiling, as if he didn't know.

'Don't let him see me,' I pleaded.

'You think he might fancy you, do you?' He stared intently at my face. 'Well you've got a point. Stay there and I'll tell you when he's gone. There's some sacks there, you can hide under them, if he comes over.'

The sacks smelt of fish, so I hoped I didn't have to. I looked at my watch and saw I had thirty five minutes before the carriages left for Normarket, and I wanted to call in at the tool shop on the way back, to see if they could tell me how I could open the rusty tin.

'It's alright, he's going on his way. You can come out now.'

I peered cautiously over the side of the boat and saw Charles Tansa walking in the opposite direction to the station, so that was good.

I climbed out next to the three fishermen, thinking there's

safety in numbers. They were all looking at me, and smiling in amusement. It was quite embarrassing.

'What's your name?' asked the young handsome one.

'Gelany and this is Ruffles'

'Hello Ruffles.' He said, bending down to stroke her. 'Mine is Gordon. Do you live round here? I've not seen you before.'

'No, I live near Wells.'

'And what brings you to Easten then?'

'I'm looking for my father, Timothy Lantern. I don't suppose you've heard of him, have you?'

'No. Is he famous then?'

'No. He disappeared eight years ago, and I'm trying to find him.'

'You've left it a long time. He could be anywhere by now,' he laughed.

'It's not funny' I said and started to walk off. He grabbed my arm, and I turned round to face him.

'I'm sorry. Have you asked at the Information Centres?' he said, trying to be more helpful.

'Yes, some of them. I'm going to the Normarket one now.'

'What about the one in Wells?'

'I asked there first. I work there.'

'Well I'm sorry I can't be more helpful. Come and see me again when you're in Easten and let me know how you got on. I'll ask around here if you like. What was his name again, Timothy Lantern? I know that the Lanterns used to have some connection to the fishing trade.'

'Thank you. Can I buy two fish?'

He wrapped up the fish and handed them to me, smiling. I paid him, said goodbye and then walked quickly off the beach to the tool shop.

The man in the tool shop suggested that I buy a bottle opener. It has a sharp metal point on the top and a lever thing underneath. He said I could also try heating the lid first, to make it expand.

I bought the bottle opener, and then ran up to the station.

We made it just in time again. It was 1pm and as soon as I sat down in a carriage, the track started moving. There was a lady sitting nearby with a crate of smelly chickens. Ruffles was very interested in them, and I thought it was going to be a difficult journey, but she did 'leave' them when I told her to.

Normarket was quite a bleak place and there was hardly anyone out on the streets. I walked in different directions trying to find the town centre. In the end I saw an old man in his garden, and he showed me where to go. The lady in the Information Centre said she didn't have time to look up my father's name that afternoon, and suggested I come back another day. I told her I had come all the way from Wells on the Electra, and I couldn't come back another day, and then I burst into tears. It was too much, because after all the searching, I still hadn't found Daddy. When I started crying, she sat me down and asked me why I was looking for him. After I had explained, she said she would have a look, and her work could wait. So that was nice of her, but she didn't find any Lanterns.

I walked back to the station, and waited for the carriages to appear. I was really fed up and beginning to feel tired. I think I must have dozed off on the journey back to Wells, because it didn't seem very long. As I was walking home, I realised I had done all that journey for nothing. I also wondered about where Daddy could be, if he isn't on the Island. I really don't know what to think.

I got home just before 5pm and was cooking the fish

when Mother arrived home from work. It was difficult not saying anything about what I had been doing that day, but she didn't seem to suspect anything. She did remark that the fish tasted nice and fresh though.

I didn't feel like walking back into Wells for the Youth Club that evening, but couldn't think of what to say, if Mother asked why I wasn't going. So I left Ruffles curled up in her basket in my room, feeling envious of her, and went. I told Sascha where I had been. It was a relief to be able to talk to someone about it. She was sympathetic, but I could tell she didn't know what to say. Peter came over and asked me to play table tennis, but I told him I was too tired, and explained where I had been. He sat down beside me, and asked me why. I explained my search for Daddy to him, but told him not to tell Rayson, who was across the room. It just might get back to Mother, if Uncle Ray's family knew. He promised he would keep quiet about it, and then asked if he could come to see me on Thursday evening, and we could go for a walk along the cliffs. I said he could, and stayed a bit longer, before coming home.

Monday, 27th June

I didn't have a go at opening the rusty box yesterday, as Mother was about and I didn't want her to see it. I wanted to see what was in it first, before deciding whether to tell her about it.

As I walked home from work today, I decided I would try to open the box after lunch, before going to the allotment, as Mother would be out at work then. I got the box out from under the floorboard, and tried levering up the lid with the bottle opener. It seemed like it was going to lift the lid, but it kept slipping off. So whilst I ate my lunch, I put the tin upside down on top of the range oven in the kitchen. A bit later I picked the box up, and took it outside, and started trying to lever the lid up again with the tool. When my fingers touched the lid, it was so hot, it burnt them. I yelled 'Ow' and chucked it away. It hit the wall of the house hard, crashed to the ground and when I went over to pick it up, I saw that the lid had come off!

Inside the box was some soft material wound round and round, and it smelt of the sea. The material must have been waterproof, because inside was a sheet of paper with writing on it, and the ink hadn't run at all. I was disappointed that it was just a sheet of paper, that didn't seem like treasure. I was going to leave reading it until later, but then I noticed it was a letter, and it was dated 100 years ago. So I decided the allotment could wait a bit longer and peered at the scrawly handwriting.

Actually it is quite an amazing letter. I thought I would copy it into my journal, as the paper is very fragile and it is breaking up the more I touch it. Here is what it says -

21st June, 1821.   *Dogland Island*
Dear Reader

We are fleeing from this Island in a boat, as our lives are in danger. Reginald Tansa has claimed rulership of the Island, and no one is allowed to believe in God anymore. He says God has not helped us, so he is going to. We are not allowed to speak of God, and he has burned down our churches, where we were meeting. But we cannot keep quiet about God, who is real and is our friend. Our lives are meaningless without Him. There are twenty of us, in two boats. More will be leaving, if they can get away.

Reginald Tansa says God does not exist, but we know He does. We know that he created everything that we can see, including the sky, the land, the sea, the plants, the animals, the birds, the fish and all the people. We know he especially loves the people He created, and He wants to be our friend, and help us with our lives down here. Although we can't see Him, He talks to us, and we know our spirits will go to be with Him when we die. We are not afraid of dying, but we are not giving RT the privilege of killing us. We may perish in this boat if we do not find another Island to land on, but that is up to God.

We decided to risk our lives by finding a cave to leave this letter in, because we want people on the Island to have a chance of finding God again. We know RT will tell everyone there is no God and make them believe it by penalty of death. We don't know how anyone will find the letter, but if God wants someone to find it, we know it will happen.

We wish you dear reader, the joy that we have, in our relationship with God. He does exist, just turn your heart and mind towards Him, believe in Him and talk to Him. He loves you and wants to help you. He is your Father.

God bless you dear Reader.
Solomon Temple.

After reading it, I went off to work on the allotment feeling in a bit of a daze, just thinking about what it said. I'm still feeling amazed about it all. It felt like Solomon Temple, from 100 years ago, was talking directly to me. Did they survive and where did they go? I wonder if it is true, and there really is a God?

Tuesday, 28th June

I got the letter out again, at lunchtime today, to have another look at it. It is disintegrating and has nearly turned to dust, I can't pick it up anymore. I am so glad I copied it before it broke up.

But I can't show it to anyone else now, so even if I told them about it, I don't think they would believe me.

After dinner I thought I would ask Mother whether she thinks there is a God. It seemed a hard subject to bring up, to suddenly start talking about God. So I started with flowers.

'Isn't the countryside looking lovely now, with all the flowers out?'

'Yes, it is,' she answered, sounding surprised at my remark.

'Mum, do you think there could be a God even though we were taught at school there isn't one. You know, one who made the flowers and things?'

She looked startled.

'No, Gelany, I don't. What on earth put such an idea into your head?'

'Oh, I just wondered.'

'Well, don't. You know what you were taught at school, there is no God. Thinking there could be one, will only get you into trouble. The Tansa law says that we're not allowed to speak about God. You know that don't you?'

Yes. But what if they're wrong.'

'That doesn't come into it. We are not allowed to believe in a God or talk about it. It will only get you into trouble with the police. Why have you started thinking about God?'

I didn't know what to say. I didn't feel like sharing about the letter.

'I don't know. I just did.'

She started clearing the table, and it seemed like it was the end of the conversation. But as she went over to the sink, she turned round and faced me.

'Gelany, please don't talk about God again. I don't want

you to get into trouble with the police.'

I didn't say anything, I just looked as if I had heard the warning. I want to ask one or two other people what they think first, so I didn't make a promise.

Thursday, 30th June

Peter came over this evening. My mother opened the door to him and was quite friendly towards him, and asked how his family are. She knows his mother. Sascha and Peter live near the town of Wells, on a farm. They look a bit alike, in that they both have dark hair and are quite tall. He is 20 and works on their farm with his father. They have a younger brother, Jack.

I fetched Ruffles, and we walked to the cliffs. We could hear the sound of the waves turning over on the shore down below. I pointed out to Peter where the cliff had fallen with Ruffles on it. He said that I was very lucky to have got her back and for her to be unhurt. We walked about two miles along the cliffs, towards Soumarket, and then back again.

Peter talked mainly about the farm. It sounds like hard work, they have cows, as well as wheat, and he is not keen on it. Most farms have one type of animal, cows, sheep, pigs, chickens or rabbits, and different types of crops. He likes the Youth Club, especially the sports. I think he is good at them all.

It was a really beautiful evening to be walking along the cliffs. Both the sky and the sea were a deep blue, the green grass was lavishly decorated with red and white flowers, and birds were flying above our heads, calling out to each other. I was still bursting to ask someone else about God, so before I could stop myself, I blurted out,

'Peter, do you ever think there could be a God who made all of this?' I pointed to it with my arms circling round and added, 'It's all so beautiful.'

'Not really. I suppose I believe what we were taught at school, that everything developed by itself. It's seems a bit primitive to believe in a God you can't see. It seems made up. What do you think then?'

'I'm not sure. Do we have to believe what the Tansa family tells us? Supposing they are wrong and there is a God.'

'Well it will just get us into trouble with the police if we start talking about God. So I suppose it's not worth thinking about.'

I wasn't sure that he was right, but I wasn't ready to share with him about the letter I had found yet. We had reached the path that turned inland, and he changed the subject, talking about a skittles competition and suggested I join in. When we reached my house, he said he hoped I wouldn't be tired this Saturday evening, then we could play table tennis. I watched him walk up the same road I used to wait for Daddy to come down. It is nice, in a way, to have another man in my life, but no one can replace my father.

Friday, 1st July

I received unwelcome news at work today. The Tansa family have announced that there is going to be a Parade Day in Easten on Sunday, 7th August, for the people of Wells. The three other towns have to go to Parade Days too, but on different Sundays. They are celebrating their 100 years of ruling the Island.

On the Parade days, all the police are going to march past in their uniforms. The statue will be finished by then, and they order everyone to come to see it, and as they walk past it, they must turn towards it and bow. It said everyone will congregate on the beach after and sing 'The Carta' song together.

I had to put a big poster up, on the noticeboard outside, and an information sheet in the July folder, all about it. The poster has a drawing of the huge statue with small smiling people in a line walking past, and the one in front of it is bowing. People who were reading the poster outside the Information Centre weren't smiling. I heard a lot of groans. I hope I can get out of going, I don't fancy it.

Saturday, 2nd July

I worked hard on the allotment all day. There are no weeds left on it now. Mr Ditchling's patch has weeds, which is unusual, and I haven't seen him lately. I wonder where he is. All the plants are growing well, but we haven't had any rain since the river flooded. If it doesn't rain soon, I will have to start fetching water from the well, which is hard work.

I was a bit tired when I got to the Youth Club, but I played table tennis with Peter. We had two games and he won them both. I think he likes to win.

Sunday, 3rd July

This morning I went over to Uncle Ray's farm and stayed to lunch. Ruby took me to see the kittens again, and they were crawling around. She was excited because her Daddy has said she can have one of the kittens as her own. She showed me which one. It is a black one with a white bib, four white paws, and a white star shape on its forehead. She said she didn't know whether to call her Sooty or Beauty or Star. I said 'She certainly is a Beauty.' So Ruby decided to call her that.

As we walked back to the house, we saw Jimmy up a huge oak tree with some planks of wood. Ruby said he is building a tree house. Aunt Pearl was in the kitchen and she asked Ruby to lay the table, and asked me to go and tell Uncle Ray that lunch was nearly ready. I found him in the cow barn, inspecting a cow's foot. I wanted to ask him if he thought there could be a God, but wasn't sure I could bring the subject up anymore. However, he wanted to talk to me about something.

'Hello Uncle Ray. Aunt Pearl says lunch is nearly ready.'

'Hello Gelany. How are you today?' He asked, looking up.

'Fine, thank you.'

He straightened himself up and looked more serious.

'Your mother called in on her way home from work on Friday. She's a bit worried about you. She's concerned that you're asking questions about your father, and wanting to find him. And she said now you are asking questions about if there could be a God, who created everything. I told her it's probably normal at sixteen to be a bit unsettled. I think she would just like you to get married to Peter, and settle down.'

He was now smiling, but I didn't know what to say.

'Are you alright? Are you really wondering if there is a God?'

'Yes.'

'Well you learnt at school how things came into existence. Why should you question it? It doesn't really matter if there is a God, we can't see him.' I was going to tell Uncle Ray about the letter, but before I could, he carried on.

'It will get you into trouble, if the Police hear you are talking about God. If you were a child, they would probably give you a warning and scare you. Now you're sixteen they could deal with you more severely. So keep your thoughts to yourself, won't you Gelany. Come on let's go in for lunch,

I'm feeling hungry.' He put his arm around my shoulder and we walked back to the house, chatting about Ruby's kitten.

I suppose Mother asked him to have a word with me. Oh well, that's that then. I can't tell anyone about the letter. But I don't feel ready to get married yet, and I haven't even thought about marrying Peter!

3

The Dove

Monday, 4th July

There was a new boy on Mr Ditchling's allotment today,
getting all the weeds out. I said 'Hello', and he said 'Hello'
back, but rather reluctantly I thought. Then he turned away
and got on with his work. He doesn't seem very friendly
either. I wonder what has happened to old Mr Ditchling.

I fetched some water out of the well for some of the
plants, which looked like they were in danger of dying. It
makes such hard work when it doesn't rain. I wished Daddy
was there to help me. I know wishing doesn't make any
difference, and it makes me feel worse somehow. That boy
didn't offer to help, even though he must have seen I was
struggling. I'm feeling a bit fed up really.

I sat on the cliffs this evening and wondered about
Daddy. As there is no record of him at the Information
Centres, does this mean he isn't on the Island. But where
else could he be? Did he go away in a boat for some reason
and now he can't get back, because they shoot at him,
thinking he is an alien? Or did he fall off the cliffs and no

one knew about it. How am I going to find out where he is?
I really don't know.

Tuesday, 5th July

After dinner this evening, I thought I would ask Mother
again about Daddy. I knew it would make her cross, but I
didn't care anymore.

'Mum, if Daddy isn't on the Island, where else could he
be?'

'What makes you think he isn't on the Island?'

'Well I thought he would come to see me by now. I
thought he'd want to see me on my sixteenth birthday. Do
you think he could have gone off in a boat and can't get back?
Or could he have fallen off the cliff and no one saw him?'

There was silence, then she took a deep breath and
replied slowly, as if she was trying to think of the right
words. 'Gelany ... that time you heard us arguing ... it was
because he had someone else ... and he had to choose. I was
annoyed that he would even consider it. But he must have
made his choice, because he didn't come home. Now, does
that satisfy you?'

I shouted 'No!', and stormed off to my room, I could feel
the tears starting. I had a good cry, then blew my nose to try
to stop myself, and took Ruffles out. I walked briskly along
the cliffs, feeling deserted and hurt, that Daddy would leave
me for someone else. But that still doesn't explain why his
name isn't in the Information Centre records. Would he have
changed his name for some reason? Doesn't he want me to
find him? And that makes me feel worse. I feel as though
my heart is breaking, and I wonder if it could break.

Wednesday, 6th July

This evening, I took Ruffles for a walk along the cliffs

and sat down in my usual spot on the grass, by some bushes. I was still upset about Daddy and feeling as if he has deserted me, now I know he has someone else. I started thinking about the letter I found in the cave. I remembered it said that God wants to be our friend and it also said 'He is your Father.' I needed a father right now, so I thought I would try talking to Him, like it said you could. I looked around to make sure no one was about, and whispered 'God if you are real, and you want to be my friend, please will you talk to me, like it says in the letter?'

I was looking up at the cloudy sky, and suddenly the clouds parted a little, and bright sun rays shone down on the sea, making it sparkle and turn to gold. Then out of the light, something started flying towards me. When it got nearer, I saw it was a graceful white bird. It landed on the ground and looked at me. It was beautiful, and pure white, I have never seen a bird like it before. Ruffles stared at it, but did not move. I tightened my grip on her collar. Then the bird flew up onto my shoulder and sat there briefly, before taking off and disappearing in the sky over the Island. I don't know why, but after that I felt happy and peaceful. It was like a sign from God to tell me He does exist.

Thursday, 7th July

I've felt happy all day. I feel as though I've got a special secret, as I'm not allowed to tell anyone. It didn't even worry me when Mrs Newsby told me off, for putting some records in the wrong files.

I said 'Hello' to the boy working on Mr Ditchling's allotment, but he still seemed reluctant to return my greeting. Perhaps he is shy. When I was fetching some water from the well, Sarah told me that the boy is looking after the allotment, because the old man is unwell. Mr Ditchling is his grandfather.

On the cliffs this evening, I walked and walked, and told God about all the things that are bothering me. I didn't say them out loud, in case anyone heard me, although I hardly ever meet anyone along there. I seem to be able to talk to Him in my head, like thoughts, but it felt to me like God could hear them. I told him we need some rain, and as He created it, could He send some for the allotment.

Friday, 8th July

It rained all last night! The allotment has had a really good soaking. Ruffles got very muddy and I had to wash her when we got home. But I didn't mind that, as I didn't have to carry water from the well. The plants have all perked up and looked much better.

Today, at work, we had a news report about a dove sighting. The headline said 'The dove is back'. It said it is a large pure white bird, and no one has seen one on the Island for over 100 years. I think that was the bird I saw, two days ago.

I thanked God for the rain this evening. I did wonder whether to ask Him to help me find Daddy, but I'm not sure I want to find him anymore. How could he leave me for someone else, and then never contact me again?

Saturday, 9th July

I worked on the allotment in the morning. Everything seems to be growing, after the rain, especially the weeds. There is quite a lot to harvest. I took home some potatoes, carrots, parsnips and beetroot, which were much easier to dig up now the ground is soft. I also picked some strawberries, they are really sweet and delicious this year. I had to tie Ruffles up because she was trying to eat them too. Sarah came over to give me some of her surplus peas, so I gave her some strawberries. I like Sarah, she is the only who talks to me on the allotment, and she is usually cheerful. The other people just get on with their work, with their heads down.

In the afternoon I went back and picked a load of broad beans, and put them in our handcart. Then Ruffles and I walked up to the Market Barn in Wells, dragging the cart behind me. Mr Mars bought the beans off me for his stall. I used the money to buy some lamb, butter and eggs in the butcher's shop and a freshly baked loaf in the bakers'.

This evening I went to the Youth Club. Sascha said I seem happier, and asked if I had got over not finding Daddy. I didn't know what to say. I didn't want to tell her I've found out he has run off with another woman, and changed his name so I can't find him. So I just said 'I think so'. She told me Peter is having a birthday party next weekend, on Sunday, and my mother and I are invited. They are going to have a fire outside and cook on it, if the weather is fine.

I played two games of table tennis with Peter, which he won as usual. Then he suggested we play doubles, and got Sascha to come over. He looked around for a fourth person, saw Mr Ditchling's grandson, and called out 'Justin, do you want to join us for a game of doubles?' So now I know his name is Justin. But he shook his head and said 'No, thanks', and I felt sure it was because I was there. How can he dislike me when he doesn't even know me. Is he just shy or what? Anyway, Rayson came and joined us, and he made it fun, although I think Peter prefers to take the game seriously. Rayson hit the ball so hard one time, it landed in someone's drink. We all started laughing. But our laughter was cut short when three Policemen came in. They sometimes turn up at public gatherings, without warning, to make sure there is no one planning anything against the Rulers. They didn't find anything, but after that, people were more subdued. It was a reminder that we are not free to do as we like.

The Police dress completely in black and look rather menacing. The have peaked leather caps, leather jackets, and their trousers are tucked into leather boots. They are given special privileges, and are not allowed to leave the police army, once they have chosen to join it.

As I walked home it started raining again, and now it is really noisy as it is beating against my window. I must get to bed, it's getting late.

Sunday, 10th July

This morning I went to Uncle Ray's farm. I always take Ruffles with me, and she goes to join the other collies whilst I am there. It's like she is visiting her own dog relations. Aunt Pearl was in the kitchen getting lunch ready. She told me Ruby was probably in the barn with the kittens, and that she was upset because her kitten was unwell. Aunt Pearl confided in me that she didn't think it was going to live. I went over to the barn and found Ruby sitting on the ground with the kitten in her lap. She burst into tears when she saw me and couldn't speak. I took the kitten from her. It was floppy, and did not respond to me. I told her to go and get it some warm milk and a dropper, and she ran off.

I stoked the kitten, it felt soft and warm, and looked so perfect and cute, with its symmetrical black and white markings. I rubbed it for a while, trying to revive it, but it didn't respond. Then my eyes filled with tears, and they dropped down onto the kitten.

'Oh God,' I whispered, 'you made this beautiful kitten and you can make it well again. Please, please, please, let it live. Please.'

Then as I was stoking its little silky head, it's eyes

opened. It shook its head, said 'miaow' and started wriggling about.

'Gelany!' I turned round and saw Ruby standing in the doorway watching. 'Is the kitten alright?' She came over, put a small bowl of milk on the ground, and stoked the kitten.

She stared at me with eyes full of wonder. 'Gelany, I saw a bright light around the kitten. How did you do that?'

I couldn't tell her I asked God to heal the kitten, so I answered 'She just perked up that's all. Now let's give her some milk.'

Ruby fed the kitten with the milk, it drank lots, then it started to climb out of my lap. She picked it up and cuddled it, before putting it in the basket with the others.

As we were walking back to the house, she told me 'I'm going to tell Mummy that you healed the kitten, and that you have special powers. You can make a bright light shine to do the healing.'

'No, I don't have any special powers. The kitten just perked up and the light was the sun, shining through the doorway.'

'I don't believe you,' she argued.

'Alright then, let it be our special secret.'

She seemed to like the idea of us having a secret together, so she agreed. I'm quite surprised she saw a bright light, because I wasn't aware of one. Perhaps she has special powers to see things!

We got to the kitchen at the same time as Uncle Ray and Rayson, who had been working in the fields, and were looking rather muddy. Ruby happily told everyone, that the kitten was better. I'm not sure they were convinced, but they acted pleased and didn't question us about it. After lunch I went to see Jimmy's tree house. Uncle Ray is helping him to make it, when he has the time. We climbed up the ladder, onto the platform, and up there you can see right over the farm. He still has to make the walls and the roof.

Ruby followed me about more than usual, and didn't let me out of her sight. I think she was expecting that I might do something else with my 'special powers' and she didn't want to miss it. I'm glad she kept quiet about what she saw, as I didn't want Uncle Ray asking me awkward questions.

Just before I left, Uncle Ray came with Ruby and I to take a look at the kitten. It was lying on the top of a heap of kittens. We stroked it and it stretched and yawned contentedly. Uncle Ray said it did indeed look fine now. Ruby looked like she was bursting to say something, but instead, she looked up at me and smiled. She walked to the gate with me and said in a whisper 'Thank you Gelany'. I gave her a hug. When I got to the bend in the road, I looked back and she was still watching me, so I waved goodbye, before she went out of sight.

Monday, 11th July

A news sheet came today, that said Charles Tansa has found a wife, so that is good news for the rest of us girls on the island, but probably bad news for her. Her name is Emerald Cohen, and she is living on their estate, being prepared for marriage. I wonder what that involves. I do feel sorry for her, I expect they captured her. The wedding is going to be on 30th July. There was also a poster for the noticeboard, to announce the wedding, and tell people they could go and see a parade of carriages. I think I'll give that a miss. I don't think many people will go.

Tuesday, 12th July

We had a news report at work today, that said it has only rained on our western end of the Island. The rest of Tansay is still very dry and people are struggling with their food crops. It has rained here every night since Friday.

This evening when I was walking with Ruffles on the cliffs, I saw Justin walking towards me. He had some binoculars round his neck. I would have talked to him, but he just nodded his head as a sort of greeting, and walked on quickly. Then I felt annoyed, it felt as though he was invading my cliffs.

I sat down in my favourite spot, by the bushes, and looked at the dark clouds hanging low over the sea. I thanked God for the rain, and for healing Ruby's kitten. I wondered how many people on the Island believed in God before the Tansas took over. The letter said their churches had been burnt down, which must have been buildings where they met together.

Soon some big drops of rain started falling, so Ruffles and I ran home. Maybe I'll be asking God to stop the rain soon!

Thursday, 14th July

I was working at my table this morning, sorting out the news items, when Mrs Newsby came over and told me there was a man at the front counter asking to see me. My immediate thought was 'Daddy!', and my heart skipped a beat. My legs felt like jelly as I walked over to the entrance desk. I was totally expecting to see him. So I was very surprised to see Gordon, the curly-haired fisherman there.

'Hello Gelany. It was my turn to bring the fish to Wells today, so I thought I'd come to see you, before I go back on the Electra. Have you found anything out about your father yet?'

'No.' I felt awkward as I could see Mrs Newsby looking over at us, and she was not looking pleased. So I said in a low voice 'I finish work in fifteen minutes. Can I talk to you then, outside. I'm supposed to be working now.'

'Yes, fine. I'll go and get myself a pie from the butcher's. I'll see you outside then.'

As I walked back to my table, Sascha was looking at me, her eyes full of questions. But she waited until we were getting ready to leave, to ask me who he was. I told her he was a fisherman I met in Easten, and I had to go as I was meeting him outside. She said jokingly not to let Peter see, or else he might be jealous.

Gordon was sitting on the seat outside, with a brown paper bag in his hand. I suggested we walked to the station, where there are some seats on a grassy area. I wanted to get away from the busy town centre, where I thought everybody would be looking at us.

As we walked along, he pulled an empty box on wheels behind him, which he had carried the fish in. He asked me about my father, and what I had found out at the Information Centres. I told him how my father had just disappeared, and that there was no record of him, but I didn't tell him that he had gone off with another woman. He was very sympathetic. Then I said I had given up trying to find him and I didn't really want to talk about it anymore. Which is true.

We sat down on a seat near the station, and talked about Easten, the statue which is nearly finished, rain or lack of it, and fishing. He asked me if I knew that Charles Tansa has found a wife, and joked that it is safe for me to go to Easten again now. Then it was time for him to get in the carriages, as the Electra was due to start moving.

I walked home, and changed my clothes. After lunch, I took Ruffles with me to the muddy allotment, and picked some more broad beans. I decided wait until tomorrow and take them to the Market Barn on my way to work, I didn't feel like walking back to town today.

Friday, 15th July

On my way to the Market Barn, I noticed an overgrown area, with bricks and blackened timber sticking out amongst the weeds. I have walked past it before, but have not taken much notice of it. This time I began to wonder if it could have been a church. I asked Mr Mars what used to be there, and he said he didn't know, it has always been rubble. He said it has got the remainder of a wall at the back, so it must have been a building of some kind. When I left the barn, I took another look. Climbing over the low remaining wall, I pushed some of the weeds back with my feet. Underneath were some very large bricks that were partially black, broken roof tiles and more charred wood. So it probably was a building that was burnt down by fire. I wonder how I could find out if it was a church. Records only go back 100 years, so I don't suppose I can.

Sunday, 17th July

I went to Uncle Ray's farm this morning. The kitten is fine now, and even looked as though it had grown bigger. Ruby followed me about more than usual, like my shadow. We helped Jimmy and Uncle Ray, put up the walls of the tree house, by handing up long planks of wood to them.

When I went to say goodbye to Aunt Pearl, there was a lovely smell of freshly baked bread in the kitchen. She said Rayson had just made some bread rolls. She took them out of the oven, and gave me a couple to bring home. Rayson was in the sitting room, drawing a picture of cows in a field. I think he draws animals really well.

In the afternoon, I left Ruffles behind in the porch, and walked to Peter's farm. My mother came a bit later, on her way home from work. Peter is 21 today, so I took him a card I had made and a box of mixed sweets.

The weather was fine for an outdoor party. People were gathered on the large grassy area, by the house. A fire was burning surrounded by walls of bricks, and lumps of meat were cooking on metal racks that were resting on top of the bricks. There were quite a few people there, and I didn't know some of them. I felt a bit shy, so was glad to see that Rayson had come. He is Peter's best friend I think. I sat down with him, on one of the old tree trunks that were lying on the grass, and Sascha came over and joined us.

Later Peter came over and he and Rayson started talking about farm work. Peter said he didn't like it and wasn't keen on taking over his father's farm. Rayson agreed with him, and said he would like to be a baker instead, as he likes cooking. I wonder if Uncle Ray knows that. He should have trained as a baker whilst he was at school, I don't think he can be one now. I was surprised to hear that they don't like working on farms. I would love it, being outdoors all the time with animals and plants. Peter told Sascha not to say anything about it to their parents, as he didn't know what other job he could do. I don't know either.

Monday, 18th July

Two policemen came to the Information Centre today, and told Mrs Newsby that she has to make a list of everyone in the Wells area, from her records, and it is her responsibility to make sure no one is left off. This list is going to be collected next Monday and taken to Easten. It is for 'The Unveiling of the Statue' Parade Day. When people have bowed to the huge statue, they will pass a desk and have their name checked off the list. I hate the thought of this, I really don't want to bow to a statue of Ferdinand Tansa. I spent all morning trying to think up a way of getting my name left off the list. It distracted me from my work, but Mrs Newsby didn't notice, as she was too busy. She didn't look happy about it, but I suppose orders are orders, and she doesn't want to get into trouble. Sascha has the records, so she was helping.

When Sascha and I left, I asked she could leave my name off the list. She said, 'No, it would only get Mrs Newsby into a lot of trouble if it was found out. It is just easier to go and do as they want, it won't hurt to bow to a statue'. I said, 'What about people who are ill, or just can't get there that day?' She told me that their names will not be checked off the list, and they will have to go another day. I think it is awful that they can make us do things like that. I'm not sure what to do.

Thursday, 21st July

Peter came over this evening, and we went for a walk on the cliffs. There were big clouds in the sky, but it was warm. He held my hand, which I quite liked. It reminded me of my father holding my hand when I was small, and I almost wanted to pretend it was my father. But when he started moaning about working on the farm again, it brought me back to reality. I asked him what work he would like to do instead. He said he didn't know. I suggested Woodalls, making furniture, but he said he should have been trained for something else at school. He started working on the farm when he was 13, as his father just assumed he would want to take over the farm one day.

Further along the cliffs, we came across Justin, who was looking intently through his binoculars at something out to sea. Peter called out 'Hello Justin', which made him jump. He turned round and his smile at Peter quickly disappeared, when he saw me. I felt awkward holding Peter's hand and pulled it away.

Peter asked him what he was doing, and he said he was looking at some birds which were diving into the sea. He told Peter that his grandfather had given him the binoculars, and they are wonderful for bird spotting. He has been looking for the rare dove that was recently reported in the news, but he hasn't seen it yet. I didn't say anything about my encounter with the dove.

We left him to his bird watching and continued along the cliff. He wasn't there when we walked back again.

Saturday, 30th July

At the Youth Club this evening, we all went to a local field to play rounders and cricket. I was on the same team as Sascha, Peter and Rayson. Jimmy and Justin were on the other team, and they won both games. Justin and Peter were both very good at throwing the ball and got lots of people out, but Jimmy could really run fast. He amazed us all. I thought Justin seemed embarrassed when he got me out, but he still didn't say anything to me. He's not that shy with other people, I wonder why I have that effect on him. Anyway it was good fun, I wish the Youth Club went out together more.

When we were all walking back, three policemen stopped us to ask what we were doing. They don't like to see groups of people, in case they are plotting against the rulers. They don't seem to realise that if the police keep annoying us, it might make us want to revolt. Mr Bunny told them about us going to the field to play games, and they wanted to see our bats and balls before they believed us.

Friday, 5th August

When I went down to the allotment this afternoon, I

found that someone has taken lots of my vegetables and fruit. Where there should have been rows of crops was just mud, and most of the ripe fruit had gone. I felt really annoyed and upset.

As I was staring at the allotment, wondering who would do this, Sarah came over. She put her arm around my shoulders, and told me three Policemen had come with two other men. One of the Policemen had told the men what to take and made them do it. They put the vegetables and fruit into sacks and boxes and placed them in a horse-drawn cart. Only the Rulers and the Police are allowed to have horses.

Sarah was brave enough to go over and ask them why they were taking the crops. One of the Policemen told her that the Rulers needed them for a feast on Parade Day, as their own crops were not good enough, because of the lack of rain. They gave her some money to give to the owner, which she handed over to me. She said she was sorry, she couldn't have stopped them if she tried. If I was short of anything, she would see if she could help me out. That was nice of her.

When she went back to work on her own allotment, I had to try hard not to burst into tears. I had a good look to see what was missing. They have taken all of my carrots, and although I have some at home, they won't last long. Carrots are my favourite vegetable too. I had grown enough to last the winter. Some potatoes and onions are missing. The runner beans, tomato plants, strawberries and raspberries have all been stripped of anything that was ready to eat.

When I got home I counted the money, it isn't much. I worked out that it is not anywhere near the amount I would have got, if I had sold it all to Mr Mars. And anyway, I wouldn't have sold it all, because we need it for food. I thought of all the hard work I had put into making the crops grow, and the water I had carried from the well, and I did cry then.

I told Mother when she got home from work. She said, 'The Rulers are getting worse in the way that they treat people on the Island'. I don't know how I can stop them taking anymore. She suggested I harvest as much as I can and bring it home and hide it, as there are still two more parade days in August for the other towns. Easten has had theirs. I wonder who I could ask to help me, everyone is busy with their own work.

Saturday, 6th August

This morning I went up to Uncle Ray's farm early, to ask if anyone could help me to gather in some crops on the allotment. Ruby said she would and looked excited about it. Uncle Ray said I could have Jimmy for the morning, but he was needed in the afternoon, to clean out the cowshed. Aunt Pearl said she was really sorry to hear what had happened, then added that she hopes the Rulers don't start helping themselves to things on the farm.

It was nice to have Ruby and Jimmy come and help me. Ruby ran on ahead, playing with Ruffles, and throwing a stick for her to fetch. Jimmy chatted to me about school and the farm. He will be leaving school soon, but loves working on the farm, so is quite happy about it.

We stopped at the cottage to get the handcart Daddy made, and Jimmy pulled it along behind him, by the 'U' shaped handle. We dug up all the rest of the potatoes, beetroot, turnips, parsnips and swedes. We were all rather muddy after, including Ruffles who joined in the digging, although not actually digging anything up.

I noticed quite a few other people were hurriedly harvesting their crops on the allotments, including Justin.

He said 'Hallo', then got on with his work, glancing over at us occasionally. I don't think the thieves will be back until next Friday, if they are coming at all. Normarket's Parade Day is next weekend.

On the way home, the cart was quite heavy, and Jimmy went the other side of the handle to push instead. Ruby and I helped by pushing from the back of the cart. We all had to push even harder when the wheels got stuck in the holes in the road, several times. We have put all the crops in the shed for now. I will find somewhere to hide them during the week. Ruby and Jimmy were cheerful and made it all fun, I wish they could come down more often.

When my cousins left to go home, Jimmy turned back and shouted 'See you tomorrow on the Electra'. I groaned. I have been so busy I forgot it is Parade Day tomorrow.

In the afternoon, I went back to the allotment on my own, and pulled up some cabbages, leeks, and lettuce. I also picked sweetcorn and peas. I left some at home and the rest I took up to Mr Mars in the Market Barn.

I was really tired this evening, and so I didn't go back into town for the Youth Club, I just took Ruffles for a short walk on the cliffs. I sat down and told God I don't want to go to Parade Day tomorrow, and I definitely don't want to bow to the statue of Ferdinand Tansa. I have such a strong aversion to doing so, it makes me feel sick when I think about it. But I can't see any way of getting out of it.

4

Easten

Sunday, 7th August

My mother and I got up early this morning, put some lunch and cushions into our backpacks, and walked up to Uncle Ray's farm with Ruffles. I left Ruffles with the other collies, as I couldn't take her to Easten with me this time. Uncle Ray's family were all ready to leave, so we walked up to the station together.

We knew the Electra was going to be crowded, as the whole town of Wells had to get on at 8am or 9am when it stops, otherwise they would arrive too late in Easten. We got there about 10 minutes before 8, and the carriages were nearly full. A large notice said that the carriages were for the elderly and the rest of us were to sit on the track. As we went past, I saw Mr Ditchling sitting in a carriage. He didn't look well, and was bent over, looking down at the floor.

We walked along by the track, until we saw some space, and climbed up onto it, got the cushions out of our backpacks, and sat down on them. Ruby snuggled up against me and said she was scared of falling off when it moved. I put my arm around her and said it would be fine, it doesn't move very fast, and the low railing along the side was to stop things falling off anyway.

At 8am a horn sounded and the track started moving. I held on to the railing at first, until I got used to the movement. I liked sitting there listening to our family chatting, and watching the countryside go past. It could have been a nice family outing, if the Parade Day hadn't been waiting for us at the end of journey.

The track stopped moving for 15 minutes, when we got to Soumarket, but no one was waiting at the station. I expect lots more people climbed on in Wells though. We got off for a little while to stretch our legs which had become quite stiff after an hour of sitting down on the track. We got back on for another hour, and were glad to get off in Easten.

We followed lots of people down the road to the beach. A long queue had already formed, winding its way up and down on the sand, to the huge statue of Ferdinand Tansa. Next to the statue, was a policeman watching the people, making sure that they bowed as they passed it. Then there were several tables, with notices showing letters of the alphabet, which we guessed was where you got your name ticked off the list.

Uncle Ray suggested we go to join the queue straight away, and get it over with. I reluctantly joined the queue with them, still trying to think of a way I could get out of it. Ruby looked shy and grabbed my hand and held on to it tightly.

The queue moved along slowly. At one point it went near the fishermen at the water's edge, and Gordon saw me. He came over and everyone looked round in surprise when he said 'Hello Gelany'. I felt quite embarrassed, I don't know why, and I am sure my cheeks turned red, which made me feel even more uneasy. He talked about fishing and the Parade and then went back to his work, when the queue moved on. I saw my mother looking at me, and I looked away quickly, and started talking to Ruby. I knew she was probably going to ask me how I knew that man. I needed time to think of an answer, that didn't involve me coming to Easten without her knowledge, to look for my father.

It seemed to take ages for us to reach the statue. When I saw it close up, I had a strong desire to run away, but then Ruby started tugging at my hand and pointing up to the sky.

'Look Gelany. There's a beautiful white bird up there.'

I looked up where she was pointing and saw the dove. It was flying back and forth overhead, riding on the breeze. Then it started flying towards us. My attention was taken from it, by a stern voice saying 'Move along there. Stop holding up the queue'.

I looked at the policeman, who was pointing towards the statue with his hand, indicating that it was our turn to go past. As we walked towards the statue, the dove came swooping down over the policeman's head and knocked off his peaked cap. He gasped and bent down to pick it up, behind him. As he did so, I quickly walked past the statue and pulled Ruby with me. Scanning the tables, I saw one with a label 'K-L-M' on, and went to have my name ticked off. Then took Ruby to her table. She tugged at me trying to say something. I told her to 'shush', and got her name ticked, then quickly led her away to where we could talk in private.

'Gelany, I didn't bow,' she whispered.

'I know. It doesn't matter, I didn't either. I don't think anyone noticed, they were looking at the bird. Let's not tell anyone.'

'Yes, it can be another of our secrets. I didn't want to bow to that silly old statue anyway,' she said looking pleased.

We went over to the others, who were looking for a place to sit down on the beach to eat lunch. We found some dry sand near the sea, and I was glad it was a safe distance from where Gordon was working. But as soon as we sat down, my mother asked me questions.

'How did that fisherman know your name? How do you know him?'

'He brings the fish to Wells sometimes, and I've met him there.' I had plenty of time to think of an answer whilst we were waiting in the long queue. She seemed satisfied with this.

Jimmy talked about the dove knocking off the policeman's hat, and I think everyone wanted to laugh, but we didn't dare to, because of the policemen around. No one mentioned how Ruby and I hadn't bowed, thank goodness.

At 1pm we heard a band in the distance, the drums booming out the loudest of all. Everyone on the beach stood up. Gradually the sound got nearer, until we saw the front of the procession. They were coming down the road, that we had walked down, from the station. At the front was a band, mostly with drums and trumpets. They were dressed up like policemen, and had red tassels on their shoulders. Next came the four Tansa brothers, all dressed in long colourful robes. They climbed up onto a some large wooden boxes, that had been placed on the beach, to make a stage by the statue. Then came lots of policemen, their arms swinging and legs marching, all in unison. They had different coloured badges on their hats. It made me feel quite frightened, to see so many of them altogether. Some of the band came round to the front of the stage, whilst the policemen stopped all along the road and faced the crowd of people on the beach.

I felt Ruby's hand slip into mine, as the music for the 'Carta' started. People began to sing it, but as I went to join in, my throat went dry and the sound wouldn't come out. It was as if I had lost my voice, like can happen when you have got a cold. I coughed to try to clear it, but it didn't make any difference. So I just made my mouth move up and down, with no sound coming out at all. I could see the police looking at us to make sure we sang, and I didn't want to get into any trouble.

The words of the horrible 'Carta' song go like this:

Tansa is great
Tansa has saved us
Forever we will so grateful be
He is our King
He is our Saviour
We will bow down and worship him.

Thank you King Tansa
Thank you for saving us
We love you Tansa and your family
We are your servants.
Tell us your will
We gladly surrender to you.

You rule this Island
Tansay is yours
You have made it a great place to live
We are so glad
You are our ruler
Accept the honour we give to you.

This song was written 100 years ago, when Reginald Tansa did rescue the people on the Island from possible starvation. But I don't think it applies now, quite the opposite.

The Tansa brothers all smiled as we sang it. I saw Emerald, standing next to Charles, and she wasn't smiling. She has got lovely long black hair. She looked like she was trying to hide behind Charles, I think she didn't want to be up there with them. A policeman got up on the stage and told us to give three cheers for Ferdinand Tansa, which the crowd did. But I am sure it was from fear of what might happen if they didn't, and not because they wanted to.

Then the Tansa brothers left in horse-drawn carriages. I thought to myself that they were probably going back home to their feast, to eat my carrots and crops that they stole, and it made me feel cross. When most of the police had left, we decided to go back to the station. Uncle Ray wanted to get back to his farm work. Just by the stage was a large notice that hadn't been there before, and we stopped to read it. It said that there was going to be a large recruitment of policemen and any men interested should fill in forms, available at the Information Centres. Then they should attend a recruitment day for interviews.

Uncle Ray exclaimed 'Oh no, not more police, as if we need anymore,' and we all agreed. The Electra had stopped, so we climbed up, and sat down on our cushions again. After the track started moving, Ruby laid her head in my lap and fell asleep, and I wished I could do the same. Everyone seemed quieter on the way back. We got off for 10 minutes and stretched our legs in Normarket, and then climbed back on for the final hour. We were glad to get back to Wells. I collected Ruffles at the farm, who gave me a big welcome, nearly knocking me over.

I took her for a short run on the cliffs later and sat down to look out to sea. I thanked God for sending the dove to distract the policeman, so that I didn't have to bow to the statue. He must really care about me to do that!

Wednesday, 10th August

The last few days I have been busy storing all the root vegetables that we dug up last weekend. I thought if I just put them in the shed, the Tansas may come and find them if they are short of crops. Maybe I should ask God for rain for them, so they don't come to steal our food anymore. Anyway, I dug a big hole in our garden, put a thick layer of straw down and laid the root vegetables on top. Then I covered them with more straw and strips wood, and put a thin layer of earth on top of that. I marked where I had put them with some stones. I hope they keep alright like that.

No mention was made of the dove in the news sheet we received at the Information Centre today. It just said how successful the Parade Day had been for Wells people, and that the people had enjoyed it. I wish I could write the news myself and tell the truth.

Friday, 12th August

I had an interesting conversation with Mother after dinner this evening.

She told me 'I heard at work this week, that they are going to build cottages in a field near the hospital. They will be for people who work there. I've been thinking, if I could get one, you and Peter could have this cottage when you get married. I would like to live nearer the town anyway.'

I was so surprised I didn't know what to say.

'What do you think?'

'I don't know. I want to stay here, but I'm not sure about marrying Peter yet.'

'Why not? He's a nice boy. I've been friends with his mother for years. Has he asked you or said anything about it?'

'No.'

'I'll have a word with his mother.'

'No! Please don't. I'm sure we can sort it out ourselves.'

'His mother and I have been hoping you two will get married, as we've watched you both growing up.'

I started clearing the dishes away, hoping that would end the conversation. I really liked the idea of staying at the cottage. It is full of memories of my father, and all I have left of him. The garden he planted, the furniture he made and painted, the porch I watched him build, and especially the times I spent with him. I can still sense his presence here. That is the old Daddy though, the one who loved me, not the one who ran off with another woman. The thing I'm not sure about is Peter living here with me. He is always moaning about farm work. I would love to be a farmer's wife and help on a farm, I think. But it would have to be a farmer who enjoyed his job, and liked the animals.

Tuesday, 16th August

Mrs Newsby told me that she wants me to go to Easten tomorrow, to collect a Police recruitment poster for the Information Centre, and some application forms. I don't know why they can't send them in the post. But I don't mind, it will be a day out. I have to take the letter she received about it, to prove I am entitled to collect them. She said I can take a morning off work another day, as the Easten trip will take all day.

Wednesday, 17th August

Ruffles and I got on the Electra just after 9am, and there was plenty of room in the carriages. I hadn't asked Mrs Newsby if I could take my dog, but I didn't see why I couldn't. We arrived in Easten at 11.30am, and I went straight to the beach to eat my packed lunch. I sat down on some lovely warm dry sand, whilst Ruffles ran about on the wet sand, chasing birds. After I had eaten, I saw a boat coming in, and as it got nearer, I could see Gordon and another man on it. When they got closer to the shore, I went to meet them.

'Hallo Gelany. What are you doing here?' shouted Gordon.

'I'm working. I've come to pick something up to take back to the Information Centre.'

'Well you don't look like you're working. Looks like you're having a day off at the beach to me,' he laughed.

'Have you caught lots of fish?' I asked.

'No, none. It's been like this for days. I don't know what we're going to do. We can't really go out further, or around the Island, we just have to wait for them to come into the bay.'

'What about over there?' I pointed to the sea behind them, where I could see lots of movement in the water, and fish started leaping in and out of the sea, in arc shapes.

Gordon and the other fishermen looked to where I was pointing, but they couldn't see the fish.

'There, there's loads.' I pointed again.

'Well, I can't see any, but just to make you happy, we'll cast our nets once more. Got nothing to lose.'

They took the boat out again and put the nets in the water, as I continued to point and shout directions. Suddenly the net got very heavy. It was so heavy, they couldn't get it back in the boat. Instead, they pulled it along behind them, and came back to the shore.

'Here Gelany, come and help us,' Gordon shouted as he jumped out and waded through the shallow water. He gave me a corner of the net. I held on tight , but it was so heavy I couldn't move it. We had to wait for the other fisherman, whose name is Frank, to come and help. When we got the net on the beach we saw that it was absolutely full of fish.

'Well Gelany, I could kiss you. How did you do that?'

'I could see them. I don't know why you couldn't.'

'Go on, give her a kiss,' said Frank.

Gordon kissed me on the cheek, and I felt my legs go weak.

'Can I have some fish?' I asked quickly, to change the subject.

'Yes, how many would you like, and of course no charge for you today, my dear.'

I chose six big fish, which Gordon wrapped up in brown paper, and I put them in my backpack. Mother and I can have them for dinner today and tomorrow, and also a treat for Ruffles.

I watched them busily getting all the shiny, slippery, fish put into boxes that were waiting on the beach. Some other fishermen came over and admired the catch and asked them how they did it, as they hadn't caught much lately either. Gordon and Frank told them how I had seen the fish leaping out of the water. I didn't like the attention turned on me, so I said I had better get back to work. Gordon walked with me to the road.

'Thanks Gelany. Thank you for helping us out. I'm glad you came today. I still don't know how you saw all those fish. We've never had such a big catch before.' He bent down and stroked Ruffles on the head.

I said goodbye and went to the Information Centre. Ruffles waited outside, whilst I went in. The poster was in a large tube, and the forms in an envelope. I was going to put the forms in my backpack, but thought the fish might make them wet or smell. So I carried them in one hand, holding them against my chest, and tucked the poster tube under the other arm.

As I travelled back on the Electra, I could still feel the touch of Gordon's lips on my cheek. I wondered what it would be like to be a Fisherman's wife. I think I would like going out to sea in a boat, that must be fun. But I've not seen a woman in a boat. I think the wives probably stay at home to look after their houses and children. I'm don't think I would like living in the town. I wonder if Gordon would live in the countryside.

We got back to Wells at 4.30pm, and the Information Centre was still open, so I left the poster and forms there. I was glad Mrs Newsby didn't notice Ruffles sitting outside.

When I sat down on the cliffs this evening, talking to God, I told Him that I liked the fish miracle.

Monday, 22nd August

At work today, I put the large poster, about the recruitment of police, on the noticeboard outside. It has big smiling policemen on it, and smaller people all looking happy. I would have liked to have torn it up or burned it, but knew that would get me into trouble. There was also a smaller notice to put in this month's news folder.

Friday, 26th August

A strange thing is happening with the carrots. I had some at home, when the Tansas pinched all my carrots off the allotment. I thought they would only last until the end of this week, but when I looked in the store cupboard today, it was as if we hadn't eaten any at all, as there are still plenty there. But we have been eating them as usual. I'm sure God has got something to do with it.

Saturday, 27th August

At Youth Club this evening, Peter and Rayson were talking with each other, on the opposite side of the room to where Sascha and I were sitting. Then they went out somewhere together and didn't come back. Peter didn't even ask me to play table tennis. Sascha and I had a game ourselves, but she can't play very well, so I kept on winning. We tried darts, but I kept missing the board, and when I noticed Justin was watching me, that put me off even more. He looked away when I looked at him. We watched Jimmy playing skittles for a while, he is really good at that. He knocked all the skittles down with one hit of the ball quite a few times. He told me they have finished the roof on the tree house and to come to see it tomorrow.

Sunday, 28th August

When I went up to Uncle Ray's farm this morning, I saw Ruby waiting for me, by the gate. She was holding her kitten tightly against her chest, and looked as if she had been crying. I thought her kitten was ill again, until she spoke.

'Gelany, don't go to the house. There's a big row going on. Come to the tree house. Jimmy's there.'

'Why? What's the matter?' I asked as we walked along.

'Rayson has told Daddy that he wants to join the police. And Daddy is cross and shouting at him. And Mummy is crying. I ran away and got Beauty to cuddle. I've been waiting here for you, I hoped you would come.'

We put the kitten back in the barn with its siblings, and left Ruffles with the other dogs. The tree house looked splendid with its roof on, and I eagerly climbed up the wooden ladder. Jimmy was sitting on some hay on the floor, eating an apple. We sat down beside him. The room was bare except for a bowl filled up with apples. He pushed it over to us, and asked us if we'd like one.

'What's happening at the farm house?' I asked him.

'Rayson told Dad that he doesn't like working on the farm, and doesn't want to do it for the rest of his life. He's seen the poster about police recruitment, and said he is going to get an application form. Dad is cross and doesn't want him too, and Mum is upset.'

'I don't want him to either. How can we stop him?' I asked.

'I don't know. He seems pretty determined. I don't think he will listen to anyone, if he doesn't listen to Dad.'

I stayed for a while with them, talking about other things, like furnishing the tree house, to try to take their minds off it. Then when it was lunch time, they started feeling hungry and decided to go up to the house. I said I would go home.

As I walked along with Ruffles, I wondered if I could hide the application forms when I got to work tomorrow. I wish I could rip them up and the posters too. But I know I can't. Mother was surprised to see me back so soon, and I told her about Rayson. She just said 'Oh, no'.

In the afternoon I took Ruffles on the cliff and sat in my favourite spot, next to the bushes, and thought about it. I really don't want Rayson to join the police. He would be on the other side, against us. And I like Rayson. He is really gentle, I don't want him to turn into a brute. It's horrible to think about. So then I started talking to God earnestly.

'Please God, don't let Rayson become a policeman. Please stop him,' I cried out.

Monday, 29th August

This morning at work, I saw Mrs Newsby put the police application forms on the reception desk. That is out of my view, where I sit, so I can't see who comes in to ask for one.

After work, Sascha and I walked home together. She was very quiet and I asked her if she was alright.

She said 'I'll tell you when we get out of the town.' I wondered what she was going to tell me, and she kept me in suspense until we sat down on a grassy bank.

'What is it?' I asked.

'Peter is going to apply to join the police. I thought you should know.'

'Oh, no. Not him too.'

'Why, who else?'

'Rayson. There was a big row at the farm yesterday. His father doesn't want him to.'

'Oh dear. Will he stop him?'

'I don't know if he can. He doesn't like farm work. What does your father say about Peter?'

'He doesn't want Peter to join either. But I don't think that will stop him applying. He wants to get out of farm work too.'

'What do you think?' I asked Sascha.

'Well I suppose I wish they both liked farm work, but they don't.'

'You realise they would be on the other side from us. You know, against the ordinary people.'

'Maybe it would be good to have someone we know on the other side,' she suggested.

'Not if they have to follow orders against us.'

'Well, I don't know. We can't do anything about it.'

'Perhaps we should ask them not to. I'll ask Rayson, and you ask Peter,' I suggested.

She agreed to do that, so on my way home, I stopped at the farm. I found Rayson in the house making soup for lunch. He said that he had been sorting vegetables for storage this morning, and was using up some that had been damaged, and wouldn't keep so well. He seemed pleased to see me. His mother was out visiting someone, and Uncle Ray and Jimmy were working on the farm.

'I hear you want to join the police, Rayson. I wish you wouldn't.'

'Why? It's a good job with lots of privileges. I really don't want to do farm work anymore, and I've not been trained for anything else.'

'But you would be against us, on the other side. You may have to do some nasty things?'

'Like what? They only warn people about things. I could do it in a friendly way.'

'But they took my fruit and vegetables off the allotment. Would you do that?'

'I know which is your allotment. I could make sure it is someone else's,' he joked.

'Please don't be a nasty policeman, Rayson,' was all I could offer to try to dissuade him. I felt a bit defeated.

He put his arm around my shoulders and gave me a friendly squeeze. 'Don't worry Gelany, I'll try to be a nice one.'

He asked me if I would like to stay for lunch, but I declined saying I had to get home. I really was upset and just wanted to get away.

This evening on the cliffs, I pleaded with God again, this time for Peter and Rayson, not to join the police.

Tuesday, 30th August

I had a quick chat with Sascha after work today. She said she couldn't persuade Peter to change his mind about joining the police. He told her that he really likes the idea of being a policeman. I told her Rayson wouldn't take any notice of what I said either. So we don't know what else we can do.

Thursday, 1st September

When I left work today, I found Gordon waiting outside for me.

'Hallo Gelany. I've brought you some fish,' he said as he handed me a brown paper package.

'Thank you. How much do I owe you?'

'Nothing. You helped us out the other day with your amazing catch, so as I was delivering the fish today, I thought I would bring you a present.'

'Are you going back on the Electra now?'

'Yes.'

' I'll walk with you to the station.' I felt that people were looking at us, so I wanted us to talk somewhere else.

We walked to the seats, on the grass by the station, and sat down.

'How are you?' Gordon asked.

'Okay. Well, almost alright. We have trouble in the family.'

'What's up now?' he asked looking concerned.

'My cousin, Rayson, is going to apply to join the police. He doesn't like working on his father's farm. His family don't want him to be a policeman, neither do I.'

'Maybe he won't get in. I don't suppose everyone who applies will get in. I think they have quite strict rules about who can join. I knew someone who was turned down, and he never found out why.'

I was pleased to hear him say that and I hope he is right. For some reason I didn't feel like telling him about Peter as well. We talked about fishing, and Gordon told me how much he likes his job. He feels so free when he is out in the boat, well away from the coast. Sometimes he feels like sailing away, but he doesn't know if he would find any more land. It wouldn't be much fun sailing on the sea forever, he might get fed up with fish and feel hungry. I said I would like go with him if he did, I'd like to find out if there is any more land. He laughed, and said I was quite the adventurer. Then he started talking about the Rulers and how he sees them quite often in Easten. I'm glad we live far away from them, and they don't come to Wells. It was soon time for him to get back on the Electra. I waved goodbye, watching him, until he became a small speck in the distance.

5

A Proposal

Friday, 2nd September

When I was walking back home from the cliffs this evening, I saw Justin coming towards me.

Suddenly, before I could stop her, Ruffles ran ahead, sat down in front of him, and waited to be stroked.

'Ruffles, come here' I shouted, but she didn't take any notice.

Justin bent down and stroked her on the head. I went over and put her lead on.

'Nice dog,' he said.

'Yes' I replied, as I pulled her away, and started walking home quickly. I felt annoyed with Ruffles. Justin has never been friendly to me, so why should we be to him.

Saturday, 3rd September

I worked on the allotment most of today. It has been a lovely day, with the sun shining and a cool breeze. The runner beans are doing really well, so I picked a lot, and will take some to the market barn on Monday, on my way to work. There was a lot of weeding to do. Ruffles laid down on the grass and enjoyed the sun.

Justin came late afternoon, and picked some crops. His plot could do with weeding. I told Ruffles to stay where she was, as I didn't want her to run over to him. He did say 'hallo' at one point when we couldn't really ignore each other as we were working quite close, and now it was my turn to grunt back.

I gave Ruffles a run on the cliffs before going home, as I was going to the Youth Club in the evening. Mother was home from work when I got back, and she cooked the dinner for a change, which was nice.

I sat with Sascha at Youth Club and Peter came over looking quite happy. I had a couple of games of table tennis with him, and I needn't mention who won, of course. Rayson was now sitting with Sascha, and we joined them. Rayson told us that he was glad to get away from the farm, as it felt like everyone was cross with him.

'I think my family are getting used to the idea,' said Peter.

'We don't want you to join the police,' replied Sascha. 'we just know we can't make you change your mind.'

I didn't think I could make any difference, so I just kept quiet. I plan to keep pleading with God to stop them getting accepted for the police.

Sunday, 4th September

I went to Uncle Ray's farm this morning. Everyone seemed a bit subdued, but the police topic was not talked about. It felt like people weren't talking to each other. Rayson was on his own in the sitting room, painting a picture of Maplehurst Forest. He can paint trees really well. I stayed to lunch, and left soon after. Ruby was busy helping Aunt Pearl with some baking.

Monday, 5th September

Sascha has always been my best friend, even though she is a year older than me. We were in the same class at school, and walked home together until we reached her farm. I got to know her before I went to school, as I went with my mother when she visited Sascha's mother. I didn't really get to know Peter then, because he seemed so much older than me. He's only started taking notice of me since I went to the Youth Club. It's funny how age gaps seem smaller when you get older. I think Justin was in the class below mine, so I never got to know him. I only knew the children in my class, and not very well, as we were doing school work most of the time.

When school was over, we all went home for lunch, and most children worked with their parents in the afternoons. I used to help my Mother with her chores. We had chickens in the garden then, and it was my job to look after them too.

After Daddy left, Mother went to work, and I spent the afternoons with Aunt Pearl helping her. We gave our chickens to Uncle Ray, as Mother said we couldn't manage chickens, as well as her going out to work and us doing the allotment. She said there was too much to do. My mother and I did the allotment between us, but we could only work on it in the evenings and at weekends.

When I was 13, Sascha helped me get the job at the Information Centre. She was already working there, and someone was leaving, so she told Mrs Newsby about me. It was then that I started to look after the allotment on my own. Mother was spending even longer hours at the hospital, and she said I was old enough to look after it myself.

I went to Uncle Ray's farm a lot and liked being with my cousins. When I was there, it felt like I was part of a large family. There was just Rayson and Jimmy at first, and then it was lovely when Ruby was born. It was soon after the Daddy incident and she helped to take my mind off it. She has always been so cute. Aunt Pearl used to let me help look after her, even when she was a baby.

I don't think my mother has ever got over Daddy disappearing, and neither have I. She didn't want to talk about it, which I found hard. I think it has come between us. I still love Daddy, but I don't think she does anymore. I suppose I understand that more now, since she told me he ran off with another woman. I guess I would be cross if that happened to me. It hurt a lot to hear that, so perhaps that is why she hasn't told me before. It made me go off Daddy for a while, but now I am beginning to want to see him again. I still remember how he was before he left, and how much he loved me. Maybe he can't come to see me, because of seeing Mother. I wish I could find him.

Tuesday, 6th September

This evening, when I took Ruffles for a walk on the cliffs, instead of turning left, I turned right and went into Maplehurst Forest. The last time I went there was with Daddy, and the trees grow right to the edge of the cliff. I am fed up with seeing Justin turn up, when I want to sit down to have a quiet time talking with God or just be by myself. He always has the binoculars round his neck, he must really like bird spotting. I used to have the cliffs to myself, and it seems like he is invading my territory.

Anyway, it was quite nice in the wood, although the trees obstruct the view of the sea.

After walking for about five minutes, Ruffles went to the edge of the cliff and disappeared. I thought Oh no! I hope she hasn't fallen down again. I went cautiously to the edge and saw that there was a path going down the side of the cliff, and Ruffles was on it. I called her to come to me and put her lead on, then went to investigate. It was quite a wide path so I didn't feel unsafe even though there was a sheer drop to my left. The path led down to a little cave in the rocky cliff face. There were some flat rocks just inside it, and I sat down on one, near the entrance. I made Ruffles lie down beside me, and looked out at the sea. It felt safe and away from prying eyes, and I knew Ruffles would growl if anyone was coming. I really doubted that they would, as it was far away from any houses.

I told God that I think I do want to find Daddy again and I want him to still love me. It was lovely to know God loved me, but I can't see him or hug him. Then I saw the dove. It flew down onto the edge of the path in front of me. It looked at me and cocked its head on one side, as if it were listening. Then it flew away. So it found me even though I was hiding in a cave!

Wednesday, 7th September

At work today, Mrs Newsby received a letter, saying that Oswald Tansa is coming to Wells on 27th September. He is going to the Bank and Taxation Office in the morning to check that people are paying their taxes. In the afternoon he is coming to the Information Centre, to check that we are keeping our records correctly. Mrs Newsby looked really worried about it, and she said she wants Sascha and I to have a meeting with her tomorrow morning, to discuss what we are going to do.

She gave me a large poster to put up on the board outside and a smaller one to put in this month's news folder. They were headed, 'Attention All Citizens' and said that if people haven't paid their taxes that are due, they should do so before the 27th, when Oswald Tansa is coming to check the records.

It said they would be put in prison and made to do work for the Rulers, until all their debts are paid, if they have not paid them.

I didn't know there was a prison on the Island. I wonder if it is true or if they are just saying it to scare people. I asked Sascha, but she said she didn't know either. We are glad he is coming in the afternoon to the Information Centre, because we go home at lunchtime, and won't have to see him.

Thursday, 8th September

Mrs Newsby, Sascha and I had a meeting together this morning, around the table where Mrs Newsby works. She said I have to go through every file and make sure nothing is in the wrong place. I must make sure all the news folders, the noticeboard and all the areas the public use are neat and tidy. Sascha has to tidy her records about people in this area. We also have to do some cleaning. She is going to get a man in to do some painting of the walls and woodwork. The worst thing is that she wants us to be there on the afternoon that Oswald Tansa comes. She says we can have another morning off work instead afterwards. Also if we need to work any extra time to make sure everything is alright, we can have time off later for that too. Sascha and I thought we probably would have to work some afternoons, as we don't usually have much spare time.

Saturday, 10th September

I went to Youth Club this evening. Peter and Rayson were talking about the police recruitment day, in Easten. They have both received letters asking them to attend on Monday. Peter said there are to be individual interviews, as well as a meeting telling them about joining the police.

I decided not to go up to Uncle Ray's farm tomorrow. I

think it will be a bit awkward, with Rayson having the police interview the next day. I could do with some extra time on the allotment, as I probably will miss some afternoons in the next couple of weeks, if I have to stay on at work.

Saturday, 17th September

I haven't had time to write in my journal this week, I have been so busy. I went to Youth Club this evening, and asked Rayson and Peter what the recruitment day had been like.

They said they didn't know if they had got in yet. Rayson seemed a bit quiet, but Peter told me about it. First they had been given a talk about what it meant to be a policeman, and how they could help the people. They were told that they had to obey orders, and that once they joined they couldn't leave. There are lots of privileges, like free uniforms and houses to live in, and good wages. They have special days with feasts together, and social events.

They were taken outside to do some marching together and were told exactly what to do. Although it was difficult at first, Peter said he soon got into the rhythm. Reginald Tansa was giving the orders, and some other policemen were watching them. They had name tags with big numbers on, so they could be identified. The policemen who were watching, were making notes.

Peter said Reginald Tansa interviewed them, and he asked them questions like why they wanted to join the police, what they would do in certain situations when they were a policeman, and about their families.

I think they said there had only been three other men from Wells, ten from Normarket, only one from Soumarket, and all the others from Easten. Most of the new policemen would live in Easten, and a few in each of the other towns.

I felt really sad as I was walking home, and a few tears ran down my cheeks. It sounds so awful in the police. I'm going to work on the allotment again tomorrow, and not go to Uncle Ray's farm. If they ask me why I've not been coming, I will just tell them that I had to make up time on the allotment. I have missed two afternoons this week, as I worked at the Information Centre. It takes a long time going through all the files. It is rather annoying and feels like a waste of time, as most of them are alright.

Monday, 19th September

I had just finished eating my lunch today, when I was surprised by a knock on the door. I opened it and there was Peter . He asked if he could come in, as he wanted to speak to me.

I made him a drink and we sat down at the table. He seemed very excited about something.

'I got a letter today, to say I've been accepted by the police Gelany.'

'Oh,' was all I could manage. And I thought, why hadn't God taken any notice of my pleadings for Peter to be rejected.

'This means we can get married now. I'm going to get a lovely new house in Easten. I think you will like it there, it is only about five minutes away from the beach. What do you think?'

'I'm sorry, I can't marry you Peter.'

'Why? What do you mean?'

I looked down, I couldn't look at his eyes anymore, and replied, 'I don't want to marry a policeman. And I don't want to live in a town, especially not Easten.'

'But I thought we were going to get married. I like you a lot and I thought you liked me.'

'I do like you Peter. But I can't marry a policeman.'

I thought about how I would never be able to speak of God again. I knew God, how could I keep that from my husband? But I couldn't say any of this to Peter.

'What have you got against policemen? If you are in the police, you're on the right side, they look after you. People have nothing to fear if they don't do anything wrong.' I could sense he was getting angry now.

'I just don't want to be a policeman's wife. And I really don't want to live in Easten.'

'You know I don't like working on the farm. I thought you'd be pleased.'

He got up from the table, and went out of the door. I watched him from the window. He walked up the road briskly, and didn't turn round.

I sat back down at the table, put my head in my hands, and tried to make sense of it all. I hope this doesn't mean that Rayson has got accepted in the police too.

I called Ruffles, went to the allotment, and did some vigorous digging to try to get rid of my mixed up feelings.

I didn't say anything about it to Mother this evening. I feel a bit frightened of Peter now. I have made him angry and he is going to be a policeman. Still at least he will be living in Easten.

Tuesday, 20th September

I worked all day today, and was glad to get out in the sunshine when I left this evening. I could see Sascha wanted to talk to me, so we had our lunch break together on the seats by the station.

'Peter is really upset that you told him you didn't want to marry him.'

'It's not that I don't like Peter, I do. I don't want to be

married to a policeman, and I don't think I want to go and live in Easten either.'

'I want you to marry Peter, then we would be sisters. I could come to see you in Easten.'

'You know I don't like towns much, Sascha. Yes, it would be nice for us to be sisters, but I hope we can still be friends.'

'Yes of course we can. Would you marry Peter if he got a job in Wells as a policeman?'

'No. I don't want to marry a policeman.' I nearly told her that it was because I believe in God. I wanted to. But I stopped myself. I couldn't have that getting back to Peter.

'You are strange sometimes Gelany,' was all she said and left it at that. I was glad she would still be my friend, even though I had upset her brother.

But worse was waiting for me at home this evening. Peter's mother had spoken to my mother about it. She was very quiet whilst we ate dinner, and I thought it was because she had had a hard day at work. After we had cleared the dishes away, I was about to go out with Ruffles, when she stopped me and said,

'Gelany I want to talk to you. Peter's mother was waiting for me, when I left work this evening. She told me Peter asked you to marry him, and you refused. Why Gelany? He's a nice boy. What's wrong with you?'

I could only repeat what I seem to be telling everyone. 'I don't want to marry a policeman and I don't want to live in Easten.'

'Do you want to marry Peter?'

'I don't know. But now he's going to be a policeman, it doesn't matter.'

'Why don't you want to marry a policeman?'

This was a difficult question. I couldn't talk about God,

so I had to be evasive.

'They are on the other side. I don't like them. They scare me.'

'Perhaps if you married one, you would feel differently. You would be on the other side too, and you would have a nice house. They are new and much better than this one. They even have electric power.'

'You know I like the countryside. I don't want to live in Easten.'

'It's got a sandy beach. You've always liked that. That is where you spend all your time when we go there.'

'I'm sorry Mum, I don't want to.'

She turned to the sink to wash up the dishes, then looked round and added, 'You only think of yourself Gelany. You're just like your father.'

Then she started washing up and I assumed our conversation was over. I knew she was annoyed with me, and I felt rejected and misunderstood. I called Ruffles and we walked to the cliffs. I wondered which way to go, and decided to go to the left. I missed my favourite spot by the bushes, looking out to sea. It didn't seem right that Justin should keep me away.

I wondered if I did just think of myself and if that was bad. But surely she is just thinking of herself, when she wants me to marry Peter. She certainly is not thinking of my feelings.

So I am like my father am I? I know she meant it in a bad way, but somehow it made me happy to think that! It makes me want to see him even more.

I stayed out until it was dark and she was in her bedroom when I got back.

Wednesday, 21st September

Mother is cool to me today, not saying much. I think she wants me to marry Peter so she can move to a cottage in Wells. I want to stay here, but I don't think I would like living on my own. Now I have spoilt her plans. But how can a policeman have a wife who believes in God? It is their job to stop people talking about God. How can I tell anyone the real reason why I can't marry Peter? I'm not sure I would have wanted to marry him anyway, even if I hadn't found God. But I suppose he should be more cheerful when he is not working on the farm, but there is no guarantee of that.

I don't want to move to Easten either. At least I think I don't. People are right when they say I love the beach. But what about Gordon? I would see him there. Oh I feel so mixed up, but at least the God thing helps me to make up my mind. I can't marry a policeman and that is that.

Thursday, 22nd September

Gordon brought me some fish again today. He was waiting outside when I went out for a lunch break, as I worked again this afternoon. Sascha was going to have lunch with me, but when she saw Gordon waiting, she said she wouldn't come with us as she had some shopping to do. We took our lunches to the seats by the station.

'So how are you Gelany? Did your cousin get into the police?'

'I don't know about Rayson yet. Peter has got in though, he's Sascha's brother. It has been rather awkward, as everyone seems to think I should marry him. But I don't want to marry a policeman.'

Gordon laughed. 'Is that the only reason? Do you love him?'

'No, I like him.'

'Well you have to do what you think is right. You know if you want to live with him or not.'

'Everyone is cross with me. It seems like my mother, Peter's mother, Peter and Sascha all had my life planned out, unknown to me. I was supposed to marry Peter.'

I was quite surprised I had told Gordon this, but he is very easy to talk to, and it was good to be able to share it with someone, who wasn't cross with me.

He leant forward, with his arm resting on his knee, and looked back into my face, smiling at me. There is something about his tanned face, surrounded by a frame of dark curls, and his smile, that makes my legs go weak. I wished he would hug me, but not where people might see us.

'Gordon, do you believe there's a God who loves us, and made everything?'

'What a funny question, Gelany. I've not thought about it much really. Although when there's a beautiful sunset over the sea, and the bright colours in the sky look like an artist has gone wild with his paint brush, I have sometimes wondered if someone created it all. It does seem harder to believe it all happened by itself really. Anyway we shouldn't be talking like this,' he said looking behind him, as if someone might be listening.

'Well I have these thoughts, so that is why I can't marry a policeman. Please don't tell anyone will you?'

'No. My lips are sealed. But be careful who you talk to about it, there are Informers around. You will be glad to know I am not one of them.'

'What are Informers?'

'People who listen to what others are saying, and if it goes against what the Rulers allow, they tell the police. They get paid for information like that.'

'Oh, I didn't know. What do they look like?'

'Just like ordinary people. Anyway, I think I had better get on the Electra, it is nearly time for it to move. Goodbye Gelany, and don't let anyone push you into doing what you don't want to do, will you?'

'No. Goodbye.' I was sorry to see him go.

Saturday, 24th September

I haven't gone to the Youth Club this evening. I don't feel as if I can face Peter yet. My mother has been quite cool to me since Tuesday, and I expect Peter will be the same. Even Sascha is a bit subdued, and not as chatty and friendly as usual.

I have worked four afternoons during the past two weeks. So I am due five days off from work now (including the day I worked when collecting the poster and things from Easten). Mrs Newsby says she doesn't want me to take them all together, just a day here and there. She said, as I already have plenty of days to take off, I can have some extra money for staying the afternoon Oswald Tansa comes, instead of more time off.

I am going to Uncle Ray's farm tomorrow, even if things aren't good with Rayson. I miss them all.

Sunday, 25th September

When Uncle Ray's dogs saw Ruffles and I coming, they all started barking. It sounded like a greeting, perhaps they have missed Ruffles. Ruby heard the barking, looked out of the window, and came running out of the house to meet me. She had cream round her mouth. I guessed she was helping Aunt Pearl with the cooking.

'Where have you been Gelany? Why haven't you come to see us?'

'I've been catching up on the allotment at the weekends,

as I had to work some afternoons at the Information Centre, the past couple of weeks.'

Aunt Pearl was in the kitchen, surrounded by bowls of food she was preparing. She also asked me why I hadn't been to see them for a few weeks. I was surprised that they both sounded quite cheerful.

Then she said 'Have you heard that Rayson didn't get into the police? He got a letter on Friday. We're all so relieved.'

'Oh Aunt Pearl!' My immediate reaction was to give her a hug and Ruby came up and put her arms around my waist too. I felt tears of relief trickling down my cheeks.

'Go and see him. He's in the sitting room.'

I found Rayson painting a picture of some ruins, with lots of old bricks covered by tangled weeds.

'Hallo Gelany.'

'Hallo. I heard you didn't get into the police. Do you know why?'

'No. But I don't mind. The recruitment day put me off. You're right, they are nasty policemen!' he said, smiling at me.

'Oh Rayson I'm so glad you didn't get in.'

'Well so am I now. After the recruitment day I've been worrying I would get in, and I didn't know if I could get out of it. Peter didn't see anything wrong with it and was still keen on the way home.'

'You know he got in?'

'Yes.'

It was a happy lunch we all had together when Uncle Ray and Jimmy came in. Rayson was one of us again. I was glad no one mentioned Peter asking me to marry him. Perhaps they haven't heard.

I told Mother when I got home that Rayson hadn't got into the police.

'Oh that's good,' she replied.

I wanted to make some comment about it being bad that Peter had got in, but I didn't want to bring the subject up again about marrying Peter, so I just left it.

Monday, 26th September

Everything is ready at work, for the big day tomorrow. I have never seen the place look so neat and tidy.

Sascha said she missed me at Youth Club on Saturday. She said Peter is fine, and I don't have to stay away. So I promised I would go this week. I'm still a bit scared of seeing Peter though, and hope I don't end up agreeing to marry him, just because it seems the easy answer, and will make everyone happy. Except me, of course.

Tuesday, 27th September

Oswald Tansa came to the Information Centre this afternoon. I was dreading it all morning. I had a glimpse of him as I arrived at work. He was going into the Bank and Taxation office building, which is just up the road from us. There was a horse drawn carriage outside, and I saw him get out wearing a colourful cloak. It wasn't so big as the one on Parade Day, and it didn't have a hood down the back.

He was a bit late coming to us, I guess the Tax office took up his time. Mrs Newsby fussed about him, and showed him everything he wanted to see. Sascha helped to find some files too. He didn't seem to notice me and I began to wonder if I was invisible. I sat down at my desk and watched him. Under his cloak he had a waistcoat with gold buttons on. His black trousers were tucked into long socks, with red ribbons tied under the knees, and he had gold buckles on his pointed black shoes. His bushy black beard hid most of his face, except for his dark peering eyes. After two hours, he said the records were satisfactory and left. Thank God for that.

I peered through our window and watched his carriage leave. It drove past with two strong, beautiful, horses at the front. I would love to have horses like that, and a carriage would be nice, but I don't want to marry into that family to get them.

Friday, 30th September

Mother started to talk to me again this evening.

'Have you thought anymore about marrying Peter?'

'I still feel the same. I'm not marrying a policeman.'

'What will you do if I get a cottage in Wells? Will you come with me or stay here on your own? I've been to look at the cottages they are building. They have long gardens, so there is room to grow vegetables in them, but there are also going to be allotments in a field nearby.'

'What about if Daddy comes home. How would he know where to find us, if we've left?'

'He could go and ask Uncle Ray where we are. He knows where the farm is.'

So she does still think there is a possibility he could come back then. I was pleased to hear that.

'I would like to stay here, but I'm not sure I want to live on my own.'

'Well have a think about it. I've been told by Matron that I am likely to get a cottage if I apply for one. I don't really see the point in living out here anymore, if I can live near the hospital. It will save me having to keep walking back and forth to the town.'

'Okay.'

I called Ruffles and went down to the cliffs. I needed to think and have some time talking to God. I wish things didn't have to change. It seems since I became 16, I have to leave childhood behind. Now I have to think about who I want to marry and where I want to live.

I saw Justin, the bird man, in the distance ahead of me. So I sat down and tucked myself into a bush as far as I could, pulling Ruffles in beside me. When he came back, he walked past, and I don't think he saw us. The sun was sinking low in the sky, making long golden streaks across the sea. I told God I didn't know what to do.

6

Unwelcome News

Saturday, 1st October

I went to the Youth Club this evening. Peter said 'hallo' and then went over to the other side of the room, and didn't ask me to play table tennis. He talked to another girl, and they ended up playing table tennis together. I think he was trying to make me jealous. Sascha and I chatted, but I felt awkward being there. I decided I'm not going anymore until he has left to join the Police. Rayson wasn't there.

On the way home, I decided to ask Mrs Newsby, if I can have a day off on Tuesday. I will have a day out in Easten. It will be nice to get away. I was given the extra money in my wages, yesterday. It's not much, but I think it is enough to buy me a new hooded top. The green one is alright, but I would like a blue one. So I could buy that, and keep it for best. Gordon told me that there are caves in the cliffs along the beach, and you can get to them when the tide is out. Ruffles and I could explore the beach, then when Gordon comes in from fishing, I could give him a surprise.

I have been wondering, if I married Gordon, whether we could live in a cottage on the edge of the town. Then I would still live in the countryside, and would also have a sandy beach nearby. I think I would like that, especially with Gordon.

Sunday, 2nd October

When I arrived at Uncle Ray's farm this morning, Ruby came running out the house to meet me. She helps her mother in the kitchen a lot more now, and saw me through the window, as she was preparing beans at the sink. She told me excitedly that Rayson is going to be a baker.

Aunt Pearl was in the kitchen and also Rayson, who was making bread rolls.

We all greeted each other affectionately. It is so lovely to see everyone cheerful again.

'Ruby told me you are going to be a baker. I wondered what she meant. But I see now. What a lot of rolls.'

'No, I *am* going to be a baker.' replied Rayson. 'Mother went to the shops in Wells last week, and Mr Baker mentioned that he could do with extra help, as his father is getting too old to do the job now. Mother offered me!'

'Yes, Mr Baker is prepared to train him. Rayson just has to work there in the mornings, so he can still help on the farm in the afternoons for now,' said Aunt Pearl.

'Well I don't mind that. At least it isn't all day, and I get to do something I enjoy in the mornings.'

'And Jimmy is doing more farm work, now that he has left school. It is good that he actually loves working on the farm,' added Aunt Pearl.

'That's great' I replied. I am so glad things are turning out well for Rayson. I hope God sorts things out for me next.

Uncle Ray did mention that he had heard from my mother, that I had refused to marry Peter. I said 'Yes that's right.' He looked concerned but didn't say anymore about it. So I guess he has accepted it.

Monday, 3rd October

Mrs Newsby said I can have tomorrow off work. She said as everything is so neat and tidy, it is a good time. I am planning to get on the Electra at 8am. I feel quite excited about it.

When I told my mother I am going to Easten, she was quite surprised. She thinks it is a good idea to get another top though. I told her about the caves on the beach, but not about intending to meet Gordon.

Wednesday, 5th October

I had my day out in Easten yesterday. Not everything went as planned. It started out well. It was cool walking up to the station early, but the sun soon came out and warmed things up. Ruffles was pleased to be coming with me, and trotted enthusiastically by my side. After travelling on the Electra for just over two hours, we arrived in Easten about 10.30am.

I went straight down to the beach and was pleased to find the tide was low. I let Ruffles off the lead and we walked along the wet sand, until we reached the tall cliffs. There we found several caves in the black rock which had white swirly stripes running through it. Ruffles ran into every cave, sniffing excitedly. There were small shallow caves, and some really deep ones, with sandy floors. The rocky walls often had shelves of rock, and alcoves like cupboards in them. They would have made interesting houses, if they did not get filled with water at high tide.

I sat down inside one of the caves to eat my lunch early, as I was feeling hungry. I could see fishing boats out on the sea, and I could pick Gordon's out with its distinctive blue and white stripes. I was feeling impatient to see Gordon again and give him a surprise. But as the boats didn't seem to be getting any nearer the shore, I decided to go and buy my new top first.

On leaving the beach, I walked inland, along the road that has most of the shops in it. It was a long time since I had been to the Clothes Factory with my mother, and it was further than I thought. After a long uphill trek, passing all the shops, I found the big factory building on the left hand side, with its own shop at the front.

I left Ruffles tied to a post, before going inside. The shop assistant showed me a little room where I could try clothes on, and I spent quite a bit of time doing this. I knew I could only buy a top, but it was nice to try on other things as well. I might be able to buy something else another day.

Then I walked back down the road to the beach, clutching the parcel with my new, bluebell coloured, top inside. As I got nearer I could see that some of the fishing boats had come in, and Gordon's was one of them. I stopped to look for him, saw his curly black head, and started to walk over to him. But as I did, a girl, with long black plaits, got there before me. She said something to Gordon, he laughed, put his arm round her and pulled her towards him. Then he kissed her on the lips, rather lingeringly. Whilst I was stopped in my tracks, staring disbelievingly, unsure of what to do, he saw me over the girl's shoulder.

I clipped Ruffles lead on, turned around and walked quickly off the beach. He called out my name, but I ignored it, and ran up the road that leads to the station. I started crying and the sobs got stronger and slowed me down. When I got to a field, I collapsed on the grass, and as I was feeling in my pocket for a hankie, I felt someone grab my arm. I looked up and saw Gordon.

'Gelany, what's wrong?'

'I came to see you.' I managed between sobs. 'Then I saw

you kissing that girl.'

He sat down beside me.

'That's Donna. She's my girlfriend. We plan to get married when I get a house.'

'I didn't know. I thought you liked me.'

'I do like you.'

'But I like you a lot Gordon. I didn't realise you had a girlfriend.'

'Gelany, I'm much older than you. I'm twenty six. I'm sorry if I've given you the wrong idea. I do like you a lot, but as a friend. I care about you, as a younger sister.'

I stood up and started to walk away, but he followed me.

'Gelany, I still want us to be friends. Come and meet Donna.'

'No.' I just wanted to cry and cry. 'Not now. I want to go home.'

He walked with me to the station silently, his arm linked in mine, as if I needed support. After helping me up into a carriage, he stroked Ruffles on the head, and looked into my face.

'I'm sorry I haven't told you about Donna. Can we still be friends? I do like you and I'll miss you. Can I still come to see you when I'm in Wells?'

'If you like,' I mumbled. Then the Electra started moving.

On the way home I managed to stop crying, but it felt as though my heart was breaking. I even got a pain in my chest and wondered again if it can break. It felt the same after Mother told me Daddy had run off with another woman. I didn't realise Gordon was ten years older than me. I suppose I have never really thought about it. I don't think it would have changed my feelings if he had told me his age, anyway. Oh I like him so much.

I don't know if I can take any more of this. Maybe I should just marry Peter, then everyone will be happy. But will I be? What about God, He wants to be my friend, and policemen are God's enemies. I think I will keep on being friends with God, and ask Him to sort the mess out.

Friday, 7th October

I wish Mother wouldn't keep talking about the cottage she wants to move to in Wells, I want to stay here. But I don't want to live here on my own, so I suppose I will have to go with her. I know I will miss walking on the cliffs, and it would be too far to walk down here very often. I wish she didn't want to leave.

Sascha told me today, that Peter is moving to Easten on the Saturday after this one. Then he starts work with the police on the following Monday.

The wind was blowing strongly this evening and it was so cool on the cliffs, I walked to Maplehurst Forest, and sat in the cave. I told God I feel so mixed up about everything. The dove came down and sat on a branch outside, and looked at me. It made me feel calm, as if everything didn't matter anymore, just the calmness inside was important. I wish the bird could speak and tell me what to do. But after it left, I felt sure it's not right to marry Peter and go to Easten with him.

Saturday, 8th October

I didn't go to Youth Club this evening. I thought it best to avoid contact with Peter. As he is leaving for Easten next Saturday, I will go again after that. I had a long walk on the cliffs. I knew Justin would be at Youth Club, so it felt like I had the cliffs back to myself.

Sunday, 9th October

I went to Uncle Ray's farm this morning. Rayson is excited, as he is starting work at the baker's tomorrow morning. Ruby said she hopes he brings home lots of cakes.

Tuesday, 11th October

I got a news item for the folder at work today, about Oswald Tansa's visit to the Bank Taxation office. It said he found five people who owed tax, and they are going to be sent to the mines to do work for the Rulers, until they have done enough work to pay off their debts. So they aren't going into prison. They will have to live near Easten though, where the mines are. One is a farmer, who Sascha knows. She said she doesn't know how his wife and young daughter will manage the farm without him.

Saturday, 15th October

Yesterday evening, I was walking along the cliff with Ruffles, when she ran off towards the edge. I called her back, but she ignored me. She lay right on the edge looking down and whining. I went over to her and heard someone calling 'Help, anyone up there?'

I laid down flat and peered over. Down on a grassy ledge was Justin. He said the cliff had fallen and he couldn't get back up. I put my hand down to him, but it wouldn't reach. I said I would go and get help, but didn't know where from. As I ran back, I saw a man coming towards me. He looked a bit unusual, as if a light was glowing around him, and he had a bundle of rope over his arm. I told him about Justin, and he followed me to the cliff edge. Then he lowered the rope down and Justin tied it around his waist. I pulled on the rope, but the man took most of the weight, pulling behind me. It was a relief when we managed to get Justin up to the cliff top. He sat down on the grass and tried to untie the rope, but his hands were grazed and bleeding. I untied it for him, and then he tried to stand up. He said his ankle hurt, but he tested it and could walk on it. Then I turned round to thank the man who had helped us, and he had gone!

Justin asked me who he was. I said I didn't know, and then realised the man hadn't actually said anything. I walked back with Justin, who hobbled along slowly, occasionally exclaiming 'Ouch!' I let him put his arm around my shoulder for support, until we found a branch that we made into a walking stick for him. He told me that he thought he saw the dove out to sea, and as he looked through his binoculars, he must have gone too near the edge. He felt the cliffs give way underneath him, and was very relieved when he landed on a ledge, but wondered how on earth anyone was going to find him. Then he stopped, bent down, gave Ruffles a hug, and said 'Clever dog'.

He talked to me in such a friendly way, even though he was wincing in pain some of the time, that I began to like him.

When we got near to my cottage, he said 'Thank you Gelany.' But then he added, 'I'm surprised you helped me, after what happened to your father. I wouldn't have blamed you if you'd left me down the cliff.'

Now it was my turn to be surprised. 'What do you mean?'

'Well, you know, after my Grandfather told on your father, to the police.'

'I didn't know he did. What was it about?'

'Oh. Well, he ... he kept talking to my father about God, when they worked at Woodalls together. My grandfather didn't like it and warned him to stop, but he didn't. Grandfather thought he was putting my father in danger, so he told the police. That was why they arrested him when he left work.'

'I didn't know. I thought he had just disappeared.'

'Well he did, but my grandfather thinks they shot him, because a policeman standing nearby told him that's what they would do. I'm so sorry Gelany. I've wanted to be friends with you, but I've felt so bad about it.'

'I didn't know. I didn't know where he'd gone.' I was shocked, and could feel the tears welling up in my eyes. As I turned towards our cottage, I felt his hand grab my shoulder.

'Wait Gelany. I'm really sorry.'

'Go away. I hate you. And your family.' I turned and ran indoors.

Mother found me later, sobbing on my bed.

'What's the matter Gelany?'

I couldn't talk I was so upset, I just kept crying.

She put her arm round me. I can't remember the last time she did that.

Ruffles is alright, isn't she?' She looked over at Ruffles curled up in her basket.

'Yes,' I managed, then pulled a hankie out of my pocket, blew my nose rather loudly, and told her 'It's Daddy.' Then I burst out crying again.

'What about him?'

'He was shot. He's dead!'

'How do you know that?' I blew my nose again and took a deep breath.

'Justin told me.'

'How does he know he was shot?'

Now it was my turn to ask some questions.

'Why didn't you tell me the truth? You said he ran off with another woman. Justin told me Daddy talked about

God at work, and he was warned not to, but carried on talking to Justin's father about it. Then Mr Ditchling told the police. They saw him being arrested when he left work, and a policeman told them he would be shot.'

The colour drained from her face, and it turned white.

'I didn't say he ran off with another woman. I said he had someone else and he had to choose. That someone was God. I knew he was in trouble at work, and I told him to stop talking about God, that was the night you heard us arguing.'

'Why didn't you tell me the truth?'

'I didn't want you to believe in God, and get into trouble too. Daddy didn't have to carry on talking about God, even if he believed in Him, he could have kept it to himself. He chose God over us Gelany. He knew it would get him into trouble. I warned him.'

Now it was her turn to burst into tears. She added 'He left us Gelany. He didn't have to. It was his choice.'

'He's dead now. All my hopes of finding him are gone.' I replied.

Then we both sobbed together. I wondered about sharing with her that I knew God now, but didn't think it was a good idea. It might increase her pain, and worry her too. Perhaps I can just keep God to myself, although He does keep popping out sometimes, what with the miracles that have been happening.

'I didn't know what happened to Daddy,' she continued. 'When I went to see his parents, they said a policeman they knew, told them he'd been arrested. Gelany all he had to say was that he didn't believe in God anymore, and pretend he didn't. I'm sure they would have let him go. Why didn't he?'

She cried again and it was as if all her pain of the last eight years came pouring out at once. I temporarily forgot my anguish, and put my arm around her. It felt strange and awkward, but the frostiness I felt towards her before, began to melt inside me.

'Let's go to bed,' she said 'We can talk about this more tomorrow.'

She kissed me on the forehead and left the room. I sat on my bed for a while, hugging my knees, and staring at the wall, just feeling stunned. Then I laid down and immediately fell asleep, exhausted.

Sunday, 16th October

I didn't go to Youth Club yesterday, and I haven't gone to Uncle Ray's farm today. I don't feel as if I can face anyone yet. I worked on the allotment yesterday, and was worrying all the time what I would do if Justin came. But he didn't, so I was glad about that. Perhaps his ankle still hurts.

Mother hasn't said anymore about Daddy, but she is being extra nice to me, and I feel closer to her too. I went down to the cave in Maplehurst Forest this morning, and had a good think about everything. I tried to remember what Daddy looked like and I couldn't, and I got upset about it. There's a big hurt inside me, as if Daddy has died inside me, it's an awful feeling. I think I will move with Mother to the cottage in Wells. I don't like Justin and his family. How could they do that to Daddy? If I stay here I will have to keep avoiding him on the allotment, and on the cliffs, and I will be alone in the cottage. There is nothing to keep me here now. Daddy isn't going to come back.

I told Mother this evening that I will move with her. She was pleased. She said it will be a few months until the cottages are ready, but she will put her name down for one. I wish it was sooner, I want to get away.

Monday, 17th October

Sascha and I walked home together after work. She asked me why I didn't go to Youth Club, and told me that Peter had moved to Easten on Saturday morning, so he wasn't there. She was feeling lonely without both of us, but Rayson came over and sat with her. He told her all about his new job, working at the bakers'. He's really enjoying it, even though he has to get up very early to start making the bread. She wished Peter could have got another job, instead of joining the police. She wonders when she will see him again and what he will be like. Will he be more like a policeman and less like a brother now?

I told her about rescuing Justin off the cliff, and then him telling me about Daddy being shot. She was horrified to think anyone would tell the police that someone was talking about God, and that the police would shoot them. I said I was too upset to go to Youth Club. It was awful to lose hope, that Daddy might still be alive somewhere. I could tell she didn't know what to say, but we had reached her house by then. She just said 'I'm sorry Gelany', and gave me a hug, which was nice. Perhaps I will like living nearer Sascha, although we won't be walking home together anymore, when I live in Wells.

Tuesday, 18th October

I walked along the cliffs this evening, hoping that Justin's ankle will keep him away for a while. I came across the rope that we had used, lying on the cliff. It made me wonder about the man who brought it, just when we needed it. I think it must have been God who sent him. It had a miracle feeling about it.

I sat down by the bushes, and stared at the sunlight glittering on the sea. I realised I have been so busy being upset that Daddy is dead, I hadn't thought much about why he was killed. He knew God! How fantastic is that. It made me feel sort of connected with him, and warm inside.

I wonder who else believes in God but can't say because they would get into trouble. Wouldn't it be nice if we could get together and talk openly about it. I suppose that was what they did in those churches 100 years ago, before the Tansas took over. I wish I could find someone else who believes in God.

When I got home, I re-read the copy of the letter I found in the cave. It says our spirits go to be with God when we die. So Daddy is still alive, but with God. That makes me feel a bit better. It means I shall see him again one day. Won't that be lovely.

Wednesday, 19th October

Mother told me this evening, that she is going to Easten for training. She will be away for five days next week, and a nurse from Easten will come to take her place, as they can't manage without her. She said they are discovering new methods of treatment and she is going to be taught some of them. She asked if I will be alright on my own. If not, she thinks Aunt Pearl would have me to stay.

I said I thought I would be alright here, I've got Ruffles to keep me company.

Thursday, 20th October

Gordon came to visit me after work today.

'Here's two rare bream fish just for you,' he said as he handed me a brown paper parcel.

'You don't have to do that.'

'I like giving you some fish. I'll never forget that miracle catch you showed us.'

I took it from him and we went towards the station,

walking in silence until we sat down on the seat.

'Am I forgiven?' he asked.

How could I resist that smiling handsome face, with his dark eyes looking straight into mine.

'There's nothing to forgive you for. Why do you come to see me Gordon?'

'I like you. But as a friend you understand,' he said smiling at me. 'How are you?'

'I've found out my father was arrested by the police and shot. That was why he didn't come home that day.'

'Oh, Gelany. I'm so sorry. Why did they do that?'

'He talked about God at work.'

'Oh, that's awful. Did you know he believed in God?

'No. But I believe in God too. I found Him for myself.'

'Shush Gelany,' he said looking behind us, but there was no one around. 'You will be careful who you talk to about God, won't you.'

'Of course. Don't you tell anyone will you Gordon. I've only told you.'

'No never. But it is something you need to keep to yourself.'

We talked about fishing, Donna, and the house they are hoping to get. He said he wants me to go and meet her. Then we heard the horn that sounds before the Electra starts moving.

'Oh, I have to go. Bye Gelany,' He rushed to the station, but by the time he got there, the carriages were moving away. So he jumped onto the track, put the fish box over the back of a seat into a carriage, climbed over after it, and then waved his arm at me.

I wished we could have had more time together. It always seems too short. I'm not sure I want to meet Donna.

Saturday, 22nd October

There was a man working on Justin's allotment this afternoon, and I think it was his father. He said 'Hallo Gelany' in a friendly way. I mumbled 'Hallo' back, and then ignored him. How can I be friends with someone who got my father into trouble? As soon as I had finished picking the runner beans, I went home.

I went to the Youth Club this evening, and sat with Sascha. Justin was across the room and I could see he was still limping. I thought, good, he won't be back on the allotment or the cliffs for a while. I saw him look over at me, but I looked away and started talking to Sascha. They haven't heard from Peter yet, and I could tell she's worried about him. Rayson came and sat with us. He said he misses Peter too. We played table tennis together, and each had turns at one against two. I was relieved Rayson didn't call Justin over. I haven't told him yet about what Justin's family did to Daddy, and I couldn't do it there.

Sunday, 23rd October

I went to Uncle Ray's Farm this morning. Aunt Pearl was in the kitchen with Ruby, who had her arms in a bowl of flour. She had flour up to her elbows, on her nose, in her hair, and also over the table. She said she was making pastry.

Aunt Pearl asked 'Why didn't you come last weekend? Rayson wanted to tell you about his job at the bakers'. We missed you.'

'Yes and I wanted to show you how Beauty comes when I call her name and give her some food. I'll show you later.'

'I didn't come because I was feeling upset. I found out Daddy was shot after he disappeared. So now I know he's dead.' I just about stopped myself from crying again.

'Oh Gelany. Is that what happened to him?' said Aunt

Pearl.

'Why was he shot dead?' asked Ruby, and I began to wonder if I should have said it in front of her.

'He talked about God at work. Someone told the police. The Rulers say that no one must speak about God.'

'We thought something like that might have happened, but we hoped he was still alive somewhere,' said Aunt Pearl.

Ruby didn't say anymore but looked thoughtful. Aunt Pearl told Uncle Ray, when he came in with Jimmy. Uncle Ray just said 'I'm so sorry Gelany'.

After lunch Ruby took me to the barn to see her kitten. Holding a small dish with some chicken that was over from our meal, she stood at the door of the barn and called 'Beauty!'

The kitten's head popped up out of the basket and she came running over.

'See. And she does it with just a tiny piece of food too. The other kittens don't.'

'That's great. She really does know her name.'

She gave Beauty the meat and then picked her up to cuddle her. We sat down on the hay, where a warm shaft of sunlight was streaming in through the door. Then the dreaded question came.

'Gelany, what is God?'

'Well some people believe He created everything, you know all the animals, plants, trees, sea, sky and people.'

'And the flowers. He must have made the flowers, they're so beautiful.'

'But the Rulers don't believe in Him, and say we mustn't speak about him.'

'That's silly. Just because they don't believe in Him, it doesn't mean it's not true.'

'Yes that's right. But you mustn't talk about God to

anyone, not even at school, because it will get you into bad trouble.'

'You mean like your Daddy. I think that's awful.'

I was getting a bit worried, now that I had started Ruby thinking about God.

'Ruby you must promise me you won't talk about God to anyone, except your family or me. And if you do say anything to us, make sure no one else can hear you. I don't want anything bad to happen to you. Do you promise?'

'Yes, I promise. I don't want to be shot dead.'

7

A Grand Reunion

Tuesday, 25th October

Mother went to Easten early yesterday morning. It seems very quiet here on my own, even though she doesn't make much noise. I'm glad I have Ruffles to keep me company.

After work today, when I was walking past the Post Office, a lady who was standing in the doorway, called out to me 'You're Gelany aren't you?' After I said I was, she told me that she had a letter for me, that arrived yesterday. I was surprised to hear that, never having had a letter before. She asked why my Mother hadn't been in to collect the post, as she usually comes to see if she has got any, after work. I told her about the course she had gone on.

She went inside the Post Office and came out holding a small brown envelope. I looked at the name on the front, and it was definitely for me. I thanked her, put the letter in my bag and started walking home. I thought it was from Peter and I wanted to wait until I was indoors before I opened it. Sascha was not with me as she had some shopping to do. She would have made me open it straight away.

When I got home and opened it, I got a surprise. It wasn't

from Peter, it was from my Grandmother. Yes, I have a Grandmother! This is what it said:

The Old House
Gleethorpe Road
Easten.

Dear Gelany
I am writing to you because I am ill and will probably die soon. I do so want to see you before I go. I have sent you a birthday card every year, but I have never heard back from you. I can understand if your mother doesn't want you to see me anymore, but as you are 16 this year, that means you are old enough to make up your own mind about it.
Please will you come to see me. I have always loved you and longed to see you again. I know your mother is upset about what happened to Timothy, and thinks he should have kept quiet about his beliefs. I expect I would feel the same as your mother, if it had happened to me. I don't know what else I can say. Please at least write to me, even if you can't visit.
With much love from
Grandma Lantern.

I will ask Mrs Newsby if I can have some time off work this week. Then I could go and visit Grandma, without having to tell Mother. I don't suppose she would want me to go. But I want to go.

Wednesday, 26th October

I told Mrs Newsby my Grandmother is sick and asked if I could take some time off this week, to visit her in Easten. She said I can have Thursday and Friday off, as I may want to stay there overnight. That was nice of her. Sascha was surprised to hear that I have a Grandmother, and I told her it was a surprise to me too.

Saturday, 29th October

I've got two long exciting days to catch up on in my journal, so I am writing this in the morning, before I go down to the allotment. On Thursday morning, I put some overnight things in my backpack and set off, to get on the Electra at 8am. Ruffles trotted along at my side and I hoped my grandmother liked dogs.

When we got to Easten, I went to the Information Centre, and asked a lady there if she knew where Gleethorpe Road was. She said it was on the other side of the town. She told me to go past the beach and up Cliff Road to the top, where I would find Gleethorpe Road on the left. I thanked her, collected Ruffles and walked along the road by the beach. I could see Gordon's boat out on the sea, and felt a pang of sadness about what happened last time. But then I quickly turned my mind back to the anticipation of seeing Grandma and I hoped she was still alive and that I was in time.

I found The Old House at the end of Gleethorpe Road, on the edge of the countryside. I knocked on the door, but as no one answered, I tried the door handle and it opened. I tied Ruffles up to a post, and went cautiously inside, calling 'Hallo Grandma, are you there?'

A faint voice called back 'Is that you Gelany?' I opened a door to the room where the voice came from, and there was Grandma lying in bed. Her face broke into a wide smile when she saw me and she put out her hand towards me.

'Is it really you Gelany?'

'Yes'

'Come closer my dear, here sit down by my bed. No,

give me a hug first.'

I bent over her and she put her arms around me and pulled me towards her. I was a bit overwhelmed, so pulled away and sat on the chair.

'Well, at last. How lovely to see you. What a fine young lady you've grown into.'

'What is wrong with you Grandma?'

'Oh just old age I expect. The doctor doesn't really know and says he can't do anything. I'm so glad you've come. I've been longing to see you for years. Did you get my birthday cards? I sent you one every year.'

'No. I didn't know you were still alive.'

'I suppose your mother didn't let you have them. She didn't want anymore to do with us when your father was taken. I think she blamed us for bringing him up to know God.'

'Do you know God Grandma?'

'Yes. So did your Grandfather. What about you Gelany?'

'I've got to know Him recently.'

'I'm so glad.'

'Is Grandfather still alive?'

'No. He died two years ago. When I die I shall go to be with him again, and with God, so I'm not scared.'

'It's only recently I found out that Daddy was arrested, and shot, for talking about God. I thought he had just disappeared and I didn't know why.'

'How do you know he was shot?'

I told her what Justin had told me.

'They may not have shot him,' she replied. 'A policeman, who went to school with Timothy, told us that he saw Tim in the Prison, about a year later, when he took another prisoner there. I've carried on hoping that he is still in the prison, and one day will be allowed to come out.'

'Do you really think he might still be in the prison? Where is it?'

'He might be Gelany. But I don't know where it is.'

'I wish I could find out, then I could go there, and if he's still alive, they might let me see him.'

'We have some relatives in Soumarket. One of them was in prison once, Daniel Lantern is his name. He is married to Susanne. They might know. But don't get yourself into any danger Gelany.'

I made Grandma and I some dandelion coffee, and sat by her bed. We chatted about where I worked and the allotment and then I remembered Ruffles was outside and asked if she liked dogs. She said she loves them. So I fetched Ruffles, who put her front paws on Grandma's bed, and she got lots of strokes.

A lady who lived nearby came in at lunchtime, and brought Grandma a bowl of soup and some bread. When Grandma told her who I was, she asked if I would like some soup. But I had some sandwiches with me, so I ate those.

After lunch we carried on chatting, catching up with the last eight years, until Grandma looked sleepy. I left her to have a nap and took Ruffles out in the garden. I could tell it once had been a lovely garden, but now was rather overgrown with weeds. Only the vegetable plot looked cared for. Grandma told me they had moved there six years ago.

I found a path leading into the fields and went and sat down on a log with a view over the valley. The river ran along the bottom, going out to the sea. Inland, I could see the rooftops of the settlement of houses, where the Rulers live.

When Grandma woke up, she gave me some money and asked me to go and buy some food for dinner and to stay the night. I said I would. I was aware this may be my last chance to spend some time with her. In the evening, she pointed to a picture, which was leaning up against a vase on a shelf, and asked me to get it for her. She looked at it and then handed it back to me and told me it was my father. Someone had drawn it, and given it to Daddy, and he had passed it on to her.

As I stared at the picture, she told me it was just like Daddy. There was something familiar about it and I began to remember what he looked like. It was as if he was in the room with me again. I started to cry, and Grandma said come and have a hug, so I went over to her and let her hug me. She said I could have the picture if I would like it. I told her I would love to have it.

That night I slept on the sofa in her sitting room. It was comfortable and I was tired, so I soon fell sleep. But in the morning I had a very vivid dream. I dreamt that I went to the settlement where the Rulers live. There was a very high wall all around it, with a big gate in it, which was shut. Next to the wall, were some tall plants with bright red flowers and large seed pods on. I collected some seed pods, and took them back to Grandma's house. After grinding them up, I put them into Grandma's drinks and she became well, and got out of bed. The dream was so vivid, that when it was finished, I sat up fully awake, wondering if it had really happened.

Looking at my watch, I saw it was time to get up. I got washed and dressed, and went to see Grandma. She was awake and I told her all about my dream.

'That would be the Kampala flower seeds. People used to grow them, to use as medicine for many ailments. Now only the Rulers grow them, inside their compound, and no one else is allowed to. They sell the seeds in a shop in town, but they are very expensive, and I can't afford them.'

My dream had left such an impression on me, I told her I would go and see if I could find any plants.

'No Gelany, that is too dangerous. Anyway you won't be able to get into their settlement.'

'In my dream, some plants were growing outside their wall. I'd like to go and see if it's true. I've only just found you Grandma, I don't want you to die.'

'But I don't want anything to happen to you either, Gelany.'

'I'll be very careful. Just go and look to see if there are any plants growing outside, like in my dream.'

I decided to leave Ruffles behind, as it would be easier to creep up to the wall on my own, without wondering what my dog was doing. I walked down the hill into the town, over the bridge, and then followed a path beside the river, as I knew it would lead to the Tansas' settlement. The path ran through a wood for a while, until it came to a clearing, and then I could see the high wall around their land. I looked out from behind some bushes, trying to see if it was safe to go any nearer. There was a watchtower on the wall in front of me, but I couldn't see anyone in it. I pulled my hood up over my head, and crept nearer, looking all the time to make sure I wasn't being watched. I was really pleased to find some plants growing next to the wall, with large red flowers and seed pods on, just like in my dream. The plants must have grown from seeds that had blown over the wall. As I was picking the last pod and was about to put it in my backpack, I heard a shout. I looked up at the watchtower, and saw a man pointing at me.

Pulling my hood further over my head, and putting my backpack on, I started walking quickly, back to the riverside path. Then I heard a voice shout 'There he is,' so I started running. It wasn't easy with stones and tree roots sticking up out of the path. At one place, I tripped over, looked back, and saw two men running towards me. I got up and tried to run faster, but could hear by their pounding feet, getting nearer. I felt so scared, and was getting out of breath. 'Help me God,' I gasped. Then a very weird thing happened. My tense body suddenly felt light and I started feeling sleepy. Oh no, I thought, I'm going to faint. I did seem to pass out briefly, and when I came to, I was still running! But instead of being by the river, I was already in Grandma's road. Anyway I was aware a miracle had taken place, and there was no sign of the men.

After entering Grandma's house, I took off the green hooded jumper and hid it under the sofa, just in case they should come looking for me. It is a good thing that lots of people wear the same tops, and I don't think they saw my face. I told Grandma what had happened and showed her the seeds. She said she was very glad I got back safely, and told me where I could find a bowl and pestle in the kitchen, to grind them up in. I locked the doors first, just in case the men should come, and threw all the pods on the fire as soon as I had got the seeds out. It didn't take very long to grind them to a powder, and I put it in a bowl and showed it to Grandma. She asked me to give her a spoon, a jug of water, and a bottle of her elderflower cordial, and she would stir it into her drinks.

It was hard to say Goodbye to Grandma, but I had to get home before Mother came back. Grandma thanked me for what I did, and promised to write to let me know if the Kampala medicine worked. I said I would ask the Post Office lady to keep any letters for me there, and not give them to Mother. I had a spare pair of trousers in my bag, which were a different colour to the ones I was wearing when

I was chased, so I put them on. Grandma let me have an old top of my father's to wear home, in case the men were still looking for someone wearing a green hooded top. I packed my jumper and trousers in the backpack under my other things, and put on Daddy's brown top. She said Father had worn it when he was a bit older than me. It was rather large, but I liked it.

There were quite a few policemen standing around in the town, and I wanted to look at them to see if one was Peter. But I thought it was better to keep my head down and keep moving. I held Ruffles lead and kept her close to my side and walked quickly up to the station. I was glad I had left her behind when I went to the Tansas' place, otherwise they would be looking for someone with a dog. She probably would have given me away.

It was a relief when the Electra started moving at 3.30pm, and no one had stopped me. I took the picture of Daddy out of my bag, and stared at it for a long time. It helped me remember what he looked like, and lots of memories about him came flooding back. I spent the journey trying to remember those times when I was young and he was around. I got home just after 6pm.

Mother's not come back yet, but I expect she will be here soon. I just realised I'm not sure how I can explain the brown top, so I think I had better hide it, and the picture too.

Sunday, 30th October

I was on the allotment yesterday afternoon, when I saw Justin coming down the road. I quickly put Ruffles on her lead, grabbed the beans and headed home the long way round, in order to avoid him. I don't need to go to the allotment much now, just a few things left to harvest. I know what times Justin usually goes to there, so I will try to avoid them. I think I will start going to the Craft Barn to make baskets.

Mother was at home when I got back. She seemed tired but said she learnt some new things. She said she was glad to be home, but is still looking forward to moving to Wells. I would have liked to have told her that Grandma said Daddy could be alive, and in prison. But she doesn't know I visited Grandma, and I don't want to give her false hope about Daddy. I need to find out if he is alive first.

I went to the Youth Club in the evening and managed to tell Sascha about my trip to Grandma's, before Rayson came over. I didn't want to tell him, in case it got back to Mother. I told her I went to get some medicine for Grandma and about being chased. I didn't tell her about being transported from the wood to Grandma's road, when I was running away from the men. I don't think she would understand about miracles. She said she was glad I didn't get caught. I wondered if I had said too much and made her promise not to tell Peter. She said of course she wouldn't, she would never put me in danger. I felt a bit uneasy, and wished Peter hadn't become a policeman, it seems to complicate things. I hope it will never come between us, and that she doesn't have to choose whose side to take.

This morning I visited Uncle Ray and family. They all seem fine. How I longed to tell them about finding Grandma, but I knew they would probably tell Mother, and I don't want to upset her. I am getting on better with her at the moment and it is nicer that way.

When I took Ruffles on the cliffs this evening, I sat down and started thinking about Daddy. What if he is still in prison and Justin was wrong about him being shot? I wish I could find out. I asked God, 'How can I find out if Daddy is in the prison?' Then a plot started hatching in my mind. I need to find out where the prison is. Grandma said the relatives in Soumarket might know, so I'll go there and ask Isabella if she knows Daniel Lantern who went to prison. That means I need to ask Mrs Newsby for another day off. I have two days left, so I'll ask her tomorrow.

Monday, 31st October

Mrs Newsby said I have only just had some days off, so she wants me to wait a few weeks. I think she was in a bad mood. She wants me to make sure I have caught up with all my work first. It's so hard to wait, I just want to find out where the prison is, visit it, and see if Daddy is in there.

I went to the Post Office after work, and asked the lady who gave me the letter, if she would keep anymore letters for me there, to pick up myself, and not give them to Mother. She said she would and winked at me. I felt embarrassed as she obviously thought the letter would be from a boyfriend, but I let her think it. She said if she got one, she would look out for me when I go past.

I called in at the Craft Barn to ask Mrs Strawler if I could come and make baskets again. She said that I could, and she had plenty of straw, but she was waiting for some more willow twigs to be delivered. She told me to go back on Saturday afternoon.

Thursday, 3rd November

This evening, I went to the cupboard where I keep the carrots, expecting to find the last few to use for dinner, but there were still lots there. They should have run out ages ago! I haven't really missed the food the Policemen took for the Rulers, it is as if God is making up the difference, and looking after me. Isn't that amazing. He must know how much I like carrots too.

Saturday, 5th November

In the afternoon, I went to the Craft Barn, and started making baskets again. Sascha wasn't there, as she only makes baskets on weekday afternoons. She works on the farm on Saturdays, usually making butter. Mrs Strawler said I can come in any weekday afternoon too. Two older ladies were there, busily making baskets and chatting continuously to each other, but I didn't have anyone to talk to. Mrs Strawler came in sometimes, but most of the time she was in the shop, which is attached to the barn.

I was a bit slower at making them, than last time I went, but I expect I will get quicker with practice, I usually do. My fingers were rather sore when I left, they need to toughen up too. I managed to finish one small fruit basket, and Mrs Strawler inspected it, then paid me for it. She gives me half the money that she charges in the shop.

This evening, I went to the Youth Club, and played table tennis with Sascha and Rayson. There was a skittles match, which Rayson and Jimmy played in, and Sascha and I watched. Jimmy beat everyone, he is really good at it. Next Saturday, there is going to be a country dance, and I feel quite excited about that. Sascha said there are some dances where you start with one partner and then you keep moving on to other partners, and do the dance routine again. She says those are fun, but I am a bit worried I may end up dancing with Justin.

Sunday, 6th November

After I had lunch with Uncle Ray's family today, Ruby asked me to go down to the barn with her, to take some leftovers to the kittens. She said to me on the way that she wanted to tell me something. She handed me a kitten, and then picked up Beauty and we sat down on a bale of hay cuddling them.

'Gelany, I've been thinking about God. I think it's true that He made everything, and He made Beauty.' She lifted up her kitten and kissed it on the nose, then continued, ' I wanted to talk to Him, but was scared someone would hear me. But I've found I can talk to Him in my head and I hear Him speaking back to me! It feels like He's speaking to me down here.' She put her hand on her chest, near her heart.

'That's really great Ruby, but keep it all to yourself won't you.'

' The other day I saw a beautiful white bird flying around over our fields, like the one we saw on the Parade Day. I started running around underneath it, and the dogs came over and joined me. I put my arms out like wings, and it felt like I was a bird too. It carried on flying above me for a while, getting close sometimes, and then it flew off. It made me feel so joyful.'

'Oh Ruby. Have you told anyone else about it?'

'Only Hanily. She's my best friend at school. I haven't said anything about God, like you told me, only about the white bird.'

'That bird is a special one, it's called a dove. I don't think you should tell anyone about that either, because I think God only sends the dove down to people who know Him.'

'Do you really think that? Then God knows I know Him.'

'Of course He does. But you don't want anyone else to know you know Him. If the Police get to hear about it, you will be in trouble. Don't even tell Hanily anymore, okay?'

'Alright. I can tell you though, can't I?'

'Yes, but only when no one else can hear. Let it be a secret between you and God, and only me if you want to share it with somebody. Alright?'

'Yes. It's hard to keep it to myself, but I know I have to.

I know your Daddy was shot for talking about it.'

It is lovely that Ruby has found God, but I feel a bit worried. I asked God to keep her safe, and stop her talking to anyone else about it.

Wednesday, 9th November

I received a horrible news sheet today at work. It was headed 'All Doves to be Shot' and said 'There have been sightings of the dove on Tansay again. Since this bird is a pest, the Rulers have decided it should be shot and eradicated from our Island. Anyone seeing a dove should report it to the Police. A reward is offered for any information.'

I felt like tearing it up and didn't know what to do. I sat at my desk and asked God, and heard Him whisper 'Don't worry, I will take care of the dove.' So I put the sheet in the folder.

As I walked on the cliffs this evening, I looked for the dove. But all I could see were seagulls, who were calling out with their piercing shrieks, breaking the silence. They looked like they were enjoying the wind, keeping their outstretched wings completely still, and gliding on it. I wish I could do that.

It gets dark early now, and I haven't seen Justin walking on the cliffs lately, thank goodness.

Thursday, 10th November

Gordon came to see me today, and gave me some fish again. We automatically walked to the station. It was drizzling with rain, so we went in the shelter at the station and sat down there.

'Since I last saw you, I found out I have a Grandma living in Easten. She wrote to me and I went to see her. She told me that my father was seen in prison, a year after he was arrested. So he wasn't shot, at least he wasn't straight away. Anyway it has given me hope that he may still be alive.'

'That would be good. He might come home one day.'

'Yes. But I'm going to try to find out where the prison is, and see if he is still in there.'

'How will you do that?'

'Grandma told me about someone in Soumarket who could tell me where it is, because they've been there.'

'Be careful, you don't want to end up in prison too.'

'No, I've got to find out though.'

'I wish I could help. It's a man's job really.'

'What do you mean? I've only got to find the prison, then ask someone guarding it, if he could tell me if my father's in there.'

'You're a brave girl Gelany. Either that or naïve.' He laughed.

'Stop laughing at me,' I said, pushing him playfully with my hands.

He grabbed my hands, and it felt so nice. I laughed too. I wished he would put his arms around me. Then he talked about how rough the sea has been lately, until the horn sounded.

'Well I'd better get on the Electra. See you again soon Gelany.'

Friday, 11th November

I have been to the Craft Barn three afternoons this week. Sascha was there too and it was nice to have someone to chat with. We sit on the opposite side of the barn, to the older women. They talk practically non-stop, I don't know how they find so much to talk about. Sascha said her family still haven't heard from Peter. I wonder why he doesn't write to them.

Saturday, 12th November

I went to the country dance at the Youth Club. There was a band with a father and his two sons. The father and one son played fast music on violins really well, and the other son had two hand drums, that he beat furiously. I really liked the music, and it did make you want to dance. Mr Bunny called out the steps.

Sascha and I danced together for some of the dances, then Rayson came over and asked her to dance with him. He said sorry to me for taking her away. But when Jimmy saw I was sitting on my own, he came over and asked me to dance. He is so much fun, he made me laugh. He did all the steps in an exaggerated way, leaping about. It made me quite tired, so I was glad to sit down for a couple of dances. I saw Justin dancing with a girl, whose name is Sunita.

The next dance was one where you kept changing partners, and Jimmy came over to get me. I was going to protest that I was too tired, because I didn't want to dance with Justin, when I saw him sit down and rub his ankle. So I let Jimmy pull me up by my hand and lead me onto the floor. Sunita tried to get Justin up again, but he pointed to his foot, so I guessed it was hurting. Everyone, except Justin, was up on the floor, and I must have danced with half of them. Some were quite awkward at dancing, and others pushed you about confidently. We did several dances, but I didn't like changing partners all the time, so I was glad when it was over.

The next dance was for four couples and I danced with Jimmy, and Rayson with Sascha, and two other couples. It was so complicated that we kept making mistakes, and we were laughing so much, it made us make more mistakes. In the end my sides hurt, but it did feel good to laugh.

I saw two policemen come in and watch for a little while,

then they went out again. Just checking I suppose. I wondered if they ever have any fun, as they always look so serious.

I walked back with Rayson and Jimmy, as far as their farm, then had to go on in the dark by myself. I was glad the moon was shining, as I had forgotten to take my torch. On my way home I wished Daddy was there, so that I could tell him all about my first dance. Mother asked me what the dance was like, so I told her. She looked wistful and said that she met Daddy at a dance in Wells. I didn't know that.

8

Death and Life

When I was at Uncle Ray's farm yesterday, he mentioned at lunch, that his friend had told him about the news sheet, saying the police are going to shoot and eradicate the dove. He said it is a shame because it is such a lovely bird, and he doesn't think it does any harm. He said he has seen it flying over the farm lately. I looked at Ruby, and saw her face screw up. As soon as we went to the barn she started crying.

'It's my fault Gelany, I shouldn't have told Hanily. Now the dove is going to be shot. I can't bear it.'

She cuddled up to me and cried into my jumper, making a big wet patch.

'It's alright Ruby. You don't know that she said anything. I've seen the dove lots of times, and I expect other people have noticed it. There could be more than one dove too, as they would all look the same.'

'You don't think it's my fault?'

'No. Anyway God can look after the doves. He is cleverer than the police.'

'I hope so.'

I sounded more confident than I felt, as I secretly hoped so too.

Wednesday, 16th November

I received a news sheet today, that said the Tansa family are pleased to announce that they have designed a flag for the Island. I wasn't pleased when I saw a drawing of it. It has a face of one of the Tansa brothers at each of the four corners, with their names written underneath, and in the middle is the Island's name, 'Tansay'.

Mrs Newsby told me that she had had a letter, from the Easten Information Centre, saying we have to put a flag up on the roof of our building, and use a rubber stamp with the same symbol on, for documents. She said future news sheets are going to have the flag in the top right hand corner. I don't think I will like to be reminded, all the time, of who rules our Island. I expect other people will feel the same.

Saturday, 19th November

I worked on the allotment this morning doing lots of digging. So I didn't go to the Craft Barn this afternoon as my arms and legs were tired, and anyway I prefer going on a weekday afternoon when Sascha is there. As the sun was shining, I decided to go for a walk along the cliffs with Ruffles.

We walked down the road from our cottage, and when we reached the cliffs, I could see two figures in the distance. Thinking one might be Justin, I walked in the opposite direction, going towards Maplehurst Forest. The seagulls were flying and calling out in an agitated way, as if they had been disturbed. Then I noticed another white bird flying on its own, and as it came towards me, I saw it was the dove. It flew along beside me, until I reached the forest, where

Ruffles carried on into the trees, but I stopped to look at the dove.

Then a shout behind me, made me look round and I saw the two men running towards me. One of them had a long gun in his hand. Oh no, I thought, it's the dove murderers. I waved my hands at the dove frantically shooing it away, then ran into the forest to look for Ruffles. As I ran along, I could hear twigs snapping behind me, so I knew they were following me, and I thought I was in deep trouble. Ruffles went down the track that led to the cave, and I followed her, thinking it was a good place to hide.

As I was cowering at the back of the cave, holding onto Ruffles, a dark figure appeared at the entrance. The sunlight was behind him, so I couldn't see his face, and I felt scared.

The man looked at me, came towards me, then exclaimed, 'Gelany! I thought it was you.'

It was Peter! I was speechless. He didn't have a gun, the other man had it, and I hoped he wouldn't be coming into the cave next.

'You mustn't scare the doves away, we have orders to shoot them. Anyone who tries to stop us will be arrested. Do be careful Gelany.'

Then we heard the other man call,

'Anyone down there Peter?'

He went to the cave entrance and shouted back 'No, there's no one here.'

He started to leave, so I whispered 'Peter.' He turned round and I said 'Thank you'. Then he turned his back on me and walked out quickly.

Soon after that, I heard a gun fire.

I stayed in the cave for a while, waiting for them to go, then put Ruffles on a lead and crept out. To my horror, on the ground above the cave, I found the dove lying on its back, with blood on its feathers where it had been shot. I picked it up and cradled it in my arms. It was still warm, and its feathers felt soft and silky. As I walked home carrying it, I started crying, and my tears fell onto the bird, washing all the blood away, until it was pure white again. 'Oh God, I loved that bird. You said you would take care of it,' I said.

Suddenly the dove coughed, shuffled upright onto on my hands, and stood up on its feet. It looked up at me and then flew away across the sea. I was amazed and relieved.

I walked home thinking about what had happened. Peter didn't tell on me, and risked getting himself into trouble. I feel so grateful to him. He could have still been cross with me, for refusing to marry him, and got his own back. I wish I could have talked with him.

In the evening, I went to the Youth Club and I couldn't wait to tell Sascha that I had seen Peter. But she was very excited, and told me that she had seen him too. He called in at the farm on his way back to the station, just to let his parents know he was alright. He had only been able to stay for about fifteen minutes, but enough time to have a drink and a chat. He said he had been sent with an armed policeman, because he knew the area, and there had been reports of dove sightings around here. I wondered if Justin would have reported it, then dismissed that thought, as he is a bird lover. But someone could have overheard him, if he has spoken out about seeing a dove.

Peter didn't tell his family he had seen me in the cave, so I told Sascha. She was pleased to hear he didn't give me away, and said perhaps he won't turn into a nasty policeman after all. She didn't understand about the dove miracle, she thought it couldn't have been dead, but I know it was.

Tuesday, 22nd November

When I walked past the post office today, the post lady was waiting by the door. She called out that she had got a letter for me, and went inside to get it. Then she handed it to me with a big smile, as if she thought it was from a secret boyfriend. I thanked her, and put it in my bag, and found I was blushing. I was pretty certain it would be from Grandma, as I didn't expect anyone else to write to me. I waited until I got out of the town, sat down on a grass verge and opened it. This is what it said.

Dear Gelany

It worked! I am well. I got out of bed a week after you left, and now I can walk outside. I am going to try to walk to the post office this afternoon, to post this letter.

Thank you so much for coming to see me, and for risking your life to get the Kampala seeds. Come to see me again when you can. I know it's not easy.

With much love from

Grandma. x

I was so delighted, I wanted to share the good news, but didn't have anyone to tell. So after lunch, I took Ruffles down to the cliffs, and spent some time talking with God. I thanked him for making Grandma well and asked that I would be able to see her again soon.

Wednesday, 23rd November

Mrs Newsby told me today, that she wants me to go to Easten to collect a flag and a stamping kit. She suggested I go on Friday.

If I get on the Electra at 8am, I might have time to visit Isabella in Soumarket and Grandma in Easten. So I don't mind going to Easten, but I don't want to bring that flag back, or the stamping kit, which I will probably have to use.

Friday, 25th November

This morning, I took Ruffles with me to the station. She looked pleased to be coming with me, instead of being left at home when I go to work, and walked along beside me with her tail wagging madly.

I got off the Electra at Soumarket and walked to Isabella's cottage nearby. After I knocked on the green door, it was a while before the old lady opened it. She looked surprised to see me, peered at me and said,

'You're that girl who called on me before, aren't you? What's your name ... um?'

'Gelany, it's Gelany Lantern. I was looking for my father before.'

'Oh, have you found him?'

'No, not yet. That's what I've come to see you about.'

'Well, you'd better come in. Would you like a cup of mint tea?' I followed her into her kitchen.

'Yes, please.' She put some dried leaves into a teapot, and poured hot water over them from a kettle on her stove. Then she put two cups and the teapot onto a tray.

'Come and sit down.' I followed her into a small dark room, which had a cheery fire burning. We sat down in chairs either side of it, and I was glad to feel it's warmth. I hadn't realise how cold I had got, sitting in an open carriage. Ruffles laid down on the rug in front of the fire, and Isabella didn't seem to mind.

'Now what can I do for you?'

'Well, I found out I have a Grandma in Easten, and I went to see her. She thinks my father may be in the prison, but we don't know where it is. She said that a relative named Daniel

Lantern was in prison once, so he would know. Do you know Daniel?'

'Yes he's my nephew. He was put in prison a long time ago. He had a bad year on his farm, and wasn't able to pay all his tax. His wife was struggling to run the farm on her own, and she had two young children, so all our family got together and managed to pay his debt for him. He wasn't in there for long.'

'Did he tell you where the prison was?'

'No, I never heard him speak about it.'

'Can you tell me where to find him?'

'Yes, probably best if I draw you a map. They live at Baytree Farm, which is on the other side of the town.'

She got up and found some paper and a pencil in a drawer. When she sat down, I went to look over her shoulder, whilst she drew a map and gave me directions. Then she handed me the piece of paper.

'Thank you. I haven't got time to go there now. But I will come back another day.'

As we drunk our tea, she asked me more about my family and we tried to work out how we are related. She thought she must have married one of my grandfather's cousins. The time went quickly, and I had to get back to the Electra. I thanked her and she told me to come and see her again.

At the next stop, Easten, I decided to go and see Grandma first, before picking up the flag as I didn't want to carry it around with me. As I walked past the beach, I could see Gordon's boat and some others out on the sea. The waves looked very choppy, so I was glad I wasn't out there with him.

I knocked on Grandma's door, and this time she came and opened it.

'Oh Gelany, how lovely to see you,' she exclaimed.

'What a lovely surprise.'

It is so nice having a Grandma. She looked well, quite normal in fact. She made me some blackberry tea and we went to sit by her fire. I had two hours there, and we chatted nonstop. I told her about my visit to Isabella and that she had given me Daniel's address. Grandma told me not to get my hopes up too high. I shared with her about the dove being shot, and when she heard it came back to life again, she laughed and clapped her hands. She was delighted to hear about Ruby running round with the dove and believing in God, and would like to meet Ruby. Grandma told me about how she slowly got better when she drank the Kampala medicine, and felt stronger each day. When I started talking about work and mentioned I had come to Easten to collect the flag to go on the Information Centre roof, I realised it was time to go and get it. The time had flown by.

Grandma walked back down the road with me, then she hugged me and kissed me on the cheek.

'Goodbye Gelany. Come and see me again when you can. And I hope you can bring news of your father.'

'I will Grandma. I'll go and look for him soon.'

As I walked back past the beach, I could see Gordon emptying out his net. He didn't notice me, which made me feel sad. But I knew I hadn't time to stop anyway.

At the Information Centre, I collected the large flag, which was rolled up and covered in brown paper. She also handed me a smaller parcel, which she told me was the stamping kit, and I put that into my backpack. Then I struggled up the hill to the station, hoping the Electra wouldn't start moving before I got there, but I made it just in time.

I got back to Wells at 4.30pm and left the flag and kit at work, before walking home. Ruffles looked as tired as me on the way back, not as bouncy as when we had left that morning. I told Mother about my trip to get the flag, but not about seeing Isabella or Grandma. I would have liked to have shared everything with her, but she would probably try to talk me out of going to the prison, and I know I just have to go. I want to know where my father is, and I will search as long as there is a chance that I can find him.

Thursday, 1st December

Gordon came to see me again today. He always gives me some fish now, and I don't have to pay for it, because of the fish miracle. He said he will let me know if they ever get short of fish, and I can go to the beach and look for fish in the sea, to see if it would happen again! He says Donna wants them to get married as soon as they can get a cottage. I don't think he realises how painful it is for me, to hear him planning to marry someone else. But I suppose I have got to get used to it and cope somehow. I don't know if I want to carry on seeing him or not. I do like the way he comes to see me, and smiles at me, and is interested in me. It makes me feel special. And I like his handsome face so much.

Friday, 2nd December

Mother told me that she has to work tomorrow, as another nurse is off sick. She said she doesn't mind, even though it should have been her day off, because she will get extra money and can buy some things for the new cottage. I think I will take the chance to go to Soumarket, I don't like making baskets on Saturday's anyway, as Sascha isn't there to talk to.

Saturday, 3rd December

Ruffles and I got on the Electra at 8am. When we

reached Soumarket, I got the map out, that Isabella had drawn for me and followed it carefully. The road led through the town centre, where there were lots of people busy shopping. I wondered if any were Lanterns that are related to me. I continued along the road on the other side of the town, until I found Daniel's farm. When I knocked on the door of the cottage, a young girl opened it.

'Hallo, I'm looking for Daniel Lantern. Is he here?'

'No, he's down there in the vegetable garden. Mum is at the shops.'

'Is it alright if I go and find him?'

'Yes I should think so.' She stared at me curiously, but didn't offer to come with me.

I thanked her, and walked along the track the way she had pointed. When I got to a large vegetable plot I could see a dark haired man, with a boy, both bent over working, and I went up to them. Daniel was pulling up a cabbage. He cut off the stalk, stood up and put it in a trug with some other vegetables, and then looked surprised when he noticed me standing there.

'Hallo, I'm Gelany Lantern.'

'Are you now? Pleased to meet you.'

'Isabella told me you live here.'

'Did she now?'

'Yes. I want to know where the prison is, and Isabella thought that you would be able to tell me. You see I think my father may be in there.' The boy stared at me with big brown eyes.

'Is he now? Well I'm just on my way to the house, would you like to come with me and I'll see if I can help you.'

We all walked off the vegetable plot together in silence, until we reached the track.

'So you know Isabella do you? I haven't seen you before,

yet you say you're a Lantern.'

'I live in Wells, so I don't come here very often.'

'Your father's in the prison, is he?'

'Well I think so. He disappeared eight years ago, and my Grandma was told that he was seen in the prison, about a year later. I want to go and find out, but I don't know where it is.'

'I was in the prison about nine years ago, so I wouldn't have seen him.'

We had reached his cottage. 'Would you like to come in and talk about it? My daughter is at home and my wife is coming back soon, or she may be there already. Bring the dog in.'

. I went into the cottage with them. It was rather like my cottage, but a bit bigger. He showed me to the living room, and the children followed us in. He told me to sit down, and then went out again. I heard the back door open and Daniel telling his wife about me. The two children came over and stroked Ruffles and told me he was a nice dog. I asked them what their names were, and they said they are Josh and Petal. Daniel came back in carrying a tray with five glasses of elderflower juice, followed by his wife, Susanne, who smiled at me.

'So you've come a long way to find us,' she said.

'Yes, and it's an even longer way back, as I have to go to Easten and Normarket, before getting back to Wells.'

They laughed.

'Now you want to know where the prison is then?' said Daniel thoughtfully.

'Yes please.'

'Well, I was blindfolded when they took me in a carriage from Easten to the prison, as I don't think they want anyone to know where it is. I know we went on the road that goes to Soumarket. On the way, the horse got a stone in its shoe, and the guard got out to help. I took the opportunity to push up my blindfold, and looked out to see where we were. I could see the Electra bending sharply to the right, but we were on a track that went straight ahead. We carried on down that for a while, so I think the prison is at the end of that track. It's called Journey's End.'

'I know the place where the Electra bends, so I may be able to find it. I don't think the prison was on the maps we had at school.' I said.

'No, it's not Dad. Is it a secret?' asked Petal.

'Yes, I think it is.'

'Aw, that was a terrible time,' said Susanne. 'The children were small, and I couldn't manage the farm on my own. Our relatives got him out of prison, by paying all the tax due. I shall always be grateful to them.'

'Yes, we will,' added Daniel. 'Was your father sent there for not paying his tax, Gelany?'

'No. He kept talking about God at work, and someone didn't like it and told on him to the police.' I saw Susanne and Daniel exchange worried glances. They didn't say anything, so I continued, 'I'm not sure if he is still alive, but he was seen in the prison a year after he disappeared. So I want to go and find out if he's still in there. I haven't seen him for eight years.'

'That's a long time,' said Susanne sympathetically.

'How could I get there?' I wondered out loud.

Everyone looked thoughtful.

'I suppose the only way is to walk from Soumarket,' offered Daniel.

'How far do you think it is?'

'Could be about seven miles, I should think.'

'I know,' said Josh suddenly. 'When you get on the

Electra at Wells, instead of sitting in the carriage, you could walk down the track as it's moving, and then when the carriages stop in Soumarket, you could jump off the track, and you would be further on. Maybe near the road that leads to the prison.'

'That's not such a bad idea!' said Daniel, 'Well done Josh.'

'Do you think you can do that, without losing your balance and falling off?' Petal asked her father.

'What do you think Gelany?' He asked.

'I could try, but it wouldn't save walking distance, would it, only time?'

'Yes I think you're right. So you have the choice. Walk about seven miles from Soumarket, or walk along a moving track and then it would be less to walk when the Electra stopped.'

'What if she'd walked too far, then she would be past the prison road when it stopped, and she'd have to walk back,' said Petal. Everyone one laughed.

'I don't think so, she would have to run fast to do that,' said Daniel.

Susanne asked me about where I lived, and my family. I told her about Mother, and Uncle Ray's family, and my job. They told me about the farm, and that Josh had just left school and was beginning to help his father. Petal said she wanted to work at the Information Centre like me, when she left school, it sounded important. I looked at my watch, and saw it was time to go.

'I'm sorry, I think I had better get going. I need to get back to the station by 11.45am. It has been nice meeting you all.'

'Oh, can't you stay longer,' pleaded Petal.

I was torn between staying, and getting to know them

better, or having time to see Grandma.

'I have a Grandma in Easten, and I want time to call on her today.'

'Come and see us again. Perhaps you could stay and have some lunch with us next time, and you could let us know how you got on at the prison,' said Susanne.

'Be careful going to the prison Gelany. It's not a nice place down there, with the guards. Best if you take someone with you,' warned Daniel.

As they all stood at the door waving to me, I was sorry to leave them so soon, and I really will try to go back and see them again one day. Since I became sixteen, and started looking for Daddy, I am finding more people to visit! I am beginning to like travelling on the Electra too.

I ate my sandwiches in the carriage, as it was travelling along and got to Easten at 12.45. I knew I didn't have much time to see Grandma, as I wanted to get home before Mother did. I ran down the road to the beach, with a surprised Ruffles trying to keep up with me. Gordon was on the beach and he saw me, called out and came over, so I had to stop. My legs still go weak when I see him, and my heart stirred up, I wonder why he has that effect on me? I half expected him to kiss me, but he didn't. He looked pleased to see me, his smile almost reaching his ears. I had to tell him I was in a hurry and why.

I had less than an hour with Grandma, but it was worth it. I told her I had found out where the prison is, and she told me to be careful. She is still well.

I didn't feel like walking back to town this evening, to the Youth Club, so I told Mother I felt tired and had a headache. It was true, although the headache wasn't that bad.

Sunday, 4th December

It has been a busy weekend. I went to Uncle Ray's farm this morning and stayed to lunch. Ruby was in the kitchen helping to get the dinner. I went to see Rayson, who was painting a bird, flying over the farm.

'I like that picture Rayson.'

He looked up and smiled at me. 'The bird is a dove, but don't tell anyone. I'm going to make it look like any bird. I've seen it flying over the farm lots of times lately.'

'Have you? I really like that picture. How is the baker's job going?'

'Very well. Mr Baker says I am learning quickly, and I do like it. Mum likes it too, as I bring fresh bread home, and Ruby likes it when I bring home left-over cakes. She says she wants to be a baker too.'

I have been thinking about when I could go to the prison. I will ask Mrs Newsby if I can have one of my days off that are due. I have worked out that I can ride on the Electra, walk to the prison, and get back in time, before the track stops moving for the night. I think I will go on Friday, when Mother is at work. I can't wait to go, and find out if Daddy is still there. If he is, I will be really close to him, and there is a chance that they will let me see him. Daniel said I should take someone with me, but I don't know who I can ask. Anyway, I would rather go on my own. I will take Ruffles with me though.

9

An Accident

Monday, 5th December

I asked Mrs Newsby if I could have the day off on Friday, but she said 'No', as we have just had a delivery of information sheets, with all the laws on. She said that there are some new laws too. She wants me to sort them into categories, and label them in different folders, so that people can find what they are looking for easily. I'm don't think anyone will want to look at them. I feel a bit annoyed, as I don't see why it can't wait. She said I can probably have Friday off next week, if it is all done.

Sunday, 11th December

Yesterday afternoon, when I had finished making a basket, my fingers felt quite sore, and I didn't feel like making anymore. I was feeling restless, so I went home, got Ruffles and took her for a walk on the cliffs. I thought I would collect some winter berries, as they look particularly good this year. I had seen some on the bushes where I often sit and talk to God. When I got there, I saw that the biggest ones were just out of reach. As I stretched my arm out, I pushed further and further into the bushes to reach them, and suddenly my right foot went down a deep rabbit hole. It twisted my foot at an angle and a sharp pain shot through it, that made me cry out. I fell down to my knees, the bushes scratching my face. Crawling out on my hands and knees, tears started running down, making it difficult to see. Ruffles ran over to me, and licked my wet face. I tried to stand up, but it was too painful and my ankle felt weak. So I just sat on the ground, hugging my knees and crying, not knowing what to do. Ruffles sat down next to me, and I put my arm around her, then suddenly she pulled away and ran off. When she came back a few minutes later, I saw Justin behind her. Oh no, I thought, I really didn't want him to see me in such a state.

He looked down at me, and said 'Ruffles ran up to me and pulled at my trouser legs with her teeth. I couldn't see you and wondered where you were, so I followed her. Is anything wrong?'

'I've hurt my ankle.'

'Can you walk on it? Here let me help you get up.'

He pulled me up to my feet. But I couldn't walk.

'Ouch!'

'Put your arm round my shoulder, and hop on the other foot.'

'No. Go and tell my mother. She'll know what to do.'

'I don't like leaving you here.'

'Just go.'

He went off. I sat looking at the sea. My ankle didn't hurt too much if I stayed still.

'Please God help me,' I whispered and then cried again.

A bit later Justin came back, pulling my truck on wheels behind him.

'Your mother wasn't there, but I saw this in the garden. I thought you could sit on it and I can wheel you home.'

I was still mad at him for what his family had done to my father.

'No, I don't want you to.'

'Come on Gelany, I can't leave you here.'

'Yes you can.'

'Come on. You didn't leave me hanging over the cliff.' He put his hands out to pull me up. He was right, I hadn't left him. But I didn't know about his family telling on my father then. 'I owe you one, Gelany.'

'Alright, just this once.' I let him help me onto the truck.

'I hope it is just this once, we don't want you hurting yourself again.'

He pushed me home, it was rather uncomfortable, but better than walking. He chatted about the birds he had seen on the cliffs, but I remained silent. When we got home, Mother was still not there. Justin helped me off the truck, but he could see I was in pain.

'Sit down again, Gelany, let me look at your ankle.' Reluctantly, I let him.

'I think you could have broken it. It has swollen up a lot. I think I had better take you to the hospital to get it checked.'

I felt really annoyed it had happened, and just because I was trying to reach larger berries too. If only I hadn't done it. But I had, and there was no one else around to help me. I agreed for him to take me to the hospital. He put Ruffles in the porch, and pushed me all the way up to Wells. I felt so miserable I didn't want to talk. Justin pushed me in silence most of the way. He helped me into the hospital, where I was examined by a doctor who said I have broken my ankle! He said he would put it in plaster straight away. Justin asked him how long it would take, and the Doctor told him to come back in an hour. When it was plastered up, the doctor found me two crutches. He said I have to go back in six weeks to have the plaster off.

Justin had gone into town, and when he came back he wheeled me home. Mother was there by then, and was quite shocked to see me with my foot in plaster and two crutches. I told her what had happened. We both thanked Justin and he said he'd better get home, as his parents would be wondering where he was.

Today I have mostly been sitting around, or trying to walk with the crutches. The doctor said not to put all of my weight on the broken ankle for two weeks. So I have been putting a lot of weight on my arms, and they are beginning to ache. The plaster goes from below my knee, to above my toes, and it has a rubber shoe thing strapped over my foot, so I can put it on the ground.

Last night, I cried myself to sleep. How can I go to find Daddy now? It will be ages before I can walk properly again. I keep crying, I can't help it. Mother thinks it's because my ankle is hurting, but it's not.

Monday, 12th December

This morning we got up early, as Mother said she would have to push me on the truck to work. We decided to leave Ruffles at Uncle Ray's farm on the way, so she could get some exercise, as I won't be able to walk her for a while. We found Aunt Pearl in the farmhouse and told her what had happened. She was shocked and sympathetic, and said we could leave Ruffles as much as we liked. Mother took Ruffles over to the barn where the other dogs live.

When we got to the edge of the town, I wanted to get off the truck, as I didn't want people staring at me. We asked Mr Mars if we could leave it at the Market Barn, and he said we could. It was then a slow walk the rest of the way. Mother came in to see Mrs Newsby and asked if I could work a full day every other day, so that she could push me to and from work on the cart, whilst I needed it. Mother doesn't work half days, and Mrs Newsby agreed.

Sascha was surprised to see my leg in plaster. When I tell people what happened, I feel quite silly, but they are usually sympathetic.

On the way home, Mother and I called at the Craft Barn and asked Mrs Strawler if I could take some basket making stuff home with me, so I can make baskets on my days off work. When she saw me with the crutches and heard about my ankle, she readily agreed.

Tuesday, 13th December

Today I was at home all day, and Ruffles stayed by my side, to keep me company. In the morning, I managed to do a few jobs, sitting down. Everything seems so much harder with crutches. Feeling quite tired after lunch, I laid down on the sofa and fell asleep. When I woke up I wondered where I was, then I remembered about the broken ankle. I started crying again. I wish I didn't keep crying, but I feel so miserable.

I picked up a basket base and some willow twigs and started to weave the straw in and out. The weather was so dull today, it didn't help my mood and soon tears were stopping me seeing what I was doing. It's no good I thought, and put the basket stuff away. Then I remembered I hadn't talked to God, since asking him to help me, when I broke my ankle. He did send Justin, so I should be thankful for that, but why couldn't he have sent someone else?

I asked God why he allowed me to break my ankle, and I felt Him whisper the answer in my thoughts. He said that He could keep intervening in the world, but when He made it, He decided to allow the people to make their own choices.

I hadn't been careful enough when I couldn't see where I was treading. But He told me He can bring good out of bad things that happen. I can't see how He can bring good out of this. I was just about to go and find out if Daddy is in prison, and now I can't. But I suppose I shouldn't argue with God.

I picked up the basket again, and managed to do a bit more. Late in the afternoon I heard a knock on the door. I wondered why Mother was knocking, I thought perhaps she had her hands full and couldn't turn the handle. So I got up, got hold of the crutches and hobbled to the door. I was surprised to see Justin there.

'I just came to see how you are.'

'I'm alright, thank you.' I was just about to close the door, when he put his foot in it to stop me.

'Gelany, please let's be friends.'

'I don't see how we can be.'

'It wasn't me who told the police about your father. What have I done? My father liked your father. It was my Grandfather who did it, and even he regrets it now.'

'It's a bit late for that.'

'He was scared his son would get into trouble, if he started believing in God. He didn't think they would arrest your father and shoot him, only give him a warning. I'm so sorry. I'd do anything to make it up to you.'

'How can you ever make up, what my Mother and I have gone through.'

'I know I can't. But I like you Gelany. Please let me be your friend. I want to help you?'

The iciness I felt towards him melted a bit. He was right, he hadn't done anything to harm me.

'I don't know, what do you want to do?'

'Be your friend. Visit you whilst you're stuck at home. Help you get to work. Walk with you on the cliffs when you're better.'

'I like walking on my own.' Even as I said it, I wasn't sure it was entirely true. It was when I wanted to talk to God though, then I needed to be alone.

'Do you really hate me. Can't you ever see me being your friend?'

'No, I don't hate you anymore. Sometimes I even find myself liking you. But something inside me fights against it. I've missed Daddy so much, it's created a big hurt, like a wound inside.'

'I can understand that. But can you try to remember, I didn't have anything to do with it?'

I found myself saying 'I'll try.'

My mother turned up then, so Justin said goodbye.

'What did he want?' she asked.

'Just to see how I was.'

She didn't say anymore. I know she was grateful to him for finding me on the cliff, and taking me to the hospital and back. But I guess she feels the same way about his family as I do, that it was their fault that Daddy was taken away from us.

Wednesday, 14th December

At work today, I finished putting all the law sheets into the files, so I probably would have been able to have the day off on Friday if I hadn't broken my ankle. How annoying.

Mother struggled to push me home on the truck today. I know she gets tired at work. I began to wish I'd asked Justin if he would do it. So I was pleased to see him when he knocked on the door this evening. Mother answered it, and let him in. He was carrying a posy, of red berries and wild clematis fluffy seed heads.

'I've just been walking on the cliffs, and as you can't get

to them at the moment, I thought I would bring something from the cliffs back to you.'

'Thank you. Justin you know you said yesterday, that you would like to help me get to work? Well Mother was rather tired this evening when she pushed me home on the truck. I wondered if you could push me home next time.'

'I'll push you to work as well, if you like. I work at Woodalls, so I can easily take you up to the town and back.'

I didn't know he worked at Woodalls, just like his father and mine. I guess I've never thought about where he worked.

I told him which days I was going in to work, and we arranged the time. Then Mother said dinner was ready, so he left. I think she was pleased when I told her that Justin was going to push the truck. She said 'He's not as bad as his grandfather then.'

Thursday, 15th December

I did some house jobs this morning and made baskets in the afternoon. I got so bored being indoors, that I went outside with Ruffles to try to walk to the cliffs. I didn't get very far, as it is such an effort to walk. I found a stick and threw that down the road for her, several times. She brought it back to me, but kept putting it at my feet and staring at it. It was hard bending down to pick it up, holding one crutch, and trying not to put my weight on the bad foot. I will have to take some biscuits with me next time, and train her to give the stick back to me in my hand.

Friday, 16th December

Justin pushed me to work and back today. I do feel silly, and am determined to walk there as soon as I can. We left Ruffles in the barn at Uncle Ray's farm, but didn't see anyone there. Justin only talked a little bit when he was pushing me, because the truck makes such a lot of noise on the stony track, that he has to shout, so most of the time we were silent. When we got home he asked me if I would like him to take Ruffles on the cliffs tomorrow, for a walk. I said 'No, thank you. She's okay'. But then I felt a bit guilty, because I thought if he had asked Ruffles she probably would have said 'Yes'. That's if she could speak of course.

Saturday, 17th December

I am glad I broke my ankle at this time of year, as I don't have to work on the allotment, and by the time I do, in the Spring, it should be healed.

Mother was at home today as she had the day off for a change, and I enjoyed having her company. She's been cooking dinner all this week and washing up. I have to hold the crutches when I am standing up, so can't do much. Most of the time I have been sitting on the sofa, with my foot up. It swells up by the evening, and the plaster feels really tight and uncomfortable. She said it will swell up less as it heals.

In the morning she gave the cottage a good clean, and handed me the cutlery drawer to sort out. I also made a basket, but in the afternoon the sun came out and then I longed to be outside. I told Mother I was going out to practice walking with the crutches, and she told me not to overdo it and to be patient. I still didn't get very far down the road, it was such an effort. Ruffles ran up and down beside me, wondering why we weren't going to the cliffs. She found the stick we had been playing with before, and dropped it at my feet, nearly tripping me up. I went indoors and got some dog biscuits, and tried to teach her to give the stick back to me, but soon gave up. It just wasn't possible to hold the crutches, bend down, hold a biscuit, and grab the stick before she dropped it, all at the same time.

I missed going to Youth Club in the evening. Mother saw I was bored and got our tin whistles. She had found them at the back of a cupboard, when she was sorting it out today. She gave me mine on my fourth birthday, and taught me how to play it. Then I used to play it at school. We haven't played them together since Daddy disappeared. This evening, we were both rubbish at first, but when we remembered how to play them, we had quite a lot of fun, and even ended up laughing when we made mistakes. It did make me miss Daddy a bit in the end, because he used to like to hear us play.

Sunday, 18th December

This morning Rayson and Ruby came to see me. They said Jimmy couldn't come because he had to work on the farm. I told Aunt Pearl I wouldn't be going to see them, when I collected Ruffles on Friday. She looked surprised to see Justin, and so I introduced him to her. She said it was nice of him to push me on the truck, as she thought my mother was finding it hard.

Rayson brought a large apple pie that he said he had made earlier. The apples were from an old apple tree growing near their house. Mother asked them to stay to lunch, and they said they would.

It was lovely having them eat with us at the table, and hear their cheerful chatter. Rayson told us about how he was now responsible for making the huge batch of bread dough at work. He said his arm muscles ached at first, really badly, after he had kneaded it, but now his arms were getting really strong. He rolled up his jumper sleeves and showed us his muscles. We all laughed. Ruby said that she got an 'A' for a story she wrote at school, about a dog that could talk to other animals.

After lunch, Mother asked Rayson if he would chop up some large logs for her, that she hadn't been able to cut herself.

When they went out to do it, Ruby whispered 'Gelany, shall we ask God to heal your ankle. He healed my kitten, so I don't see why he wouldn't heal you.'

'Okay, but we have to do it quietly, Mother wouldn't like us talking to God.'

Ruby came over to me and put her hands on my foot.

'Please God heal Gelany's ankle, and make the bone strong again and not broken. Thank you for healing my kitten.' She looked up at me. 'There, walk on it and see if it feels better.'

I suppose I didn't really expect it to feel any different, but I got up and walked around the room to please her. I realised I had forgotten to pick up the crutches, but found I could walk without them. It didn't hurt and felt quite normal, apart from the cumbersome plaster around it.

'Well, is it better?'

'It does feel better walking on it. But how can I tell? I've got this thick plaster cast around it.'

'I suppose you can't take that off, can you?'

'No, and I don't suppose the doctor will take it off early. He has no reason to. He would think it strange if I asked him.'

'Oh well you'll just have to keep it on then! How long for?'

I was walking round and round the room and it did feel good.

'Another five weeks. But it does feel better Ruby. Thank you.'

'Thank G...'

I think she was about to say 'God' when my mother

walked into the room. She looked at me.

'I was just trying to walk without the crutches.'

'Well the doctor said not to put much weight on it for another week, so I think you should use the crutches.'

I was sorry to see Rayson and Ruby go home, their surprise visit had cheered us up. I wondered what to do about my ankle. I went outside and practised walking with the crutches, and it seemed a lot easier. I said to Mother I thought I could walk to work this week. But she said I must let Justin take me on the truck for another week, so I don't put too much weight on it, like the doctor said. I could try walking to work the following week, if I really wanted to.

I am going in to work on Tuesday and Thursday this week, so I suppose I will only have to put up with being pushed on the truck by Justin two more days.

Monday, 19th December

I wrote to Grandma today, to tell her about breaking my ankle, and that I wouldn't be able to go to the prison for a while or visit her. I shall take the letter to the post office tomorrow on my way to work. I know it might not be broken anymore, but I can't go to Journey's End with this plaster on my foot, it would be too difficult to walk the seven miles to the prison and back. I certainly wouldn't be able to balance on the moving track, and walk along it to save time, like Josh had suggested.

In the afternoon, after it had stopped raining, I went outside with Ruffles, to see how far I could walk. I managed to get down to the cliffs and back! Ruffles was pleased. This evening, it has not swelled up as usual. I'm sure it must be healed, it feels fine.

Tuesday, 20th December

At work today, a man came in and gave Mrs Newsby a hand written poster, which had details about a 'New Year's Eve Singing concert'. Mrs Newsby told me to put the poster on the noticeboard outside. She told me to copy the details onto a piece of paper first, and put that in the News Folder. It said there is going to be a band in the Central Hall, and everyone is welcome, and can join in with singing. I hope I can go.

Sascha told me she misses me at the Youth Club, but Rayson has been sitting with her some of the time. She said they haven't heard from Peter, and her mother wonders if he's not allowed to write to them.

Justin pushed me to work and back. I think he likes doing it, but I feel a fraud.

Wednesday, 21st December

I made two baskets in the morning. In the afternoon, I thought I would try to walk for 20 minutes. I thought, if I can do that, then I will be able to walk to work next week, and I'll tell Justin tomorrow. So Ruffles and I walked to the cliffs and a little way along them. It was lovely to feel the fresh air on my cheeks, see the sea again, hear the thundering waves, and see Ruffles sniffing the grass for exciting scents of animal trails.

Thursday, 22nd December

Last night I couldn't get to sleep, and tossed and turned in bed. Then I lay on my back and stared at the dark ceiling, I wondered why I felt so uneasy. Suddenly I saw some words being written on the ceiling with a pen. The words were lit up, like they were written with fire, and they glowed in the dark. The writing said 'Tell Justin the truth about your father'. I couldn't think what it meant at first, then remembered Justin still thought that my father was shot dead, after he was arrested. I realised it wasn't right to let him carry on believing something that was not true, when I knew there was a chance, that my father may still be alive. I struggled with this for a while, and then said to God, 'Alright, I'll tell him tomorrow.' When I made that decision, I fell asleep straight away.

So when Justin and I reached my house this evening, I asked him if he would like to come in for a hot drink, to warm up, and he said he would. Mother was still out at work.

We went in the sitting room and sat by the fire, holding our hot mugs of milky barley drink,

'Justin, soon after you told me about my father being shot, my Grandma wrote to me. I didn't know she was still alive. I went to see her in Easten, and she told me that a policeman saw my father in the prison, about a year after he was arrested.'

'You mean ... you mean that he wasn't shot? So is he still alive?'

'He could be. I was planning to go to the prison last week, and ask if he's in there. But then I did this.' We both looked down at my plastered foot. 'So I won't be able to go and find out for a while now.'

'Maybe I could go for you. Do you know where it is?'

'Yes, I think so. But I want to go myself. I want to be the one who finds out if he's there, and if he is, I would be near him. Maybe they will even let me see him.'

'Oh I do hope he's still alive, and one day he will come back to you.'

We were both silent for a moment, thinking about it.

'I feel a bit better now I have some hope. But I am also scared, in case I find out he is dead after all. So I try not to think about that.'

'Oh I do hope he's still alive Gelany.'

'Don't say anything about it to my mother. She doesn't know I visited Grandma, and I don't want to get her hopes up, and then have to tell her that I found out Daddy is dead after all.'

'No I won't say anything to anyone, if you don't want me to. Not until you've found out.'

'I think I can walk to work next week. The doctor said I can put weight on my foot then. Thank you for pushing me on the truck. I will be glad to be able to walk again though. I feel a bit silly being pushed.'

'Okay, if you're sure. Just let me know if you find it too much and want help again.'

When Justin left I realised I was warming to him. There is still a bit of a struggle going on inside, as if two emotions are fighting each other. I think I would like to be friends with him. I do wish he wasn't connected to the family who deprived me of my father when I was a child, and caused all the pain my Mother and I have had to go through.

10

Convalescence

Monday, 26th December

I managed to walk to work and back today, although it took rather longer than usual. Now I can put all my weight on my plastered foot, it helps me to walk more normally. I'm sure it has healed really, but I'm still using the crutches, because the heavy plaster on my leg makes me lose balance easily. Mrs Newsby said I can carry on working every other day for a couple more weeks, to save me walking in every day. I said I would like to do that, and worked a full day today.

We got a news sheet to say that some new police houses are going to be built in Wells, and we are to have more policemen living here. When I told Sascha, she said she hoped Peter would get one and be able to come to live here, then her family might see him sometimes. I'm not sure if it is a good idea or not. I can understand them wanting to see him, but what if he is changing into a nasty policeman, or he may have to arrest people he knows.

Tuesday, 27th December

A day at home again and a dull one weather wise too. In

the afternoon, I took Ruffles down to the cliffs and walked a little way along them. The sky and the sea were both dark grey, and you couldn't see where one stopped and the other started. It was lovely when the sun tried to shine through, and shafts of light broke through the cloud, making patches of silver upon the sea. I haven't seen the dove lately and I miss it, I hope it is alright.

I even cooked dinner today and it was nice to be busy again. I can do lots more, now I can put my weight on my foot, and I don't have to hold onto the crutches. I was beginning to feel a bit lonely though, after being on my own all day, so was glad when Mother came home. I asked if she was going to go to the New Year's eve singing concert. She said she would like to, and hopes she won't have a tiring day on Saturday.

Thursday, 29th December

When I took Ruffles on the cliffs this afternoon, I heard the cannons firing in the distance. I put her on the lead and went as close to the edge of the cliffs as I dare, but I couldn't see anything unusual in the sea. It's amazing how far the sound of a cannon travels. I remembered how I used to cling to Daddy when I heard them firing. I still feel scared when I hear one now, and wonder if aliens are trying to invade our island. I hope I never meet one.

Friday, 30th December

Sascha told me Gordon was waiting to see me yesterday, at lunchtime, and she told him why I wasn't at work. He gave her the two fish meant for me, saying she might as well have them. He said he didn't come last week, as someone wanted to swap weeks. She said she thought he was really nice, and Peter has got competition. I told her he already has a girlfriend and we are just friends. I didn't say I wish I was his girlfriend though.

Sunday, 1st January, 1922

It's a New Year today, I wonder what it holds in store. I suppose I'll have to move to Wells, and I don't really want to. I don't feel the need to get away from Justin anymore. This year I hope to find out if my father is alive or not.

Yesterday evening, was the Singing Concert. Mother went to Sascha's house after work, to save her walking home and then back in again, and went with her family. I called at Uncle Ray's farm on the way, and walked with them. It was very crowded in the hall, but we managed to find seats together. I had Ruby on one side and Jimmy on the other, and next to Jimmy was his friend Rex.

There was a band on the stage, with two violins, two tin whistles and a hand drum. A man named Mr Archer, announced each song, and sometimes he told us the words first, if it wasn't a well-known song. He led the singing with a very loud hearty voice.

When we were about to start, three policemen walked in, went down to the front and spoke to Mr Archer. He turned to us and said that we had to start and finish the concert by singing 'The Carta'. I heard some quiet groans, and the policemen gave us stern looks. Ruby looked at me, and made a face, and I smiled back, hoping she would behave herself. I saw Rex nudge Jimmy with his elbow.

The music started for The Carta and we all stood up. I didn't want to sing it, so decided just to move my mouth up and down. Ruby had a tall man in front of her, so she probably thought she couldn't be seen, and I couldn't hear her singing either. Mr Archer's voice boomed out with 'Tansa is great' joined by a few other strong voices, and a general mumble. Next to me I could hear Jimmy and Rex, but soon realised they weren't singing the proper words. It sounded like 'Tansa's not great, Tansa can't save us' and went on similarly throughout the song. I gave him a warning look, and mouthed 'No', but he just smiled at me and carried on. I didn't know Jimmy was a rebel!

After that song, the policemen strutted to the back of the room. We thought they were going, but they took three seats from some children, and sat down. I felt annoyed. I had looked forward to having some fun, but now it felt like we were being watched. Once the singing started though, I tried to forget about them, and made up my mind to enjoy it. There were lots of the usual folk songs, about life on the farm, the sea, and some new ones about people or animals. It was really good. It makes you feel so happy when you sing. But it brought us back to earth, when we had to sing 'The Carta' again at the end.

As we were walking out, Justin came over to me and asked if I was managing to walk to work alright, and I told him I was. It was embarrassing being pushed on the truck, so I am glad I don't need him to push me anymore.

Mother and I walked back with Uncle Ray's family. Jimmy said to me, that he thought the policemen had come in to make sure we weren't having a meeting, to plan to overthrow the Rulers. I hadn't thought of that. I told him I heard him singing the wrong words and he just grinned at me.

I didn't go up to their farm today, as it is quite an effort walking with the plaster and crutches and I felt like I needed a rest. There were some heavy rain showers too.

Monday, 2nd January

I got my tin whistle out this afternoon. I felt inspired to

play it again, after hearing the music on Saturday. I was surprised at how many songs I could remember from school. I even managed to play some tunes that I heard at the singing concert.

Tuesday, 3rd January

At work, a news sheet came today about the cannons firing last week. It said three boats were spotted out in the sea, near Easten, and although the cannons couldn't reach them, it scared them away. It also said that the Rulers of Tansa feel it is their responsibility to keep the citizens of the Island safe from their enemies. Therefore, they are going to recruit more people to be Lookouts on the cliffs, and provide more cannons and guns.

I do wonder who is in the boats, it didn't say anything about that. I asked Mrs Newsby if she thought there could be other Islands like ours, in the sea, with people on like us. She said she didn't know as she has never been off the Island, and nor has anyone else, except for the fishermen, as far as she knew. I would have liked to have asked why they are thought of as enemies. I don't think they have fired guns or cannons at us. But I suppose they have never got near enough to do it. I thought I would like to be a Lookout, staying on the cliff tops all day, but I suppose it could be boring, and wet or cold sometimes.

Thursday, 6th January

Today, at work, we had a delivery of a poster asking people to become Lookouts. There are paid jobs, but it also said everyone should do their duty and be a Lookout when they are on the cliffs. There was also a sheet to put in the Information Folder. It had details of the date to go to Easten to apply for the jobs, and it said there would be more huts built along the cliffs to provide protection from the weather. Also more cannons are going to be built and placed along the cliffs.

It sounds to me like they are expecting an invasion of aliens, and are getting ready for them. How scary.

Saturday, 7th January

I felt bored at times being at home the past two days, so I will be glad to go back to work every day next week, and just for the mornings. It made a change working alternate full days, but I find whole days at work, too long really. Mrs Newsby said yesterday, she will be glad to have me in every day again too.

This evening, I made a big effort to go to Youth club. It was dark and cold walking there, but I was fed up with being indoors. Mother said she would come with me and visit Sascha's mother at the farm, whilst I was there. She said she didn't like me going on my own in the dark, especially as I couldn't walk properly.

Sascha was pleased to see me, and we walked together to the Youth Club. Rayson joined us at the table, and asked if I would be playing table tennis this evening, but I knew he was joking. Justin came over, and asked if he could sit with us. I wasn't sure about it, but didn't have to answer as Rayson said he could. They started chatting about the competitions in skittles, darts and table tennis, that are taking place soon. I found my eyes drawn to Justin and listened to what he said. I didn't know what to say to him and felt a bit shy about it, which was annoying.

I had told Mother I would only stay there for an hour, and that soon went. When I got up to leave Sascha said she would come with me, to make sure I got to her house alright. I didn't like to make her leave early, but it was nice to have her company. Then I walked the rest of the way with Mother. She said she thought I was walking really well, and you wouldn't know I had a broken ankle, except for the plaster and crutches. I probably haven't got a broken ankle anymore, since Ruby prayed for it to be healed! But of course I couldn't say that.

Sunday, 8th January

This afternoon, Mother lay asleep on the sofa, tired after her week's work. The sun made an effort to shine, and came through the window, making a bright patch on the carpet. That was where Ruffles was lying, and she looked at me expectantly. 'Okay' I said, putting on my warm coat and hat. Lying next to her lead, in the porch, was my tin whistle, and I felt a desire to play it, so I put it in my pocket.

It was quite nice on the cliffs with the sun shining, even though rather cold. I walked to my favourite bush, I hadn't been back there since I broke my ankle. I have never played my whistle on the cliffs before, but no one was around, so I thought I would have a go. At first I played a few folk songs that I learnt as a child, then I began to make up some tunes myself. They just seemed to flow naturally out of me, and I was quite surprised at how beautiful it sounded. Ruffles lay down next to me and seemed to be enjoying the music too. When I felt that I had played all that was inside me that wanted to come out, I saw the dove flying towards me, and I stopped. It landed on the ground in front of me.

'So you're back, are you? Where have you been?'

It cocked it's head on one side, looking at me, as if asking for another tune. So I played one more, and then it flew off.

I do love music. It's like another language, one you cannot express in words. It seems to speak sometimes, but I'm not sure what it was saying today.

Thursday, 12th January

Gordon came to see me today.

'Hallo Gelany. I was sorry to hear about your accident,' he said looking down at my foot. 'When do you get that plaster off?'

'One week and two days' time. I'll walk with you to the station.'

'Well you seem to be walking alright. I expect you'll be glad to get that off.'

'Yes, I really will. I found out where the prison is and was planning to go there, but then I did this.'

'Sorry I haven't been able to bring you any fish today. We're a bit short as we haven't been catching so many. I would ask for your miracle services, but can see you can't come to Easten. Anyway I think it is just the time of year, when fish aren't coming into the bay so much.'

'I expect the sea is a bit rough too. Do you still go out in it when it is?'

'Yes most of the time.'

'Well, you are brave, or maybe naïve.' I got my own back, from when he said that about me.

He gave me a friendly push.

'We don't go out if it's really stormy, my dear.'

I asked him if he had seen the boats that the cannons fired at, and he said he did, but they were much further out than the fishing boats go.

Friday, 13th January

I've managed to walk to work every morning this week, so I was quite glad to sit down at home in the afternoons and make baskets, with my feet up. Ruffles was pleased to have me at home too. On Monday, she was rather expectant of a walk though, and I didn't feel like it, after walking to town and back. So the rest of the week, I took her with me and left her at Uncle Ray's farm with the other dogs, so she could get some exercise.

Only one more week until I get the plaster off. I can't wait.

Saturday, 14th January

I haven't gone to Youth Club this evening as it is pouring with heavy rain. I think Mother was glad not to have to go with me. She said she thought I ought to give it up for the winter anyway, whilst we live here. It is so dark and cold in the evenings. She said when we move to Wells, it will be easier for me to get there. Not sure what I think about that. I really don't want to go anymore.

Today, she had the day off and we cleaned all the floors of the cottage together. Mother swept them with a broom and shook out the rugs, and I went over them with a mop and bucket.

Sunday, 15th January

No rain today, and I couldn't wait to go to see Uncle Ray's family. It seemed ages since I have been there on a Sunday morning. I arrived just before lunch, and found Ruby and Aunt Pearl in the kitchen. Ruby was very quiet which was unusual and I wondered why. Chatter round the lunch table seemed a bit subdued too.

After we had eaten, Ruby collected the leftover meat in a dish, and asked if I would go with her to feed the cats. As we walked down to the barn, she was still quiet, and so I asked her how her kitten was. She told me it's nearly as big as a cat now. She was right, Beauty had grown a lot, and was almost as big as her mother. After the cats had eaten, she picked Beauty up, and we sat down on the straw bales.

It was then I found out why she wasn't her usual cheerful self.

'I got into trouble at school on Friday.'

'Why? What for?'

'For questioning De-vel-op-men-ta-tion.' She said it slowly and deliberately, as if having difficulty with the word.

'What did you say?'

'Well the teacher explained to us how people happened. She said at first there were only fish in the water, then the fish gave birth to a creature that could walk on the land. When a creature wanted to walk on two legs, it gave birth to a man. She asked if we had any questions. I put my hand up and said 'What about the flowers, how did they happen?" She said it started with one plant, and they developed different ones in their seeds.'

'Is that all?'

'No, then I said that they look like they have been designed and created by someone, and she asked me why I thought that. So I said "Well, they are so different from each other, and are so beautiful. Maybe the Development theory isn't right, and everything was designed and created to be the way it is, by someone." I didn't say God, but she said "Come to see me after school. We are not allowed to believe in a God. The Rulers want us to believe the truth, not to believe in fairy tales." After school, she asked me why I thought there might be a God. I didn't know what to say. So then she asked me if my parents had told me, and I said "No, I just thought it up myself. I love the flowers, and think they look as if they have been made by someone who knew what he was doing." Then she told me that on this Island we believe in the Development theory, and the Rulers don't want us to speak of a God. She said "So you will stop doing it, won't you?" And I said I would. Then she wrote a note and told me to give it to my father.'

'What did he say?'

'He asked me why I was talking about God at school, and didn't I know it was against the law. So I told him what the teacher had said, and that I didn't say God, I only mentioned things might have been created by someone. Then he asked me if you had spoken to me about it. I told him you only told me about your father, when I asked why he was shot, that was all.'

'Oh Ruby, you can believe differently, but you must keep it to yourself. The law says we mustn't talk about God. They put people in prison if they don't obey it.'

'What's prison. I thought you said they shot people?'

'They don't always shoot people. Sometimes they send them to prison. It's is a building, a long way away, where they lock people up, until they agree to obey the rules.'

'I don't want to go there.'

'Then please keep quiet about it. You can only talk to me about it, if you are sure no one else is listening.'

She looked around to make sure no one was, and then said she would.

Saturday, 21st January

Plaster off today, at last! I've been so looking forward to it. Mother was working, so I walked with her up to the hospital. The doctor took me into the treatment room, and I handed him the crutches. He gave them back to me and told me I would be needing them for a bit longer, because my ankle will feel weak after being set in one position for six weeks. He was right. After he cut the plaster off, I put my weight on my foot and it felt like it was collapsing. He handed me back the crutches, and told me to use them a couple more weeks until it feels stronger. He said it looked like it had healed very well, and gave me a piece of paper with some exercises on to help strengthen it, which I am supposed to do every day.

I was rather disappointed to be walking home with crutches, but it did feel lovely to have the plaster off. When I got home, I heated water up on the stove and had a soak in the tin bath, by the fire. It was so much nicer to be able to relax and put my foot in the water, instead of dangling it over the side.

In the afternoon, I walked to the cliffs, so Ruffles could have a run. I was surprised to see Justin up there, as I thought there wouldn't be many birds to see in the winter. He came towards me, and looked down at my foot.

'Hallo Gelany, you've got the plaster off.'

'Yes, it was taken off this morning. I'm trying to get my ankle stronger, it feels so weak.'

'You're doing well. It was only six weeks ago that I found you up here after you broke it.'

'Yes, I'll be glad when I can give up the crutches though. What are you doing up here? I didn't think there'd be many birds about at this time of year.'

'There aren't so many, but there are some unusual ones on the rocks below the cliffs. I don't go looking over the edge, of course, but watch them when they fly around. Come over here and have a look.'

I put Ruffles on her lead and followed him towards the edge of the cliff. We stood there looking for a little while and then I saw them flying up. Justin handed me his binoculars. The birds were so much bigger looking through them, that I could see them quite clearly. They had pure white chests underneath and their heads, beaks, backs and tails were all black.

'They're lovely.' I said handing him back the binoculars.

'Do you know what they're called?'

'No. Perhaps I ought to name them. Maybe black headed, beaked, backed and tailed gulls?

We started walking back towards home.

'It might be easier to call them white chested gulls.'

'Yes,' he laughed. 'I suppose you'll be going to look for your father, as soon as that ankle is stronger?'

'Yes, that's the plan.'

'Are you okay going on your own?'

'I'll take Ruffles with me.'

I had a feeling he was offering to come, but I wasn't going to encourage it, so changed the subject.

'Will you be working on the allotment in the spring?'

'Yes, I expect I will. My Grandfather is still not well, and my father is usually too busy. He's not keen on outdoor work anyway, whereas I enjoy it.'

I realised I didn't feel bothered about him working next to me on the allotments anymore, which is quite a change from how I felt before.

'Are you going to the Youth Club tonight?' he asked.

'No, my mother doesn't want me to go out in the winter evenings. Anyway, I don't fancy the walk, as I've already done a trip into town today.'

When we reached my cottage, he said goodbye and went on his way.

Sunday, 23rd January

I went to Uncle Ray's farm today. There was a very cold wind, so I put on my scarf, gloves and hat, as well as my coat, and was glad to get inside the warm farmhouse kitchen. When I left Ruffles in the barn with the farm dogs, she dived into some hay and circled round several times, to make a deep nest, next to the other dogs. Aunt Pearl and Ruby were cooking as usual.

'Hallo Gelany,' said Aunt Pearl, 'It's good to see you've got the plaster off. Show us how you can walk.'

I rested the crutches against the wall, and walked briskly around the large kitchen table.

'Well that looks quite normal, not even a limp. Do you still need those crutches?'

'Just a little longer I think. My ankle felt quite weak at first, but it's getting stronger every day.'

'Look Gelany,' said Ruby, 'I'm making gingerbread men, women and children.'

I looked at the line of gingerbread people she had put onto a baking tray, and laughed.

'They look great Ruby. Very artistic. Do you want to be a baker like Rayson?'

'I'm not sure what I want to do when I leave school. There are lots of things I'd like to do.'

'What are those?'

'Maybe be a baker, breed dogs, write stories, work in a clothes shop, umm, build houses, umm...'

'I can see why you can't make up your mind. You've lots of choices.'

'Did you want to work in an Information Centre, when you were at school?' she asked.

'No, Sascha told me there was a job there. I'm glad it's only mornings, then I can be outside, working on the allotment, in the afternoons.'

'Maybe you should be a farmer's wife,' suggested Aunt Pearl.

For some reason that made me blush.

'I don't know any farmers that I'd like to marry, or that want to marry me.'

'It's a shame that Peter wasn't content to be a farmer.'

I didn't say anything, but I did wonder if I would have married him if he was going to be a farmer.

'Is Rayson in the sitting room?'

Aunt Pearl said he was, so I went to see him. He was painting a picture of winter trees.

'Hallo Rayson. That's nice. What do you do with all your pictures?'

'Hallo Gelany. Most of them are hanging up in the house, or stacked up in a cupboard. Mr Baker has said I can put some up for sale on the walls of his bakery, which is nice of him. I just have to get some frames from Woodalls.'

'Could I have one of a dove, maybe for my next birthday?'

He looked at me and smiled. 'I'll see what I can do.'

The family was cheerful, when we sat round the kitchen table for a lunch of beef stew.

I was glad that Ruby's trouble at school seemed to have been forgotten. After feeding the cats with Ruby, I stayed for a game of cards, and then took Ruffles home. She immediately went and laid down as near as she could to the fire in the sitting room. I expect she wonders how those farm dogs can live outside in that barn.

Tuesday, 24th January

There was a news sheet at work today, which said that Charles Tansa's wife Emerald is expecting a baby in June. Poor girl. They always have boys, who seem to get worse with each generation.

Thursday, 26th January

The station guard came into the Information Centre today, to tell Mrs Newsby that the Electra track isn't working. He said it had been playing up lately, jerking sometimes, and yesterday it stopped and wouldn't move again. He thought he would let her know, because it means we will not get any news sheets while it's broken. He also asked if we could put a poster up to let people know. He said he will come and tell us when it's moving again. Mrs Newsby asked me to make a poster for the noticeboard. I did it in black and red ink in my best large writing. She said it looked good, and liked the way I had written 'Electra' and 'Not working' in red, so that stood out.

I suppose that means no fresh fish either, or other food that comes on the Electra. I hope it gets mended soon, so that I can get to the prison.

Saturday, 28th January

I left the crutches at the hospital yesterday, and it felt good to give them back. A nurse examined my ankle and said it's fine. I felt so free walking home, I wanted to run or dance. But I didn't, I was just glad to be walking normally again.

This afternoon, I walked quite far on the cliffs with Ruffles, almost as far as I used to. I didn't sit down by the bush though, as it still feels so cold. I enjoyed the feeling of the fresh cool air on my face, and it smelt of seaweed and salt. The clouds were moving rapidly across the sky, and as the sun set, they became tinged with gold.

I said thank you to God for making my foot better, and it felt like He smiled at me. I asked Him to make the Electra work again, so that I can go to the prison. And please let my father be there, I added.

11

The Lake

Tuesday, 31st January

I knew the Electra was working again today, as a news sheet was delivered to us, and we hadn't had any whilst it had broken down. It was a very unwelcome one (as most of them are), as it said that taxes on the land are going up in April, to pay for the extra police and Lookouts on the cliffs, that keep us safe. It said they also need more money to repair the Electra, which is getting old and worn out. Then it had a table showing the new rates to be paid. It seems very unfair that we are the ones who have to pay for the extra police, who spy on us and make us obey the Tansas' rules. Sascha and I discussed it, as we were walking home.

She said 'I don't know how my father can pay anymore, he is already struggling to earn enough from the farm.'

'My mother and I don't have any money to spare either. Why can't they just print more money to pay for it all?'

'I don't know.'

I told Mother when she came home, and how much we will have to pay. She was very cross about it.

'The Tansas will make themselves more unpopular, then

they will need more police. It's a vicious circle' she said.

Wednesday, 1st February

Mother said she has decided that she will make some baskets at home, to help pay the extra tax. She said I must try to make more than I usually do. I said I would, but feel annoyed that we have to do more work, just to give the Tansas more money.

Thursday, 2nd February

Gordon was waiting for me when I left work today. I was going to walk home with Sascha, but Gordon handed me some fish and said he had also bought me a pie. He hoped I liked the butcher's chicken pies. Sascha said she would see me tomorrow, and didn't seem to mind, so I went to the station with Gordon.

'How are you Gelany?'

'I'm alright, look I've got the plaster off my foot.'

'Oh yes, you're walking really well too. Is it okay?'

'Yes, fine.'

'So are you planning to go and find the prison now?'

'Yes, I hope so. I don't know when yet. The Electra broke down, and it has only just been mended.'

'It still jerked sometimes, on the way,' he said, as we sat down on a seat in the shelter, out of the wind. Gordon gave me a brown bag with the pie in. I bit into it, and it was still warm.

'Mumm, this is delicious. Thank you.'

We ate our pies in silence, just enjoying them.

'That's better. I was really hungry,' he said, as he screwed up the bag into a tiny ball, and put it in his pocket.

'Have you heard that the Tansas are putting up the taxes?' I asked.

'Yes. I went to the Central Hall, yesterday. My father goes there to play Stickball and asked me if I'd like to try it. After a few games, we sat down at a table with some of his friends, and had a drink of beer. One of the men had seen the news sheet at the Information Centre and told us about it. They started talking about their dislike of being ruled by the Tansas, and what they could do about it. I was a bit worried, and looked around to see if anyone was listening, but I don't think anyone overheard.'

I looked round to see if anyone was listening to us in the shelter, but there was no one around.

'What did they think they could do about it?'

'Oh I don't know, I think it was all talk. If we don't pay we go to prison. I don't think we can do much about it.'

'What's Stickball?'

'It's a game you play on a table, hitting balls with sticks and trying to get them down holes. The holes have nets that catch the balls.'

'Oh, that sounds fun. I wish we had one of those tables at the Youth Club.'

'Yes, it's quite good. I wasn't any good though. My father says it takes practice. Oh, there's the horn, I'd better go. Bye Gelany, nice to see you, and glad you're walking normally again.'

'Goodbye Gordon.' He ran to the Electra and jumped into a carriage, just as the track started moving.

As I walked home, I thought about the prison again. I'll ask Mrs Newsby if I can have Friday off next week.

Friday, 3rd February

Mrs Newsby said I can have next Friday off, but now I'm in two minds about going. If he is in there, it will be lovely to find out that he's still alive. But what if I am told he's dead? Then I won't have any hope left.

Saturday, 4th February

I got a bit bored today. I will be glad when I can work on the allotment again. I went down to look at it, and pulled up a cabbage. No one else was there. Then I went to the cliffs with Ruffles, but it's too cold to stop there. So I came home, and tidied things up. I was glad when Mother came home. She said the hospital is full, as there is an illness going around, and some people are getting quite bad with it. She said no one has died from it though. She was very tired, so I got the dinner. I cooked a bean stew, and it was quite nice. Sascha gave me the recipe. It had some wild herbs in it, that she showed me by the roadside, and we picked them on the way home yesterday.

I played my tin whistle in the evening and then we played cards. When Mother went to bed early, I made up some card games I could play by myself. Ruffles seemed content to lie next to the fire, as close as possible.

Friday, 10th February

I got ready to go on the Electra this morning, but as Mother wasn't up at her usual time, I went in to see her. She was still lying in bed, and said she didn't feel well and thought she had a temperature. She told me to call in at the hospital on my way to work, and tell them she wasn't coming in today, because she was ill.

I didn't know what to do, I wasn't going to go to work, as I had planned to go to the prison. If I did, I wouldn't be back until the evening and Mother would worry if I wasn't home at lunchtime. So I decided I would have to go to work. How annoying.

I called in at the hospital and told a nurse about Mother,

and she gave me a bottle of herbal medicine. I could hear a lot of coughing there, and so was glad to get out. I told Mrs Newsby I had planned to go out for the day, but Mother wasn't well, so I couldn't. She was alright with me going in to work instead, and said I can have another day off.

Mother has stayed in bed all day and only wanted drinks.

Sunday, 12th February

I have had to do all the washing and cleaning this weekend, as Mother is still in bed and says she feels too weak to do anything. She didn't want much to eat, so I got all the different vegetables that I could find and made a soup and mashed it up, so it was easy to drink. She seemed to like that.

I walked up to Uncle Ray's farm, just to let them know Mother was ill, and then came home. Aunt Pearl gave me some parsnips, a squash, and some ham bones, when I told her that Mother would only eat soup.

Thursday, 16th February

Mother is still quite ill, and I'm a bit worried about her. I've been going to work in the mornings, then coming home and looking after her and doing the chores. I've been keeping the fire alight, and she has been lying on the sofa by it, during the day, sleeping most of the time. I hope she gets better soon. The medicine doesn't seem to make much difference. She has started coughing, especially at night and it keeps us both awake.

Friday, 17th February

Another night of coughing fits. This morning, I asked Mother if she thinks I should take her to the hospital, on the truck. But she said, no, the hospital is full up and they can't do any more than we are doing here, and she certainly didn't fancy a ride on the truck.

Saturday, 18th February

I had a dream last night. It was so clear, as if it was really happening. I dreamt I walked to the lake in the middle of the Island. As I looked down, into the water, I saw blue rocks and stones at the bottom of the lake, and water was bubbling up out of them. I filled up a bottle with the water, took it home, and put spoonfuls of it in Mother's drinks. At first she coughed more, but then she got up out of bed, and told me she felt fine. She got dressed and went to work. When I woke up, and heard her coughing, I realised it wasn't true, and I felt really sad.

In the afternoon, after I had given Mother her soup, the sun was shining, so I took Ruffles down to the cliffs. As I was walking along, pleading with God to make Mother better, I saw Justin ahead of me. My first reaction was to turn back before he saw me, as I had gone as far as I wanted to walk anyway. Then I realised I would like to speak to him. He had stopped to look through his binoculars and I walked up to him.

'Hallo Justin. What are you looking at?'

'Oh, hallo Gelany', he said giving me a big smile. I'm looking at that flock of birds in the sky, but I don't know what they are.'

I looked where he was pointing and saw a huge flock of birds swooping and diving together in unison, as if they were one.

'They are clever the way they fly together like that. I don't think I have seen them before,' I said.

'I've seen them a few times, but only recently. How are you? How's your ankle?'

'It's fine. It's Mother I'm worried about though. She's been ill in bed for over a week now, and doesn't seem to be getting any better.'

We started walking back along the cliffs. Ruffles had her nose to the ground, running here and there, following the rabbit trails.

'I'm sorry to hear your mother is ill.'

'I had a really vivid dream last night. I walked to the lake in the middle of the Island. I've never been there, but I saw it very clearly. In the lake were some blue rocks, and water was bubbling up to the surface from them.'

'I've been to the lake, and there is a place like that, with blue rocks.'

'Is there? Well I collected some of the bubbling water in a bottle, and put spoonfuls of it into Mother's drinks and she got better.'

'I've heard that the water in the lake has healing powers, but I thought people had just made it up, like a fairy tale.'

'I'd like to go there, and get some of that water. I think it's worth a try. Could you tell me how to get there? How long would it take?'

'It's not easy to explain the way, but I'll come with you if you like. We could go there tomorrow. It's probably about an hour and a half's walk from Wells, I think.'

'Would you? Alright.'

We walked back to the cottage, talking about it. We decided to meet on the Wells Road, next to the windmill, at 11am, and take our lunch with us. I'm not sure what to tell Mother. I don't think she would believe in healing water, and would try to talk me out of it.

Sunday, 19th February

It was a sunny day today, and no wind, so a good day for

180

a long walk. Mother coughed a lot in the night, so I didn't like to leave her, but I believed the lake water might help. I did all the chores and made sure she was comfortable, and then told her Justin had asked me to go for a walk with him to the lake, and take our lunch. I asked her if she would mind if I went. She said no, I had been indoors a lot with her, and it would do me good to get out on a sunny day. I gave her some soup and bread before I left and said I would give her some more when I got back, in the afternoon. I was surprised she didn't object to me going with Justin, but I think she was too weak to care who I was going with.

I called in at the farm, left Ruffles at the back door, and went to see Aunt Pearl and Ruby, to let them know I wouldn't be going to lunch today.

'Where are you going?' asked Ruby.

'For a walk to the lake, with Justin. He wants to show it to me.'

'Can I go?'

'No it's too far for you to walk,' answered Aunt Pearl, giving me a smile.

I felt my face blush, as I knew she was thinking he was my new boyfriend. I couldn't really explain about the healing water, so I had to let her think it. She asked how Mother was and I told her, then said 'Goodbye'. Ruby moaned about me not staying, and not coming with me. She had her hands in a bowl of flour, making pastry. I told her that if the lake was nice, I would take her to see it one day, when she could walk that far. Then I collected Ruffles, who had run off the barn to see the other dogs. She looked a bit surprised that we were not staying there.

Justin was waiting for me, when I got to the windmill. We carried on up the Wells Road, took a path off to the right and climbed over the Electra track, when it stopped moving.

Justin pointed to some pine trees ahead, and said we should aim for those. We walked through some rough grass, then found a path by the pine trees. The path, which had tall trees and thick bushes each side, took us all the way to the lake, and it was quite a long way. Ruffles enjoyed running around, exploring a new area, and seemed tireless.

Finally the lake came into view, and as we got nearer, I couldn't help exclaiming 'Oh it's so beautiful.'

The lake was huge, and the rippling water was different shades of blue.

'Is it like the one in your dream?'

'Yes, but even better in real life.'

Ruffles ran up to it and had a long drink.

'That must taste good,' said Justin.

'Yes, have you tried it?'

'No. I have only been here twice before. Once to try to catch fish, but I didn't get any.'

I bent down, scooped some water up in my hand and tasted it. It was clear and tasted fresh.

'I can't see any blue rocks.'

'They were further along, that way.' Justin pointed to the right.

As we walked along, I began to feel weak with hunger.

'Oh, is it far? I'm getting hungry.'

'So am I. I can't remember how far. Let's sit down and have our lunch.'

It was lovely eating our lunch, looking out over the lake. Geese were floating on it, occasionally honking. As we sat there, a 'V' formation of birds flew over our heads and splashed down on the lake in front of us. There was even more honking then. Justin took out his binoculars to take a closer look.

It felt good sitting there with him, I find him easy

company. I surprised myself by thinking, I don't think I would mind if he put his arm around me now. It must be the romance of the place, I told myself. Anyway I don't think he would want to, after the way I treated him, and I think he's just being nice to me, to try to make up for what his Grandfather did. When we had finished our lunch, he put his hand out, I took it, and he pulled me up off the ground.

We walked along beside the lake, peering into the water, looking for blue rocks. I could see quite a lot of fish swimming amongst the weed.

'I'm surprised you didn't catch any fish, there are so many near the edge.'

'Yes, the boy I was with caught a few. He had a fishing rod. I just had a net, and there weren't any at the edge then. I wish I had brought a net with me today! Look there's the blue rocks.'

The rocks were a turquoise colour, and a jet of water seemed to be shooting up out of them, making bubbles on the surface, that slowly popped. I got the bottle I had brought for the purpose, out of my backpack, and let it fill up amongst the bubbles, then screwed the lid on.

'It looks so refreshing, I think I will try some myself.'

I scooped some water up in my hand, and sucked it into my mouth.

'What does it taste like?'

'It tastes slightly warm and a bit sweeter than usual.'

Justin scooped some up in his hand and tasted it.

'Yes, it does, how strange.'

'Well, it's really lovely here, but I think I had better get back now, to see how Mother is.'

Justin didn't turn back straight away, he was staring ahead in the distance. Then he put his binoculars up to his eyes.

'I think it would be a good time to leave. I can see three men over there, walking towards us, and they look like policemen. I don't think we're doing anything wrong, but let's go.'

I looked ahead and saw some tiny black dots. We turned around and headed back to the path. When out of sight of the men, we ran for a while, until we felt breathless, and then walked quite fast. We didn't see them again, thank goodness. We went our separate ways when we reached the windmill.

'I hope the water works and your mother is better soon.'

'Yes, so do I. Thank you for taking me to the lake, Justin. Goodbye.'

'Goodbye Gelany.'

As I walked home, I thought I would like to go to the lake again sometime. I do wish it was nearer. The policemen spoilt it a bit though, I wouldn't like to meet them there. I will ask Mrs Newsby if she knows if it is alright to go there.

Mother didn't look any better when I got home at about 3pm. She said she is coughing in the daytime now, as well as at night. I have started putting a spoonful of the lake water into her drinks and soup, like I did in my dream. I do hope it works soon.

Monday, 20th February

Mrs Newsby said she thinks it is alright to go to the lake, people go there to fish sometimes. She said she had heard that policemen seem to be taking more of an interest in the lake lately, but she doesn't know why.

As Sascha and I walked home together, she told me her news.

'Peter called in to see us on Saturday.'

'Oh, that was nice for you and your parents. Did he have

a day off?'

'No, he came to Wells, with another policeman. He was on duty, but he said he couldn't talk about what they were doing. He said that Reginald Tansa says the people are getting more rebellious, and they need to keep them in order.'

'Oh, that's awful.'

'Yes. After he had gone, Father said he thinks he's being brainwashed.'

'What's that?'

'He said it means they get the policemen to think like the Tansas do, by giving them talks. That worried my Mother. She remarked Peter had seemed a bit cool, and wasn't his usual friendly self. I thought that too.'

'Oh, I'm so sorry.'

It must be awful for their family to see Peter changing that way.

When I got home, Mother was lying on the sofa. She didn't cough this afternoon, which was a good sign. She said she is fed up lying around feeling useless. When I got the basket making stuff out, she asked if she could try making one.

Tuesday, 21st January

When I woke up this morning, I wondered what was wrong. Then I realised I had slept through the night without waking up when Mother coughed. I quickly went to Mother's room, hoping she was still alive. She was lying awake, and said she had a good night's sleep.

This afternoon, she made a basket when I did, and said she felt much better. She said she still felt weak, but would try eating dinner with me, instead of soup.

In the evening she seemed, almost her normal self. That lake water worked quickly!

Wednesday, 22nd February

Mother said she feels stronger today and is planning to go back to work tomorrow.

Thursday, 23rd February

Gordon was waiting for me today, when I left work. He gave me some fish roe and said sorry he hadn't bought me a pie today, but they hadn't caught many fish this past week. I told him I don't expect him to buy me a pie. We walked to the station together, he seemed a bit quiet.

'Is anything wrong?'

'Yes, I suppose there is. I went to the Hall yesterday, to play stickball with my father and his friends. They started talking about the Tansas and what they could do to protest about the taxes going up. My father said we should do more than that, we should get rid of them, and rule ourselves again. Wilf said we need lots of dissatisfied people, to have enough to rise up against them, and he didn't think that many people cared. So my father got up on the stage and asked the people there if they were fed up with the Tansas ruling us. Most of the people put their hands up, and then he said we should get together and do something about it.'

'What did people say?'

'They had just started to shout out ideas, when suddenly it went quiet. We turned round and saw that two policemen had walked in the door. They asked what was going on, and no one answered. My father got off the stage and came and sat back at the table. They asked him what he was doing on the stage, and he said he was just announcing a stickball competition. I don't think they believed him, and we wondered if they'd heard him. One of the policeman got out his notebook, and asked my father his name. He was reluctant to give it, and told me after, that he was thinking of saying a false name. But before he could speak, the other policeman said it, as he knew him. My father told me not to tell my mother, as it would only worry her.'

'Oh dear. We have to be so careful. It's a bit scary.'

'Yes. I wondered if there has been an informer in there before, who has heard what they are saying, and told the police about it.'

I looked around to make sure no one was listening to us. Gordon looked too, I've not seen him looking scared before. The shelter, we were sitting in, has glass windows in it, and we couldn't see any one nearby. I told Gordon about my mother being ill and getting better at last. I didn't tell him about the dream or the lake, as I'm not sure he would believe in things like that. Then it was time for him to go.

I'm fed up with the Tansas ruling us, and all the policeman who seem to be against us. But what can we do about it?

Monday, 27th February

Mother seems her usual self now, so I decided to ask Mrs Newsby if I could have next Friday off, and she said I could. I thought I would go on a Friday, in case I'm tired after all that walking, or the news about Daddy is not good, then I have the weekend to get over it. I'm trying to believe I will find Daddy there though, only that thought will make me do the long journey.

Thursday, 1st March

I've felt awful today, headache, feel sick and I just want to go to sleep, which is what I am going to do now. I hope I feel better in the morning. I've put a few things in my backpack ready for the journey tomorrow though.

Friday, 2nd March

I didn't get to the prison today. I'm beginning to wonder if I am meant to go, as things keep stopping me. I woke up still feeling ill, and didn't want to get out of bed. Mother came in before she left, to see why I wasn't up. I told her I wasn't feeling well, and said she hoped I hadn't got what she had, and to stay in bed. The she said she would tell Mrs Newsby. So I had to tell her I had the day off, as I had some days owing. She was in a hurry, so she didn't ask me why I was having today off, thank goodness.

In the afternoon, I remembered the water from the lake, and that I had some left in the bottle. I have started putting it in my drinks, to see if it will work for me.

Saturday, 3rd March

I have been feeling a bit better today. I even made a basket this afternoon, and ate some dinner this evening, that Mother cooked.

Sunday, 4th March

I am getting better. I think that lake water is working on me. I ate normally and took Ruffles for a walk on the cliffs. I am thinking of going to work tomorrow. Mother is surprised I am better so quickly, and she said that I can't have had the same thing that she did.

Monday, 5th March

I went to work today, and felt well. A news sheet came about police raiding a meeting in the Central Hall, in Wells, on Saturday. It said that they suspected people were speaking out against the Rulers, and it will not be tolerated. They did not arrest anyone this time, but warn if they catch anyone they will be severely dealt with. Sascha told me that a friend of her father's was at the Hall that night, and he said they were meeting to form a music group, and the police are imagining things.

Thursday, 8th March

Mrs Newsby received a letter today saying that everyone is going to be required to carry an identity card. Blank cards are going to be delivered to the Information Centres. Mrs Newsby says it will be more work for us, as Sascha and I will have to write people's names, addresses and dates of birth on them. Then we will put up a poster telling people to come and collect them. We think it is so people cannot give false names to the police.

I sometimes wish I could leave this Island, but I don't know where I would go. I don't know if there are any other Islands, and if there are, would the rulers be any better? I wonder what happened to those people who left in the boats a hundred years ago.

12

Rebellion

Saturday, 10th March

I took Ruffles for a walk on the cliffs this afternoon. I had my hood up, and my head bent down as I battled my way into a really strong wind. So I didn't see Justin was ahead, and nearly bumped into him. He was looking through his binoculars, at a small flock of birds who were zooming about in the sky.

'Oh, hallo, I didn't see you there.'

'Hallo Gelany. How are you?' His face broke into a big smile.

'I'm okay. It's a bit cold in this wind though.'

'Yes. I was on my way back when I saw those birds. I think they have blue chests, but they are moving so fast, I can't really get a good look at them.'

'They seem to like the wind, even if we don't. I think I'll go back now too.'

I called Ruffles, and she came running up panting, after following some rabbit trails. When she saw Justin, she went up to him, wagging her tail.

'Hallo Ruffles. You don't seem to mind the wind either,'

he said as he stroked her silky head.

We turned and started walking home. It was much easier walking back with the wind behind us. We tried to talk, but couldn't have a conversation, as the wind was noisy and I couldn't hear with my hood up. I was pleased to see him, and enjoyed walking along with him. What a change from how I felt before! So when we got to my cottage I asked if he would like to come in for a warm drink.

'Is your mother well now?'

'Yes. I'm sure it was the lake water that made her better. She's at work now.'

'That's great, that she's better. So it was worth going to the lake then.'

He followed me into the kitchen, where I made two cups of milky barley drink. We carried them into the sitting room and sat down round the fire. He told me the Youth Club had shut down for a while, because not many people were going, but it has started again now.

Then he asked, 'I don't suppose you've been to the prison yet. Have you decided when you're going?'

'No. Every time I plan to go something happens to stop me. I'm beginning to wonder if I'm meant to go.'

'But you must go. You might find your father. I'll come with you if you like.'

'I suppose I'll go. But the weather isn't very suitable, and I seem to have lost the sense of urgency.'

'Well the weather will be better soon, with spring coming. I'll go for you if you like.'

'No it has to be me. I might find out he's there, and be able to see him. But I suppose I'm beginning to think he's dead, and then I'm scared to go.'

'I can understand that. Well let me know if I can help.'

As I looked at Justin sitting by the fire, with Ruffles at

his feet, I saw him as I have never seen him before. I felt drawn to him, the same way as I am to Gordon. Not just as a friend, but I wanted to go and sit by him and feel him put his arms around me. Justin noticed me looking at him, and smiled. I looked away quickly, knelt down and put another log on the fire.

'I'm glad we can be friends now Gelany.'

'Yes.'

'I expect we'll be meeting at the allotments soon.'

'Yes, I haven't really felt like going in this wind and rain. But I must start going soon. There is a lot of work to be done at this time of year.'

'Well I had better get going. It's getting dark, and looks like it's going to rain again.'

'I hope Mother comes home before it starts.'

As Justin became a speck in the distance on the road to town, I saw another speck pass him. It was Mother coming home. She didn't ask if I'd seen Justin. I don't think she wants me to be friends with him.

Sunday, 11th March

I went to Uncle Ray's farm today. Ruby is very excited, as it is her eighth birthday next Sunday, and Aunt Pearl says she can have a party. She told me I am invited, and my mother too.

Tuesday, 13th March

A box of Identity cards was delivered to the Information Centre today. Mrs Newsby said I must spend an hour a day working on them if I can, and let any other work that is not urgent wait. I am to sit next to Sascha, as she has the people's records. We are to use our best handwriting, and are going to start tomorrow. She said if we don't have enough time, we may have to work some afternoons. I hope it's not too many, as I really ought to start working on the allotment.

Wednesday, 12th March

It was nice working next to Sascha today. We finished all the surnames beginning with 'A'. We don't like the idea of carrying Identity cards, but Sascha said as long as we behave ourselves, we have nothing to worry about. I'm not sure I want to behave myself, if it means obeying all the Rulers' laws.

Thursday, 15th March

Gordon was waiting for me after work. I could sense something was wrong straight away, he definitely was not his usual cheerful self. His face looked sad and tired.

'What's wrong Gordon?'

'Let's go to the shelter by the station. I'll tell you there.'

We walked quickly in silence, until we reached the shelter and sat down.

'My father has been shot. He's dead.' He bent his head down in his hands, and ran his fingers through his black curls.

'Oh no Gordon. What happened?'

He looked up, and I could see tears in his eyes.

'Last week, after he left the Hall. I wasn't there, I'd gone to have dinner with Donna's family. I wish I'd been there now. Maybe I could have stopped it.'

'Do you know what happened?'

'Wilf said that the men had been complaining about the Ruler's again. My father stood up and spoke out to everyone, saying they should all get together and do something about it. I expect there was an Informer in the Hall. Wilf was walking home with Dad, he heard a shot, and my father fell to the ground. He saw two men, who looked like policemen, run away behind a building. He bent down to help my father, and then realised he was already dead. Oh, Gelany, how could they do that?' He went silent, biting his lip, trying to hold back the tears.

'That's awful.' I put my arm round his shoulders, wondering what to say. I was really shocked. 'How's your mother?'

'She's really upset. She keeps crying. She said she had warned him he'd get into trouble, if he didn't keep quiet about the Rulers. But I don't think she expected him to be shot dead, with no warning.' Then he put his arm around me and hugged me to him. 'I know what it's like for you now. We've both lost our fathers.'

I wasn't sure my father was dead yet, but it wasn't the time to argue about it. So I just let him hug me. I've wanted that for so long, but did not wish for him to lose his father, to make it happen.

The horn sounded for the Electra to start moving, and Gordon said he had to get back. He took his arm away, said 'Bye Gelany,' and walked quickly to a carriage.

I walked home feeling sad for Gordon, and worried about what might happen, if the police are spying on us, and have orders to shoot people.

Saturday, 17th March

I went to the allotment this morning. It was dry and sunny, and there were quite a lot of other people there, all working hard, preparing the soil for planting. Sarah came over and said 'Hallo', and had a chat about the weather.

I prepared about a third of the plot, digging the soil over and pulling the weeds out. I also planted a row of broad beans. My back ached after, so I decided to go home, sit down and make baskets in the afternoon. I was just leaving when Justin arrived.

'Hallo Gelany, are you going already?'

'Yes, I've been here all morning and my back is beginning to ache. So I think I've done enough for today.'

'I expect our muscles need to get used to it again, after the rest they've had over the winter. An afternoon will probably be enough for me too. I'll see you another day then.'

'Yes. Will you only come on Saturday afternoons?'

'No, I plan to come in the mornings as well. I had go to get the doctor this morning. My grandfather was worse. Then I did some jobs for him. I don't think the doctor knows what is wrong, but he left him a bottle of medicine. I managed to persuade Grandfather to take some, even though he says it tastes awful.'

When he talked about his grandfather, it made me remember that Justin is related to Mr Ditchling, the one who deprived me of my father. I wish he wasn't related.

'I'll see you another day then. Goodbye.'

I enjoyed working on the allotment again, I didn't realise how much I'd missed it. It will be nice to have Justin's company too, working alongside me.

When I got back to the cottage, I saw a policeman sitting in our front porch. Ruffles, was by my side and she started growling. It scared me, and as I stopped in my tracks, wondering what to do, he saw me and stood up. Then I saw it was Peter.

'Hallo Gelany. I've been waiting for you. I want to talk to you.'

I wondered what I had done wrong. Ruffles ran up to him and sniffed his uniform.

'Are you on your own?' I asked looking around, as

policemen are usually in pairs.

'Yes, it's my day off. I wanted to see you, so I've travelled here from Easten.'

I didn't really like asking a policeman in, and wondered why he had to wear his uniform on his day off.

'Okay, come in,' I answered reluctantly. 'Would you like a drink?'

He said he would, so we went into the kitchen and I made some mint tea. He watched me silently and I wondered what he could possibly want. Did he want to warn me about something? We took the cups to the sitting room and sat in chairs on opposite sides of the fire.

'How are you Gelany? I heard you broke your ankle.'

'It's fine now. How are you? Do you like working in the police?'

'It's alright. They're building some new police houses in Wells. So I've come to ask you again if you'll marry me. I could apply for a house in Wells, and ask to be transferred here. You told me you didn't want to live in Easten.'

'Oh Peter, it's not just where I live. I don't want to be married to a policeman either. I'm sorry.'

'I can't change my job now. We can't leave the police once we've joined. It's a good job, it pays well. You wouldn't have to work on the allotment anymore, we could afford to buy all our food from the shops and market. The houses are going to be really nice too, they will have electricity. That means clean power for lights and cooking. I think you'd like it.'

'No I wouldn't Peter. I like it here, and I like working on the allotment.'

'That's because you've never known anything different. Come to see me in Easten, and I can show you the house I live in there.'

'No Peter. I don't think you understand.'

'I'll give you time to think about it. Either come to see me, you can stay the night, I've got a spare room, or I'll come back to see you, in about a month's time. That's when we need to apply for the houses.'

'Peter, why are the police raiding meetings now?'

'The people are getting rebellious, that's why they're recruiting more police. If people are speaking out against the Rulers, we have to stop the meetings. It's our job.'

'Thank you for not telling on me when you found me in the cave. I saw the dove had been shot.'

'Yes they're pesky birds. They scare away other birds, that are good for meat.'

'Is that what you think?'

'Yes, it's what we've been told. There haven't been any doves around for a hundred years, and now they've started coming back. We have to get rid of them before they start to breed on the Island.'

I was so upset by all he was saying, I didn't know what to say. I didn't like to contradict a policeman. All I could see was his uniform, I could hardly see the Peter I used to know. I hated having a policeman in our cottage. I decided to try to get him to leave, without upsetting him.

'Have you been to see your family today. I know they'd love to see you. They miss you so much Peter.'

'No, I haven't seen them yet. I thought if I have time, I'll see them on the way back.'

'Well I won't keep you then. You must have time to go and see them.'

'Gelany you will think about it, won't you? I'm still your friend, even though I'm a policeman. It would be good for you to be on our side. Things are probably going to get tougher around here.'

Well that was a romantic speech, wasn't it! 'No, no, no Peter, I will never marry you', I wanted to say, but I didn't. I don't want to get on the wrong side of the police, so I just stood up to encourage him to go. He came towards me as if to kiss me, and I backed away.

'Your uniform frightens me Peter. I wish you'd come in ordinary clothes.'

'Well you'll have to get used to it. We have to wear it when we're off duty too, and be ready to uphold the law, if we see anyone breaking it.'

'Can't you wear you own clothes in your own house?'

'Yes, it's only when we go out, we have to wear our uniforms.' He took a piece of paper from his pocket. 'Here's my address. You can write to me and tell me when you're coming to see me. Please come.'

I took the piece of paper but didn't make any promises. I would have liked to have chatted more if he looked like Peter, but I felt as if I had an unwelcome policeman in my cottage. We said goodbye and he left. I breathed a sigh of relief. I felt like throwing the paper in the bin, but decided to keep it in my drawer, so I could write to him. Probably not to say I'm going to go to see him though.

Sunday, 18th March

Ruby's eighth birthday today. My mother, Ruffles and I walked up to Uncle Ray's farm at noon. Aunt Pearl was in the kitchen stirring a big pot of bean and vegetable soup. Evidently it is Ruby's favourite. She called to Ruby who was in the sitting room,

'Ruby, Aunt Wanda and Gelany are here. Come and take your things off the table, I want to get it ready.'

Ruby came running in carrying a rag doll in her arms.

'Look what Mummy made me. Isn't she lovely?' Look

I'll show you my other presents.' She pushed some brown paper off the table, onto the floor, and showed us a skipping rope from Jimmy, and a picture of her kitten, painted by Rayson.'

I gave her a kiss and said 'Yes they're all lovely, and here are two more.'

She opened the sweets from my mother and two blue ribbons for her hair, from me.

'Thank you Aunt Wanda, I like those. Thank you Gelany, can you tie them in for me?'

I had just finished tying them in her long blonde hair, when there was a knock at the door. Her friend Hanily was there with her mother. Aunt Pearl said that they would take Hanily back later, and her mother went home. Hanily gave Ruby an egg cup that is shaped like a chicken. Ruby was so pleased with all of her presents.

'Oh, I forgot to tell you Gelany, Daddy has made me a swing and put it up in the oak tree. He said I am old enough to hold on tight now. Let's go and see it after lunch.'

My Mother and I helped Aunt Pearl lay the table. As well as the soup, there were rolls and currant buns from Rayson's bakery, slices of ham, and a large birthday cake. Rayson had drawn a picture of a cat on it, with the icing. As soon as Uncle Ray and Jimmy came in, and had cleaned up, we all sat down to eat.

Ruby looked round the table and remarked, 'There's eight of us, because I'm eight. Perhaps next year there will be nine.'

We all laughed. 'I wonder who the ninth person will be,' said Uncle Ray.

I secretly hoped we would all be there next year, as I thought about what happened after my eighth birthday. And if there were going to be nine, I hoped the extra one would be my father.

After lunch had been cleared away, we went into the sitting room. Beauty was curled up on one of the chairs. Ruby told me the cat had been allowed in, as it was her special day. I picked Beauty up and put her on my lap. She snuggled down, and we made each other warm. Ruby and Hanily tried to skip with the rope, until they knocked a vase off a table. Aunt Pearl said she would have to use the skipping rope outside in future.

Uncle Ray got his violin out, and told Jimmy to get his tin whistle. Rayson got a saucepan and a wooden spoon to use as a drum. They played folk songs, and we all had a good time singing along. Ruby made us sing the one about a cat three times.

When Uncle Ray put the violin down, Ruby pleaded with him to come and show her how to swing. I think he would have liked to have had a doze in his armchair, but he gave in and said he would, as it was her birthday. Hanily, Jimmy, Rayson and I went too. Aunt Pearl said she would stay behind and have a chat with my mother.

The oak tree isn't far from the house and can be seen from the kitchen window. Uncle Ray had looped two strong pieces of rope over a thick branch, and made a wooden seat that he had painted blue. Ruby climbed up onto it, he gave her a big push, and told her how she could make it carry on swinging. She hung on tightly, and put her legs out straight in front, then swung them back, as it went backwards. She couldn't quite get the rhythm, and Uncle Ray kept pushing her gently from the back, and encouraging her to do it herself. It made tears come to my eyes, as I remembered my Daddy taking care of me, and my eighth birthday when he had made me a dolls' house. I said I needed to go and get my hat and walked away quickly. The tears started running down my face, as I walked up to the house. I blew my nose and wiped my eyes, and went indoors. Mother was in the hall, getting something out of her bag.

'What's the matter Gelany?'

'Oh, it's just seeing Ruby and Uncle Ray having fun on her eighth birthday. It reminded me of Daddy and me.'

She put her arm round me, and said 'Oh you need to forget all that. You're grown up now.'

I pulled away.

'I'm alright. I've just come in for my hat.'

Hanily had a turn on the swing next, then me, Jimmy and even Rayson. We laughed a lot and it made me feel better. Jimmy could swing the best, I think he will want to use it as well as Ruby. Uncle Rayson told him to remember it's Ruby's and to take care of it.

The sun was going down and it was getting colder, so Uncle Ray suggested we went indoors for a game of cards. We raced back up to the house, Jimmy getting there first. But soon Mother said we had better go home, as it was getting dark. Uncle Ray and Ruby took Hanily home too.

As we walked home, I was glad I was part of Uncle Ray's family. But seeing Ruby having fun with her father, has made me determined to go and find mine. I am going to ask for next Friday off.

Monday, 19th March

Sascha whispered excitedly to me at work, that Peter had been to see them, but she waited until we were walking home together to say more.

'We were so pleased to see Peter on Saturday. He said he'd been to see you first, and told you he could be transferred to Wells. Will you marry him now?'

'I don't want to marry a policeman.'

'Oh. Perhaps he will come to live in Wells anyway.'

'Then he will have to arrest people round here. Maybe people we know.'

'I'm sure he wouldn't do it unless they've done something terribly wrong.'

I didn't say any more about it, I don't want to worry her, or fall out with her. I started talking about the Identity cards instead.

Mrs Newsby said she wants us to work one full day this week, as we need to spend more time on the Cards. I told her I was going to ask for Friday off, and she said I could have it off if I work two full days. I didn't like to remind her she already owes me some time off, as I could see she needs the cards done. It's annoying, as I need to go to the allotment in the afternoons now. I went this afternoon, and dug and weeded another third of the plot, and I will do the rest tomorrow. Then I have to work, at the Information Centre, Wednesday and Thursday all day. At least I can go to the prison on Friday. Then I'll do some planting on Saturday. What a busy life!

Thursday, 22nd March

It's spring now, and yellow daffodils are blooming in the garden. It is lovely to see the flowers again. I am quite tired, as I have finished digging all the allotment, and have written in many Identity cards. Mrs Newsby told us there are some spare ones, in case we make mistakes, but to try hard not to make any, as we will need them when children become sixteen. Only people over sixteen have to carry them.

When Sascha went to see Mrs Newsby about something, I put a blank Identity card in my pocket. I thought it might be a good idea to put a false name and address in one, and carry it with me. It might be useful if the police stop me and

I don't want to tell them who I am. I am going to take it with me tomorrow. I'm not sure what name and address to put in it though.

I told Sascha that I am going to the prison tomorrow, and not to tell anyone else. She told me to be very careful.

I took Ruffles for a walk on the cliffs this evening and had a chat to God. I asked Him to help me find my father tomorrow and to keep me safe. Then I came home, levered up the floorboard, and got the picture out, that Grandma had given me. I stared at it, remembering what Daddy looked like. I wonder if he has changed much in the last eight years. I certainly have. I feel so excited I can hardly wait. I am going to put what I will need for the journey, in my backpack now.

13

A Visitor

Friday, 23rd March

After Mother left for work, I got the rest of my things together, putting some bread, cheese, a chicken pie, and a drink in my backpack. Also some dog biscuits and meat for Ruffles. I quickly wrote a note to Mother and left it on my desk. It was to let her know where I had gone, if I got home after her, and she wondered where I was. If I got back first, which was what I expected to do, I would throw the note away. Then I could choose whether to tell her or not. If it was good news I would certainly tell her, but if it wasn't then I probably wouldn't say anything about it. There wouldn't be any point, it would only upset her. This is what I wrote:

Dear Mother
I have been told that Daddy was not shot after he was arrested, and that he was seen in the prison, a year later. I have gone to find out if he is still there. The prison is at Journey's End, between Soumarket and Easten. Where the Electra bends sharply left going towards Easten, there is a track that goes to the right, and the prison is probably at the

end of that.
I am planning to be back this evening.
Love from
Gelany.

Ruffles and I left home at 8.40am and walked up the Wells Road. Instead of going up to the station, we cut across the fields, going past Sascha's farm, until we reached the Electra track. As I wasn't going to sit in a carriage, I thought I might as well climb on further towards Soumarket. There were a few sheep, on the track, with a shepherd and two sheepdogs. He looked surprised and said 'Good day' as we climbed up near them. Ruffles stared at the sheep. I put her lead on and pulled her away and started walking. After about five minutes, the track began to move. I wobbled about a bit at first, and felt like I could fall off, but I soon got used to it.

It was strange to go through Soumarket, without stopping. An old man on the platform gave me a strange look as we zoomed past him, whilst we were walking along the moving track. About 10.15am, the track jerked and stopped, then went forward and jerked and stopped a few more times. I had to sit down and hold on tight to avoid falling off. Then the track gave a big jolt, shook, and finally stopped. Not a good sign. I got off, hoping it would be alright when I came back.

I let Ruffles off her lead and we walked on a road, that ran alongside the Electra. After about two miles, the Electra and the road, turned sharply to the left towards Easten. There I saw a stony track going off to the right, just as Daniel had said it did, and we started to walk down it. The track had two deep ruts in it, suggesting a carriage must travel this way, so I was hopeful of finding the prison at the end.

'Nearly there now Ruffles,' I said, looking down at her.

She was trotting close by my side looking a bit tired. 'Let's stop for a drink.'

Ruffles looked up at me longingly, as if I had read her mind. Sitting down on a grassy bank, I took my backpack off to get some water out. Ruffles took a long drink out of a small dish I had brought for her, and then wandered off, sniffing in the long green grass for rabbits. As I was having a drink myself, she started to bark at something she had found.

'Come on,' I said, getting up, 'We haven't got time for rabbit hunting today. Let's get a move on.'

I started walking down the track, but she stayed where she was, pawing at something and whining, so I went back to see what she was making a fuss about. When I pulled the grass apart, I saw a shiny object lying on the ground, and picked it up to take a closer look. It was a big silver coloured key. I didn't know where it was for, so I put it back on the ground and started to walk away. Ruffles wouldn't leave it, so I went back, picked it up and put it in my backpack. That seemed to satisfy her, and she followed me down the track.

Further on, I saw two black figures coming towards us. Ruffles gave a rumbling growl in her throat, and I guessed that they were policemen. I looked around for somewhere to hide, but it was open countryside, and I knew they had already spotted me. I carried on walking towards them, trying to look confident, after all I wasn't doing anything wrong. When they got near, I started to walk past them, without looking at them, until I heard a voice I recognised.

'Gelany, what on earth are you doing here?' It was Peter. I looked at him, feeling slightly relieved.

'I'm going to the prison. Is it down this road?'

'Yes, but why are you going there?'

'I was told my father may be in there, and I want to find

out if it's true.'

'You'd better not go there, no one's supposed to know where it is. If you do, I'm sure they won't tell you anything, and you'd probably be in trouble. The chief guard isn't in a good mood at the moment anyway.'

'Why, what's happened?'

'Robert and I were bringing a new lock and key to the prison, as one has broken, and they can't lock a door. But the key must have fallen out of Robert's bag on the way, we didn't know that the stitching had come undone. The guard has sent us back to look for it, and we've just walked all the way from Easten, so it could be anywhere.'

'I found a key. Is this it?' I said, as I took off my backpack and rummaged around inside. I handed the key to Robert. As he stared at it, the worry fell from his face, and it broke into a smile.

'Yes, it is. Where did you find it?'

'Ruffles found it in some long grass, quite a way back there. She started barking and pawing at something, so I went to see why.'

'Thank you. She'd make a good policeman's dog,' said Robert.

'No, she's mine,' I said horrified, putting my arms round her neck.

'It's alright, we're not going to take her away. You've really helped us out today, we were in big trouble,' said Robert.

'Yes,' said Peter, looking at the ground, as if he was thinking. 'I know, we could try to find out if your father's in the prison for you. Can you wait around until we walk back, then we can let you know if we find out anything.'

'Oh would you, please?'

'I think I remember what he looked like. What's his

name?'

'Timothy.'

'We will probably have a meal there before heading back, if they're still going to feed us,' said Robert. 'Where will you wait, it looks like it's going to rain?'

'She could wait in that barn, near the prison. Come with us Gelany, we'll show you.'

We walked along the track until we were near to the cliff edge. Here the track continued across a spit of land that led to a small island, with a huge grey building on it. On either side of the prison were high walls with metal spikes on the top, running to the edges of the land, keeping the prisoners in and unwanted intruders out. Peter pointed to an open sided barn nearby, at the edge of a field, and I walked over to it. It had lots of hay and straw bales inside. A welcome sight, as drops of rain had started to fall, and I was feeling very hungry and tired. Sitting down on a hay bale, with Ruffles snuggled up beside me, I got out the chicken pie, and it did taste good. Ruffles looked at me longingly with her big brown eyes, and I gave her a bit. When she asked for more, I gave her the dog biscuits. I wondered if she thought it was a strange long walk we were having today.

I could see the prison from the barn. The ground floor of the building had two wooden doors, and a window that was covered in iron bars. One door was only big enough for a person to go through, and the other one was large enough for horses and a carriage. On the next floor up was a row of windows, and they all had iron bars across them. I sat there for a while looking at it, hoping that Daddy was inside, and then began to feel sleepy, so laid my head down on the hay. I must have dozed off, because I was awoken by Peter calling my name in a loud whisper. I picked up my bag, and joined them as they walked back up the track.

'Was he in there Peter? Did you find out?'

'Yes, he is.'

'Did you see him?'

'Yes. He was at another table though, so I couldn't speak to him. I asked the prisoner who was serving us lunch, if he knew if Timothy Lantern was in there. He said "Yes, he's the furniture maker, sitting over there", and pointed him out. When I looked, I recognised your father. He wouldn't have recognised me though, what with me being eight years older and dressed in a policeman's uniform.'

'So he's still alive!' Although it was what I had been hoping for, I could hardly believe it. As we walked back up the road my heart glowed with happiness. If Peter had asked me to marry him then, I think I might have said 'yes', I felt so grateful to him for giving me such good news.

They talked to each other about what they had seen in the prison, as we walked along. All I could think about was that Daddy is still alive, and I felt speechless.

When we reached the Electra, Peter said to me 'It is a good thing we met today, we were able to help each other out.'

'Yes,' I agreed.

We said our goodbyes and they carried on walking towards Easten. The track wasn't moving which was not a good sign as it should have been at that time. I climbed up onto it and sat down. Ruffles followed me and sat down beside me, leaning against me.

'At least we know Daddy's still alive Ruffles,' I said, as I put my arm around her.

Now I didn't know what to do. Easten was five miles away, but if the Electra wasn't mended, it would be a shorter walk home going in the opposite direction.

The only way I was going to get home that day, would

be if the track started moving, so I sat on it and waited. 'Please God,' I said, 'please make the track move again.' I sat there for quite a while, but the track still didn't start moving. When it was 4pm I knew that there was no way I could get home before dark.

I wondered where I could sleep for the night, and thought of the hay barn. So Ruffles and I walked all the way back down the road to the prison. The air was getting chilly, as the sun was low in the sky, so the barn was a welcome sight, and I sat down on a hay bale.

'Time for dinner, I think,' I said to Ruffles.

I gave her a juicy lump of beef, and settled down to eat my bread and cheese. I could see the prison windows, and stared at them, hoping to get a glimpse of Daddy. I did see someone near a window, but was too far away to see who it was. After we had eaten, I was thirsty but had finished my water earlier. 'What do I do now God?' I asked out loud. It would be even harder to walk home tomorrow if I hadn't been drinking. I heard God say, 'Get up and look.' So I looked around for a puddle or something. When I went round the back of the barn, I found a spring, running down a bank, into an animal trough, and along a ditch towards the sea. The water looked fresh and I eagerly filled my bottle, and took a long drink. Ruffles stood on her back legs and lapped up water out of the trough.

Going back into the barn, I pulled lots of stalks out of the centre of a bale, and made a cosy, sweet smelling, nest. Ruffles curled up with me, and I pulled some hay back over the top of us. As we lay there keeping each other warm, I started thinking about tomorrow. If the Electra track was not mended, I would have about eighteen miles to walk home. I decided not to think about it anymore, and watched the colourful sky as the sun went down, and thought of Daddy instead, and how close I was to him. Maybe he was looking out of the prison window at the same sunset. Soon after it got dark, and I fell asleep.

I was woken up, by Ruffles growling. I hoped it was just a mouse, and told her to go back to sleep. But then she sat bolt upright and stared towards the prison, still growling. I sat up and looked in the same direction. In the distance I could see a light and it was coming our way. As it got nearer, I saw that it was a person, surrounded by light. I felt really scared, thinking it was a ghost. Pulling Ruffles down, I tried to hide in the hay.

They came up to the barn and I heard someone tentatively calling my name, 'Gelany?'

I looked out and saw a face I recognised. A face I had missed so much.

'Daddy! It's Daddy!'

I climbed out of the hay, and stood in front of him.

'Daddy, is it really you?'

'Gelany, is it really you?'

He was still surrounded by a light, but it was gradually fading. It was a good thing that the moon was shining brightly, so we could see each other. I took a step back and asked worriedly, 'Are you a ghost?'

'I don't think so. Give me a hug and we'll see.'

I slowly put my arms around his waist, and he felt warm and solid, so not a ghost. He put his big strong arms round my shoulders, and hugged me to him. It was what I had longed for, ever since he disappeared. We held each other for what seemed like a long while, in silence.

Then he held me away from himself. 'Let's have a look at you. Gosh, you've grown into a fine young lady. How I've longed to see you.'

'But how did you get out of the prison?'

'Let's sit down and make ourselves comfortable, I'm sure we've got a lot of catching up to do.'

'Come up here, where I've made a warm nest.'

He followed me up to the hay bale, and we sat inside it. Ruffles looked at us wondering where she fitted in.

'Who's this?'

'She's called Ruffles and she's my dog.'

'Hallo Ruffles,' he said as he stroked her head. She laid down beside us.

'Oh Daddy, I've missed you so much.'

'And I've missed you too Gelany.'

'At first we didn't know what had happened to you, when you disappeared. Then recently someone told me you'd been shot, so we thought you were dead. Then I got a letter from Grandma, and I went to see her. She told me you might be in the prison. So I came here to find out if you were. On the way, I met Peter, who's a policeman, and he found out you are in there, but said they wouldn't let me see you. So I went back to get on the Electra, but it's broken down, and I came back to this barn to stay the night. How did you get out of the prison?'

'When I went to sleep this evening, I had a very vivid dream. I dreamt a dove landed on my windowsill. It had a large white feather in its beak, which it gave to me. Then it spoke, and told me that you were outside the prison waiting in a hay barn. It said I could walk out of the prison and go to see you, but I must come back again before daylight. In my dream, I tried the door to my cell and it opened, then I walked through another door, and got to the front door. There the guards were sleeping, so I just opened the door and walked out, it wasn't even locked. Then I found you in a hay barn, just like this one.'

'But that was a dream wasn't it, what happened next?'

'Well I woke up, feeling quite stunned, as it had all seemed so real. Soon I heard a fluttering of wings outside my window, so I got out of bed to have a look. Sure enough, a dove landed on the windowsill, and it had a large white feather in its beak. I opened the window and it gave the feather to me. Here look, I have it in my pocket.' He got out a beautiful white feather and handed it to me.

'Did the dove talk to you?'

'No, not this time. It just looked at me, cocked its head on one side, and then flew away. Otherwise it seemed like my dream. So I got up and tried my door and it wasn't locked. I quickly put my clothes on, and left the cell. The rest was like my dream, I got through the doors with no trouble, and the guards were asleep in their chairs. So here I am! How's Mummy?'

It seemed strange him calling her that, I hadn't used that name for years.

'She's alright. She works long hours at the hospital, and wants to move to a cottage in Wells.'

'Has she forgiven me?'

'I don't know. She thinks you're dead. I can tell her you're alive now! Oh Daddy, I've missed you so much.' I put my head on his shoulder and made it wet with my tears. He put his arm around me.

'I'm so sorry Gelany. I can't say I don't believe in God, when I know He's true. He means so much to me, and I trust Him to look after me and my family. Perhaps I should have kept quiet at work, but George was so interested in God, he kept asking me questions. I knew that his father was worried, and didn't want him to believe, in case he got into trouble. I didn't think anyone else was listening, so I answered his questions, but Mr Ditchling must have heard.'

'Daddy do you mind if I'm friends with Justin, Mr

Ditchling's grandson?'

'What little Justin? No, I remember him coming to see his Dad at the shop sometimes, when he came into town with his mother. Always very interested in what we were doing. Used to want to have a go himself, with our tools. He was a nice little boy.'

'He's not so little now, I think he's fifteen. And he has a job at Woodalls.'

'How do you know him?

'He works on the allotment next to ours, as Mr Ditchling is too ill to do it. Also I see him walking on the cliffs sometimes, looking at birds through his binoculars. I rescued him once, when he fell off the cliff, and then he rescued me when I broke my ankle up there.'

'Sounds like you're good friends. How's your ankle now?'

'It's fine.' I stuck my leg out, and bent my foot to show him. 'So you don't mind if I'm friends with him then?'

'No, I don't mind. I liked his father, and I've forgiven Mr Ditchling too. There's not much point in carrying a grudge against him, I'm the only one it harms. It was hard to forgive him, I had to ask God to help me do it.'

'What's it like in the prison?'

'Not as good as being outside! They let me live because I'm useful. I make furniture for the Tansas, and anything else out of wood that they want. I also make things for the prison, and a shop in Easten, where they get money for it. The food is quite basic and repetitive, but we usually get enough. There is a small farm at the back of the prison, and some of the prisoners work on it. I'm in a cell on my own, but I can talk to other prisoners when I'm out of it. There are some more people in there who believe in God, and we can talk about it freely to each other. They can't put us in prison for it, as we're already in there. We see miracles happen quite often! There's even a guard that believes in God now, but we don't talk to him about it, as we don't want to get him into trouble. He's on our side though, so that's good.'

'Daddy, maybe I could do something and get sent to prison, then I could see you every day!'

'No Gelany, please don't do that, it's too risky. Not everyone lives. If they can't find a use for them, they often shoot people. Anyway, the women are kept in a separate building, we never see them. I hope one day I'll get out. I often pray that the Rulers will be got rid of and the Island will be set free.'

'What's pray?'

'Talking to God. It's called praying.'

'Oh, I do that. He talks back to me too sometimes.'

'Do you believe in God Gelany?'

'Yes.' I told him about the cliff falling, and the letter I found in the tin in the cave, and about the dove.

'That's wonderful. Well, except for you falling down the cliff Ruffles,' he said as he reached out and stroked her. She wagged her tail. 'God really does answer prayers in amazing ways, I've prayed that you would get to know God for yourself.'

'Mum doesn't want me to. She's scared I'd get into trouble.'

'No she wouldn't want you to. She didn't want me to talk about God to you. So I didn't, because you were young, and might not be careful enough. I had an older brother, who was a baker in Easten. He was a believer, and he disappeared. A policeman told us that he'd been shot, and let that be a warning to us. He's not in the prison, so I think he must have been killed.'

'Oh Grandma didn't tell me she had another son. What

was his name?'

He looked down sadly and said 'Paul.' Then he looked up again and smiled at me. 'Anyway, tell me about everything. What have I missed these last eight years?'

I told him about my job at the Information Centre and working there with Sascha. That I've carried on looking after our allotment, and it's doing well. He was pleased about that, and said he was glad I had taken an interest in it, before he went away, so that he could teach me things. I told him about Ruby being born and how sweet she is, and that she believes in God. He was pleased to hear that, and hoped she would be careful. He said he would pray for her. He was interested to hear that Jimmy is old enough to work on the farm, and that Rayson didn't want to, and became a baker instead.

'I'm making some nursery furniture for the new Tansa baby at the moment,' he told me. 'Have you heard that Charles Tansa and Emerald are expecting a baby in June?'

'Yes, I did see that in a news sheet.'

'I used to know Emerald's father, when I lived in Easten. We were good friends. I even saw Emerald when she was very young, that was before I moved to Wells and married your mother. I feel sorry for Emerald and that she has been taken away from her family, so I'm making the best furniture I can. I want to paint it white and decorate it, but can't decide how. What do you think she would like?'

'I think I would like baby animals on it. How about blue ducks, yellow chicks, and black lambs?'

'That sounds nice, but I wish it was you I was making nursery furniture for. Do you have a boyfriend Gelany?'

'No. I like a boy named Gordon. He's a fisherman in Easten. Sometimes he comes to see me when he delivers fish to Wells. But he already has a girlfriend, and they are going to get married when they get a cottage.'

'Oh.'

'Peter asked me to marry him. Do you remember Peter?'

'Yes, Mummy's friend's son. They hoped that you two would marry each other when you grew up. Are you going to?'

'No, not now he's become a policeman.'

'Has he?'

'You agree that I can't marry a policeman, don't you?'

'Yes. That wouldn't work would it, not now you're a believer. He might have to arrest his own wife!'

'Rayson applied to be a policeman at the same time, but he didn't get in. We were so glad about that. He's quite happy being a baker now.'

'I expect the reason he didn't get in, is that he's related to me.'

'Do you think so?'

'Yes they make lots of checks on people before they take them into the police. Men who have close relatives in prison, wouldn't get in. Especially if that relative believed in God.'

'I'm glad he didn't, I like Rayson.'

'What about Justin, is he your boyfriend?'

'No, we're just friends. I don't think Mother would like me to be his girlfriend, she doesn't like the Ditchling family for what they did to you.'

'Well don't let it stop you being friends with him, if you want to be.'

'I don't think he would want to marry me anyway, I was quite nasty to him at first, when I found out it was his family's fault that I had lost you. I think he is only nice to me now, because he wants to make it up to me.'

'You're quite an attractive young lady, I wouldn't be surprised if there was more to it than that!'

He looked down at me, grinned and hugged me. 'How

I've missed you and all the family. It's so good to have you come here to see me.'

'Daddy can you come home with me?' I asked hopefully.

'No, I don't think so. In my dream I went back in the prison after I met with you. I hope I can get back in.'

'But why Daddy?'

'They would only come looking for me, and I've got nowhere to hide. Anyway when they find me, they would probably do something worse to me as a punishment. No I'll keep on praying that the Rulers will be overthrown, and we will all be let out. My window faces out to the sea, and sometimes I see a boat or two in the distance, and I wonder if people from another island are trying to rescue us. Now you've told me about the letter in the cave, I think it's quite likely. The people who escaped, might have found another island to live on, and told their children about Tansay.'

'Why doesn't anyone come to rescue us then?'

'Well, there's a cannon on the other side of the prison, and as soon as a boat is spotted, it is fired at. The Lookout gets a good view from there, across a wide area of the ocean.'

'We heard cannons firing when I was a child, and you used to tell me that aliens were trying to come here. I thought they were some strange beings, not like us.' It was nice lying with my head against Daddy's chest, talking with him like I used to, and feeling the sound of his answering voice vibrate through me. I was beginning to feel sleepy though.

'Well aliens is what we call anyone who is not from this island, and may pose a threat. But perhaps there are friendly aliens.'

'Do you really think there are other islands out there?'

'I don't know, but I think it is likely.'

'I hope if any aliens get on the island, they are the friendly ones.' I started shivering and Daddy pulled me closer to him. 'Remember Gelany, you have God watching over you and you can ask Him to look after you. I pray for you every day. It's so lovely to see you. This meeting is God's gift to us.'

I yawned and snuggled up against him. He looked towards the prison.

'I think I must go back now. You need some sleep. You may have a long walk home tomorrow if the Electra isn't working.'

'Daddy, how will I know you've got back safely into the prison, and not got caught?'

'See that window up there, the one on the left corner of the building, that's at the top of the staircase.' He pulled a white handkerchief out of his pocket. 'When I get there, I will wave this at the window. My cell is near there.'

'Okay, I'll walk back with you, and stand where I can see the window. It's a good thing the moon is out.'

'If you don't see it Gelany, remember God is still looking after me.' He pulled himself away from me, stood up and held out his hand. I took it and let him pull me up to my feet.

As soon as we started walking towards the prison, Daddy began to get a glow around him again. I knew something supernatural was happening, and felt more confident that he would be alright.

We stopped where the narrow bridge of land began, and he pointed to the prison and said, 'If you are still here at six thirty in the morning, look up at that window again. I go past it, on my way to the canteen for breakfast. I'll try to wave the hankie then as a goodbye, before you go off to the Electra. I'll pretend I'm going to sneeze or something.' He gave me a smile, just like he used to when he joked with me.

'Goodbye Gelany. Give my love to Mummy.' He

hugged me, and stroked Ruffles on the head. I saw tears in his eyes, before he turned and walked towards the prison door. The light around him became almost dazzling, as I saw him go in through the small door. I hoped the light wouldn't wake up the guards.

I stood there looking up at the window on the left corner. After a few minutes, I saw a white hankie waving madly at the window, then it was gone. 'Thank you God,' I whispered and walked back to the haystack. I was really tired and snuggled down in the hay. It still felt warm and smelt of Daddy. Ruffles curled up beside me and we fell into a contented sleep.

I was awoken by the sun shining on my face. Sitting up, I remembered where I was and what had happened during the night. I looked at the grey prison building, and wondered if it had been a dream.

'Oh Ruffles, it wasn't all a dream, was it?' Tears started falling down my cheeks as I began to think I hadn't really seen Daddy. Ruffles whined and put her nose down in the hay, sniffing at something. I looked, and there was the large white dove's feather. I picked it up, and smiled, as I carefully put it in my backpack. Then I remembered Daddy saying he would try to wave in the morning. Looking at my watch, I saw it was 6.20am.

'Quick Ruffles, we're just in time.' Ruffles barked at my excitement, and I had to stop her. We walked towards the prison, until I could see the window clearly, but I hid behind a bush, so we couldn't be seen. Just after 6.30am, I saw a white hankie wave briefly in the window, and my heart gave a leap. I looked at Ruffles and whispered to her, 'So it was true, it did all happen, didn't it?' She wagged her tail as she looked back at me. I was excited at the thought of telling Mother that Daddy is still alive, and that I have seen him.

14

Sharing News

Saturday, 24th March

I reluctantly left the prison, because I was leaving Daddy behind, and walked back to the hay barn to collect my things. Ruffles and I had a drink at the spring, and I filled my bottle with water to take with me. I wondered what I could eat and looked around. On the bank, I found a bush full of extremely large winter berries. I have never seen them so big, almost like small apples. I ate some, and was surprised that Ruffles ate them too when I offered them to her. They did taste good, and satisfied my hunger.

When we got to the Electra track, I climbed on and sat down. It usually starts moving at 8am, but when it was still stationary at 8.15am, I knew it had not yet been mended, so I started the long walk home.

I walked down the road that runs alongside the Electra track for five miles, until I reached Soumarket, at about 10.30am. I was getting weak with hunger by this time, so was glad when I came across a butcher's shop. After buying myself a nice freshly baked pie, and Ruffles a leg of chicken, we sat on a seat and ate them eagerly. I still had at least ten more miles to walk, and felt I needed a break, so decided to go and see Daniel's family.

When I knocked on the door of their cottage, Susanne and Petal opened it.

'Gelany, it's Gelany,' cried Petal excitedly.

'Hallo Gelany,' said Susanne, 'Go and get Daddy Petal, he's in the barn.'

Petal ran off and I followed Susanne inside.

'You look tired, come and sit down.'

I followed her into the sitting room and sat down by the fire. Ruffles immediately lay down on the rug in front of the heat, and shut her eyes.

'I've walked back from the prison this morning. The Electra has broken down, and I'm on my way back to Wells.'

'Oh you poor thing. I'll go and get you some hot milk.'

She went out to the kitchen, and I heard Daniel come in, and Susanne telling him about my walk. She came back in carrying a tray of drinks, followed by Daniel, Petal and Josh. Petal had a bowl of water for Ruffles, which she put on the rug. Ruffles raised a tired head and took a big drink. Susanne handed me a large mug of warm milk, and it tasted so good.

'So Gelany, you've had a long walk have you?' enquired Daniel. I was aware of four pairs of eyes on me, waiting for the details.

'Yes, I went to find the prison yesterday, and the Electra broke down, so I couldn't get home. I stayed in a hay barn for the night, and am on my way back to Wells now. The Electra still isn't working, so I have another ten miles to walk.'

'That's a long way,' said Susanne.

'Did you find out if your father's in there?' asked Daniel.

'Yes, he is. I met a policeman I know, who was going to the prison. He told me not to go there, but found out for me.

222

He actually saw him in there, but couldn't speak to him.'

'That's a shame,' said Susanne.

'Yes, but it's great to know he's still alive. Maybe one day he will get out of there and come home.' I replied.

I had decided not to tell them about seeing him, although I could hardly stop myself from blurting it out. I wanted to tell Mother first.

'Can you stay to lunch?' asked Susanne.

'No thank you, I really must start walking again soon, or else I won't get back before dark.'

'Then I'll go and make you a packed lunch, you'll need something to eat, if you are going to walk all that way.'

She went out to the kitchen. Petal knelt down by Ruffles, who she was lying on her side with her legs out straight, and she stroked her tummy.

'I wish I could have a dog like Ruffles,' she said.

'That's hard luck, the Electra breaking down, just when you decided to do that journey,' said Daniel.

I thought if it hadn't, then I wouldn't have seen Daddy that night. I wished I could tell them, but it would sound rather strange to say Daddy walked out of the prison to see me, and then went back in again.

We talked about the farm, and the taxes going up. They told me there are people in Soumarket who want to get rid of the Rulers, and I told them about Gordon's father being shot.

When I got up to leave, Susanne handed me two bags, one was for Ruffles she said. I put them in my backpack, thanked her and told her I really appreciated it. She told me to come again, when I could, and to stay and have lunch next time. They are such a nice family.

I walked back up to the Electra track, and followed the road running alongside it, as I knew that would lead to Wells. I walked as far as I could before hunger bid me to stop, after

I had been walking for about two hours. Ruffles and I sat down on a grassy bank, with a small stream running behind it. I got out the bags Susanne had given me. Ruffles had a big chunk of beef, and some biscuits. In my bag I found ham sandwiches, a big piece of fruit cake, and a large apple. It tasted like a real feast. We drank water from the stream. I felt like resting longer, but knew I must keep walking, and the food had revived me.

It began to drizzle with rain as Wells came into sight. I cut across the fields, going back past Sascha's farm. I would have liked to have stopped there, but knew I must get home. I began to think of Mother. I realised she might not know that the Electra had broken down, and would probably be worrying about me. As I walked past Uncle Ray's farm, I saw a note pinned to the fence. It said 'GELANY – your mother is here – call in at the farm.'

I walked slowly up to the farmhouse, feeling really tired. Ruby was at the kitchen window, standing on a chair by the sink. When she saw me, she jumped down and came running out to meet me. She put her arms around me and hugged me.

'Oh Gelany, we thought you were lost. Come in, your mother's here.'

She held tightly to my hand and pulled me up to the door, where Mother and Aunt Pearl were waiting. Mother hugged me.

'Gelany, I've been so worried. I wondered what had happened to you, when you didn't come home last night. I found your note. Are you alright?'

'Yes, the Electra broke down, so I've had to walk back.'

We went into the kitchen, where Uncle Ray, Jimmy and Rayson were sitting at the table. I suddenly felt overwhelmed by all the attention on me.

'Come and sit down,' said Aunt Pearl 'You must be so

tired. I'll get you a drink.'

'What happened Gelany?' asked Uncle Ray.

'Well, I found the prison, but when I went back to the Electra to come home, it had broken down. It was too late to walk home, so I slept in a hay barn, and walked back today.'

'Gelany you should have told me that you were going.' said Mother.

'I thought I would be home before you. Anyway, I did leave a note in case I wasn't.'

'Did you find out if your father is in the prison?' asked Uncle Ray.

'Yes, he is, he's still alive!'

'Who told you?' asked Uncle.

'I met Peter. He was going into the prison, and he found out for me.'

'That's great news,' said Uncle Ray.

'Yes, Peter had lunch there, and asked someone if Timothy Lantern was in the prison. They said he was, and that he was the furniture maker, and pointed him out to Peter at another table. Peter recognised him, but couldn't speak to him.'

Mother was staring at me with her mouth open, speechless.

'Peter said they wouldn't let me in to see him though. I'm really tired, can we go home?'

I didn't want to tell Mother about seeing Daddy in front of everyone else, but I was longing to tell her.

'Yes, of course,' said Aunt Pearl, 'We're so glad you're back safely Gelany.'

Mother and I started walking down the road in silence. I was bursting to tell her that I had seen Daddy, so couldn't wait until we got home.

'Mum, I saw Daddy.'

'What do you mean, I didn't think you went in the prison?"

'No I didn't. When I was in the hay barn, he came out to see me.'

'How? Surely he was locked up.'

'It was a miracle.'

I told her about Ruffles growling and waking me up, and about the shining light coming towards me, and that it was Daddy. I told her about his dream, and the dove, and finding the guards asleep and the doors unlocked. She listened to me without a word, and by that time we had reached home. We went into the kitchen, which was a very welcome sight. She turned to face me.

'Gelany, that must have been a dream.'

'No, it really happened, look I've got the dove's feather that Daddy gave me, in my bag.' I opened my bag, and got the feather out to show her.

'That could have fallen into the hay barn by itself.'

'But it didn't, Daddy gave it to me.'

'I'll get the dinner now, you must be tired and hungry.'

I went to my room, feeling angry. Why didn't she believe me? I'd been so looking forward to telling her. I filled my basin with cold water and washed my face and hands, that woke me up.

Then I laid on my bed, thinking about all that had happened, until she called me for dinner. We sat at the table together, eating in silence. When we had finished, I felt better.

'I'm sorry Mum, I didn't tell you I was going. I thought you would stop me, and I had to find out about Daddy, if there was a chance that he was still alive.'

'You're right, I would have stopped you. It was a very

dangerous thing to do. You're lucky that you're back here safely.'

'God looked after me.'

'Gelany, don't talk like that. You know what happened to your father.' She got up from the table to clear the dishes away. Then she turned back.

'Did Peter really tell you Daddy is in the prison, and someone told him he is a furniture maker? That wasn't a dream too was it.'

'No, it happened before I went to sleep. You can ask Peter if you see him. And it wasn't a dream that Daddy came out to see me either. We had a long chat and he told me what it's like in prison.'

She didn't ask anymore, but looked thoughtful. I think she does believe Daddy's alive, but she doesn't believe that I saw him.

Sunday, 25th March

This morning Mother began to question me more, after we had eaten our breakfast.

'Gelany, who told you Daddy might be in the prison?'

Oh no, I thought, now I have to tell her about Grandma. Oh well, I may as well get it over with.

'I got a letter from Grandma when you were away in Easten doing the training. She said she was ill and thought she was going to die, and she wanted to see me. I knew you wouldn't want me to go, because you're cross with Daddy, and his family, and we haven't seen them since he disappeared. So I went to see her, without telling you. She said a policeman told her, that he had seen Daddy in the prison, a year after he was arrested, when he took another prisoner there.'

'Gelany, why do you think you can't tell me things?'

'Because you would stop me going. I'm sixteen now, and I can decide for myself.'

'I've only been trying to protect you. That family believed in God. I didn't realise until after I married Daddy. I think he thought I would believe too when he told me. But I'm too scared Gelany, and I don't want to lose you either. You are all I have left, now Daddy's gone.'

'What if God is real though? We can't make him not exist, by just not believing in Him.'

'Well, I'm not saying He doesn't exist. I just know it's too dangerous to talk about Him. Look what happened to your father, and other people like him. Some even get shot.'

'Yes, Daddy told me his brother was shot. They haven't shot Daddy because he's useful making furniture for the Tansas. They keep people in prison if they are useful in some way.'

She stared at me with amazement on her face.

'Did Grandma tell you about your father's brother being shot?'

'No, Daddy did. He said his name was Paul, and he was a baker in Easten.'

'That happened before your father and I met each other. He told me about it after we were married. He said his parents were so upset, they couldn't talk about Paul, so I wasn't to mention it.'

'No Grandma didn't talk about it. It must have been hard for them, having their son taken away by the police.'

'That is why I don't want you to believe Gelany.'

'I'm sorry, but I do. I'll be very careful who I talk to about it though.'

'Don't talk about it at all. You mean a lot to me, and I can't bear the thought of you being taken away.'

I was quite touched, as this is the first time I remember

her telling me I mean a lot to her. She has been so cross since Daddy left, I didn't think she cared much about me.

I'm not sure she believes I met Daddy outside the prison, but I think she is wondering how I know some things.

I decided to go and see Uncle Ray's family. I found Aunt Pearl and Ruby in the kitchen, getting the lunch ready. Aunt Pearl told me that Uncle Ray is worried because their milk cow's feet are rotting and it's going lame. He thinks he is going to have to have it killed, because it can't walk about to eat grass anymore.

So lunch time was a bit subdued. They didn't question me much more about my prison visit, as they thought they knew all there was to know. I kept wanting to tell them I had seen Daddy, but it would involve talking about God, as it was a miracle how he came out. I knew Uncle Ray wouldn't want me to, especially in front of his children. It is enough that they know Daddy is still alive, and are pleased for me.

Monday, 26th March

Sascha knew I was going to the prison on my day off, so as soon as I went to help her with the Identity cards she whispered, 'What happened on Friday?'

I whispered back 'Daddy is in there, he's still alive!'

'That's good news.'

I saw Mrs Newsby look at us, so I said 'I'll tell you about it later.'

As soon as we left the Centre, she asked me 'Did they let you see him?'

I told her all that had happened, as we walked along, except for Daddy coming out to see me in the night. I realise now that no one will believe me, unless they believe in God too, and know He makes miracles happen. She was very sympathetic about me having to sleep in a barn and walk all the way home, but glad to know Daddy is still alive. She was also excited to hear that I had met Peter.

'When are you coming to Youth Club? I've started going again, and I miss you.'

'I'll come next Saturday, if the weather is alright.'

In the afternoon, I went to the allotment. There is lots to do there now. I prepared the soil, raking it over, ready for sowing. Tomorrow I will go to the hardware store after work, and buy some packets of seeds. I've kept some small potatoes, they are under my bed in a box and they are beginning to sprout.

I took Ruffles for a walk on the cliffs before dinner, and put my tin whistle in my pocket. I had a good chat with God, as I walked along. I thanked Him that I had found my father and he is alive. I thanked Him for getting me home safely. I even thanked Him that the Electra broke down, or else I wouldn't have been there to see my father! I thanked Him for sending Daddy out to see me and the time I spent with him.

Then I sat down by my favourite bush, out of the wind, and looked across the sea. The sea was choppy with little white crests on the waves, and black and white clouds were moving quickly across the sky. I put my whistle in my mouth and played a tune that seemed to come from my heart. I made it up without thinking about it, and it sounded quite tuneful. It expressed all my gratitude to God. Out of the clouds I saw the dove flying towards me. It landed on the ground in front of me, listening to the music, and as soon as I finished playing, it flew off. Ruffles was lying by me, and didn't chase the dove away. She was relaxed and looked like she was enjoying the music too.

Tuesday, 27th March

Mother and I have been making baskets in the evenings. I pick up the willow, straw, and wooden bases from the craft barn, on my way home from work and take the completed baskets back. We need some extra money to pay the tax, by the end of next month, but she says she still doesn't think we will have enough. She has saved some money to buy things for her new cottage, and doesn't want to use that.

Wednesday, 28th March

I worked all day at the Information Centre today. Mrs Newsby says she wants us to work a full day every week, until the Identity cards are finished, because we are not finding enough spare time. Well that's not a surprise, we don't usually have much spare time. I didn't mind as it was raining all day, and so it wouldn't have been very nice on the allotment this afternoon.

When I lifted up the floorboard this evening, to get my journal out, I saw the feather lying there and got it out, to gaze at it again. I'm glad I've got that to remind me I really did see Daddy, or else I might begin to wonder if it had been a dream, as time passes.

I remembered I need to tell Grandma the good news, that Daddy is still alive. I don't know how soon I will be able to see her, so I have written her a letter. Here is what it says:

Dear Grandma

I have been to the prison, and found out that Daddy is still alive and in there! He makes furniture for the Tansas. I will come to see you as soon as I can, to tell you all about it.

With love from, Gelany.

I didn't think I could explain in writing about him coming out to see me, but I really look forward to telling her about it. Maybe she will believe me, that it wasn't a dream. I will take the feather to show her.

Saturday, 31st March

I worked all day on the allotment, sowing seeds and planting the potatoes. When I got there, Justin was working on his allotment. He came over and told me he had lots of digging and planting to do, so his father had come to help him. His father just said 'Hallo' to me, then got on with digging. He looked a nice man, but I wondered if he was a bit embarrassed about talking to me because of what had happened to Daddy. I was longing to tell Justin I had been to the prison, but didn't like to talk about it in front of his father. So I thought I would tell him at the Youth Club this evening.

In the evening, I told Mother I was going to the Youth Club and she wasn't too keen, as she said it is still rather dark. I told her I needed a break after working on the allotment all day, and she decided to come with me and go to see Sascha's mother. I told her I was happy to go on my own, but she said she would like to go out too.

Sascha was pleased to see me, and we sat at a table drinking Mrs Bunny's special brew. I am not sure what it was, but it tasted nice. Rayson came to join us, and it was good to chat with them. Rayson seems quite happy and joked about things. Then he was called away by some other boys, to go and play skittles, so Sascha and I played a few games of table tennis, and then sat down again.

I could see Justin on the other side of the room, talking and laughing with a girl. She looked very pretty, with brown hair down to her shoulders, curling in ringlets. They had a game of table tennis, after us. When he saw me looking, he smiled and mouthed 'hallo'. I would have liked to talk to him, and was longing to tell him what I had found out about Daddy, but he didn't come over. I felt a bit cross, and then began to feel jealous, as he was giving all his attention to that girl. I asked Sascha if she knew who she was, but she didn't, she said she only started coming last week.

Sascha and I walked back together, to her house, and I was feeling rather quiet.

She took me by surprise by asking 'Do you think you could change your mind about marrying Peter? It would be so nice to have you both living in Wells, and for you to be my sister.'

'I don't know.'

'Are you still hoping to marry Gordon?'

'He has a girlfriend and he plans to marry her, when they get a cottage.'

'There's still time for him to change his mind then.'

I didn't say anymore, just changed the subject and started talking about work and how much longer we are going to have to work on those Identity cards. Then I walked home the rest of the way with Mother.

I feel upset about Justin, and also annoyed with myself for feeling upset. I suppose I thought he was my friend, but now he seems more interested in that other girl. I had been looking forward to telling him I have been to the prison, and found out that Daddy is still alive.

Sunday, 1st April

It felt like spring today as I walked up to Uncle Ray's farm. The sun felt warm, the primroses are in full bloom, and there is lots of white blossom on the bushes beside the road. I could sense the atmosphere was better when I walked into the kitchen, as Aunt Pearl and Ruby welcomed me with enthusiasm.

'We have good news,' said Aunt Pearl. 'Daisy the cow, has stopped limping and can walk. Uncle says the foot rot has gone. He says it's a miracle, and we're so pleased we won't have to kill her. She's a good milker, as you know.'

'That is good news.'

Ruby beamed at me, and then got back to her pastry making.

After lunch, Ruby collected the leftovers in a small dish, and asked me to come with her to feed the cats.

On the way to the barn she said 'Gelany, I asked God to heal Daisy. I picked up a hoof, and pleaded with God to make her better. I saw a spark of light touch her foot, and it go back to normal. So I did the same with the other hooves in turn, and the same thing happened. The next day Daddy found her walking normally and feeding herself. He could hardly believe it. I wanted to tell him what I'd done, but thought he would be cross with me, because he doesn't want me to believe in God.'

'Oh, Ruby. That's lovely.'

'Everyone should believe in God, shouldn't they Gelany.'

'Yes. But it's not easy, with the Rulers saying it's against the law.'

We entered the barn and she called 'Beauty'. She came running over, and is a lovely looking cat. Two other cats followed slowly behind her, to see what was on offer. Ruby put the dish of food down for them to eat, and we sat down on the hay.

'When I leave school, I'm going to be a nurse, then I can heal people,' she told me.

You won't be able to heal people like that in hospital.'

'Why not?'

' People would soon know you believe in God and then you would get into trouble.'

'But that's silly.'

'I know, but we have to be careful.'

'I could ask God in my head, you know, without saying it out loud, then they wouldn't know.'

'Yes, but it might cause a stir if everyone became miraculously well!'

She started giggling at the thought of it, and we both started laughing until our sides ached.

'Come on, show me the cow.' She took my hand and led me to Daisy's field. The cow was munching fresh long grass as if it was the best she had ever tasted.

I hope Ruby changes her mind about being a nurse. It is five years until she leaves school, so there is time. The temptation to heal everyone would be too great, and she may draw attention to herself, and get into trouble.

15

Relationships

Monday, 2nd April

Mother is worrying about the tax we have to pay. We are making baskets most evenings, and it gets quite boring. As we were feeling tired this evening, she suggested we tell each other stories, to keep ourselves awake and keep working. She said the stories could be true or made up. I asked her to tell me how she met Daddy. She looked a bit surprised at this request, thought about it, and then told me.

She said she grew up in Wells and he lived in Easten. When he left school, he wanted to be a furniture maker, but there wasn't a job for him in Easten. So he travelled on the Electra to the other towns, looking for work and Woodalls said they would take him on. He found somewhere to live, with an elderly couple, who had a spare room in their cottage. When my mother was sixteen she started going to the Youth Club and they gradually got to know each other there.

When they decided to get married, they had nowhere to live. Uncle Ray said they could have this cottage, on the edge of his land. No one was living in it at the time, and it wasn't in a very good state. But Daddy liked the idea of living near the sea, and the allotments weren't far away, so that is how they ended up here. She said Daddy was very good at doing things up, and she made curtains and a bedspread, so they worked hard on it, and soon it was looking really nice.

It was lovely hearing her talk about Daddy in a positive way, and I could see a faraway look in her eyes, as if she was enjoying it too. She said tomorrow I can tell her a story. I've got lots of true stories, but I don't think she will believe them!

Tuesday, 3rd April

It did seem easier making the basket yesterday, whilst listening to Mother telling a story. I thought about my turn, on the way home. I kept thinking of ones that involved God, like the dove, and thinking no, I can't tell her that one. So I decided to make one up instead.

I told a story about people living on an Island, which was all on its own in the ocean. They didn't know it, but there were other islands around with people on just like themselves. People from the other islands kept trying to make contact, but every time they came near they got shot at by cannons and guns. I went on making up ways that the alien people tried to reach the Island and how they were found out at the last minute and chased away.

Mother thought it was a fun story, and we discussed whether it could be true, and that the aliens could possibly be nice people. We talked about things that could be on the other islands. It did help to pass the time.

Wednesday, 4th April

I worked all day today. I really wanted to be on the allotment, as the sun was shining. A man delivered some Information sheets and told us that the Electra is working again. When we made baskets this evening, Mother told me about her parents lives.

Thursday, 5th April

Gordon was waiting for me when I left work today. He gave me a brown paper parcel which had two large fish in. He said that they had a big catch yesterday. He thinks it is because the fish are coming into the shallow waters to spawn.

As we were walking towards the station he said, 'I've got something to tell you.'

'What is it?'

'Let's wait until we're sitting down.'

'I've got something to tell you too.'

'Good!'

He grinned at me, then started running to the seat, so I ran after him. I was hoping he would say his father was not dead after all, but I knew that was not possible. We sat down on the seat, enjoying the spring sunshine on our faces.

'Can I go first?' He asked.

'Yes.'

'My mother's been very upset about my father, as you would expect. One day she was crying and said to herself, "Why does it have to happen to me twice?" I heard her, and asked what she meant. She looked up startled, probably didn't realise I was there. Then she said I may as well know, Sandy wasn't my real father. I couldn't believe it at first. She told me my own father was arrested by the police, before I was born, and she was told he would be shot. She never saw him again. When she married Sandy, he didn't want her to tell me. He wanted to bring me up believing he was my real father. He didn't see why I needed to know.'

'Oh dear. Did she tell you about your other father.'

'Yes, and this is the interesting bit, she told me his surname was Lantern. So you see we might be related! My real name would have been Gordon Lantern.'

'Well, we don't look like each other. Your hair is black and curly and mind is light brown and straight.'

'I get my hair from my mother's side of the family. It's just like her hair.'

'What was your father's name?'

'Paul.'

'Paul Lantern? And he was shot?'

'Yes. Why have you heard of him?'

'I think so.' Now I had a bit of explaining to do. I told him that I'd been to the prison, and found out my father is in there. He was pleased to hear that he is still alive. Then I told him about the Electra breaking down, and staying in the hay barn the night, and then having to walk home. He was very sympathetic about that.

The horn sounded for the Electra to start moving.

'Oh dear, I haven't finished yet. Do you have to go?'

'No, I can stay a bit longer today. Come on, let's go and get a drink.'

We walked back to the shops and went into the cafe. Gordon ordered two elderflower drinks and carried them to a table. We sat at the back, as far away as we could from the other customers. I put my parcel of fish on the table, hoping it wouldn't smell too much, but it didn't, as it was so fresh.

'So what else do you want to tell me?'

I told him about Daddy coming out to see me, and that he told me he had an older brother named Paul, who was shot by the police.

'But that must have been a dream Gelany.'

'That's what Mother thinks. But I know it wasn't. I still have the white dove's feather at home to prove it.'

'Well it is hard to believe that someone could walk out of a prison and then walk back in again.'

'I know.'

'I wonder how we could find out if we *are* related,' he said.

'I know! Grandma.'

'Who?'

'My Grandma in Easten. Paul would have been her son. If she says it's true then we'll know it is.'

'Can you come to Easten, and we could visit her?'

'Yes, I'll come on Saturday. I should be working on the allotment, but it will have to wait. I want to tell her about Daddy too.'

We talked about when to meet on the beach, and then walked back to the station. Before he got on the Electra, Gordon gave me a great big hug and kissed me on the cheek.

But that's not all that happened today. When I got home and was cutting the guts out of one of the fish, two coins fell out of it. Mother was home and heard me exclaim about it. She came over and saw what had happened. When she picked them up and washed them, she said that they would mean that we have enough money now, to pay all the tax that is due. She wouldn't have to use the money she has saved to furnish the new cottage.

She was amazed. I know God caused that miracle to happen. I'm sure it must make her wonder if God is true. I took Ruffles out for a walk on the cliffs after dinner, and walked along thanking God for the coins. We don't have to make any more baskets now, but I shall miss the stories.

Friday, 6th April

As I working on the allotment this afternoon, I wondered whether to tell Mother about going to Easten tomorrow. She would be at the hospital, so I didn't have to, as I probably would get back home before her. But I decided I would tell her, she can't stop me, and I don't want to keep having secrets from her.

So after we had eaten dinner I said 'Mum, I'm going to go Easten tomorrow and planning to visit Grandma.'

'Oh.'

'I want to talk to her, now I know Daddy is alive. I'm sure she will be pleased about that.'

'Yes. Will you be back in the evening?'

'I plan to be, providing the Electra works okay.'

I wondered whether to tell her about Gordon, but it was a lot of explaining to do, and I still wasn't sure he was related. So I decided to leave it until I found out. She got up from the table to wash the dishes, turned round and said 'I appreciate you telling me, Gelany,' and smiled.

So that wasn't as difficult as I expected.

Saturday, 7th April

Well the Electra was working today, thank goodness. Ruffles was pleased to be going with me on a journey, wagging her tail and keeping close to my side as we walked up to Wells. Grandma didn't answer when I knocked on the door, and I was worried that she was ill again. I opened the door and went inside but couldn't find her. I was so disappointed. I wondered what to do, and went outside. Over the road, a lady was in her cottage garden. As I was asking if she knew where Grandma was, she came walking up the road, coming back from the shops.

'Gelany!' she exclaimed as she got near, 'How lovely to see you.' She gave me a hug and said 'Come in my dear.'

We went into the kitchen where she made us drinks and put some biscuits on a plate.

'I got your letter, such good news. Now come in the sitting room and tell me all about it.'

I told her about meeting Peter, and him finding out that Daddy is in there, making furniture for the Tansas. Also that Peter actually saw him.

'Well it's so good to know your father is still alive. I wonder how he is.'

Then I told her about the Electra breaking down, and about how Daddy came out to see me. I wasn't sure how she would react, whether she would believe me, or tell me it must have been a dream, like Mother and Gordon did. She listened to me intently, and waited for me to finish before she spoke.

'Gelany, that's wonderful! What a good thing he gave you that feather, or else you may have thought it was a dream. And he even managed to wave goodbye to you from the window in the morning. Wonderful!'

'Would you like to see the feather, I have it in my bag?'

'Yes.' I handed it to her and she stroked it gently, then gave it back to me. She asked me some questions about how he was and what it was like in prison.

'Fancy you being able to see him. What a good thing the Electra broke down!'

'Grandma, I've got something to ask you. Daddy mentioned that he had an older brother, called Paul. Is that true?'

The smile went from her face, and she looked really sad. 'Yes. That was a terrible time. He hadn't been married long and his wife was expecting their first child. He never saw him. I didn't tell you about Paul, as I didn't want you to give up hope that your father was still alive.'

'Do you know what his wife called their baby?'

'Yes, she named him Gordon.' My heart leapt, this was

amazing. Before I could speak she continued, 'I saw him a few times after he was born, he had dark curly hair just like his mother. Then she got married again. When I went to see them one day, they told me they wanted Gordon to believe that Sandy was his real father. This meant I wasn't his Grandma anymore, he had a new one. Then they moved, so I don't know where they live now. I was very hurt, but couldn't do anything about it. I sometimes saw them at the shops or on the beach, and I'd say 'Hallo' but it was like I was a stranger.'

'Grandma, I know Gordon. He's a fisherman, and I'm friends with him. He comes to see me when he brings fish to Wells.'

'Really?'

'Yes. His father Sandy, was killed recently, for talking publicly against the Rulers. After that happened, Gordon's mother told him Sandy wasn't his real father, and that his father had been called Paul Lantern. When Gordon told me, I realised his father might have been Daddy's brother. Gordon would like to come to see you.'

Grandma's eyes filled with tears. 'I should like that.'

I told her that I would go and meet him on the beach in the afternoon, and bring him back with me. We had some lunch, and talked nonstop. She loves to hear about Ruby and wants to see her. She laughed about the cow's hooves being miraculously healed.

After lunch, when Grandma settled down on her sofa for a nap, I walked down to the beach. Gordon was tidying up some fishing nets.

'Hallo Gordon.' He looked round and saw me.

'Hallo Gelany. Have you been to see your Grandma?'

'Yes and she's your Grandma too. She wants to see you.'

'That's amazing. I'll come right away,' he said as he put

the nets down.

We walked up to Grandma's cottage, and knocked on the door. Grandma opened it and looked up at Gordon.

'Well, you have grown into a handsome young man Gordon. Still have those lovely black curls I see. Come in my dears.'

We went into the sitting room and Grandma carried in a tray with three mugs of hot rose hip drink.

Gordon and Grandma had a lot of catching up to do, and I sat there listening to them. After a while I realised I had to walk back to the Electra, or else I wouldn't get home today, and interrupted them to tell them.

'I'll walk up with you Gelany,' said Gordon. 'Now I know where Grandma lives, I can come back to see her another day.'

'Yes you do that young man. Now I've found you, I don't want to lose you again.'

'I'll be back, don't you worry.'

'Sorry I have to go Grandma,' I said.

'You come back soon too Gelany, and bring that Ruby with you. I'd love to meet her.'

'Yes. I'll try to do that.'

Grandma gave Gordon and I hugs and waved to us as we walked down the road together.

Mother asked how Grandma was, when I got home, and I told her about Gordon. She remembered him talking to me on the beach, and was surprised to hear he had been coming to see me when he came to Wells, and that we are related to him.

I didn't go to Youth Club, I was too tired to walk back into town.

Sunday, 8th April

I told Aunt Pearl about going to see Grandma.

'Could I take Ruby with me next time I go. I've talked about your family, and she would like to meet her.'

Ruby jumped up and down with excitement, 'Oh yes, can I go with Gelany, Mummy?'

'Well, we will have to ask your father. Do you know when you are going again Gelany?'

'No not yet. I need to work on the allotment for a few Saturdays. I'm a bit behind with it.'

She didn't ask him whilst I was there, but I expect she will. I do hope Ruby can come with me next time.

Monday, 9th April

Sascha and I walked home together, after work, and I told her about Gordon and visiting Grandma.

'So he's your cousin then Gelany, how funny. But it's also a shame, because there's a law saying cousins can't marry. Are you disappointed?'

'No, I didn't expect to marry him. He has someone else. I'm pleased he's my cousin though. Perhaps we can be even better friends now, and I will see more of him. I like him.'

'I know you do, I can see that!'

'No, but now I can like him like a cousin. He's a good friend too.'

'Well maybe Peter has more of a chance now.'

'Maybe, but he's still a policeman, and he can't stop being one, can he.'

'Maybe you need to get over your phobia of policemen.'

She laughed and poked me in the ribs, and made me smile. I thought I would get the focus off me, and turn it on to her.

'Who would you like to marry Sascha? You're older than me, it's your turn first.'

'Don't you know?'

'No, who?'

'Rayson of course.'

'Really?'

'Why, is there something wrong with him that I don't know about?'

'No, he's lovely. I suppose I thought you were just friends. Do you think he knows?'

'Knows what?'

'That you like him that much, that you want to marry him.'

'Well I suppose it's whether he feels the same way about me.'

'I could ask him.'

'No, don't. I want him to think it up for himself.'

'Okay.'

But I'm very tempted to say something to Rayson. I don't know how I would bring the subject up though.

Wednesday, 10th April

Mother says we ought to go and pay our taxes on Saturday, now that we have got the money. The Bank and Taxation office is open on Saturday mornings this month. She said they have finished building some of the new cottages in Wells, so we could go and see one. She told me she won't have to pay taxes on the land, when she moves to the cottage, only rent. I didn't like to point out that rent is just another way of paying money to the Tansas, and the cottage won't belong to her either.

I said I'd go, although I don't really want to, and I have so much to do on the allotment.

Saturday, 14th April

Mother and I paid our taxes this morning. There was a really long queue outside the Bank and Taxation Office. I was pleased to see that other people have got the money. There was a lot of grumbling about the rulers as we waited though. It feels nice to have got that over with for another year.

The cottages are being built quite near the hospital, and we went inside a finished one. It was very neat, with a little wall built around the front garden. Inside, although it had the same number of rooms as ours, I thought they were a bit smaller, and it didn't have the useful glass porch on the back like ours. The garden out the back was just virgin soil, so it would require some work to make that into a garden.

I asked Mother if we could go and see the allotments. At the end of the row of cottages, was a rough field, and she told me that is where they will be. She said they would probably plough it up first, ready for people to use.

We walked home mostly in silence. I am going off the idea of moving. I can see it would be nice to live nearer the town, for work and the Youth Club, but I would be far away from the cliffs and the sea. I like our garden and allotment, and don't want to have to start again from scratch. Also Daddy built an extra porch room on ours, and I'd miss that. No I don't want to go, but how can I tell Mother?

I spent the afternoon on the allotment and enjoyed it. After that I felt even more reluctant to leave. Justin and his father were there, and both said 'Hallo'. When his father was doing some planting at the other end of the allotment, Justin came over to me.

'Hallo Gelany. Where were you last Saturday, I wondered if you had gone to the prison?'

'No, I went to see my Grandma in Easten.'

'Oh. Will you be coming to the Youth Club tonight?'

'I might, I'll see how tired I am. I've already been into town today.'

'Okay, I might see you there.'

He went back and got on with some digging. I felt a bit mean not telling him I'd been to the prison. But it didn't seem like the right place or time. I also still feel a bit cross with him for not coming over to talk to me at Youth Club, when I wanted to tell him. When he was with that other girl.

I went to the Youth Club this evening, and saw him across the room with the girl again. He came over and said he was glad to see me and asked Sascha and I to play table tennis with them. Rayson was playing skittles. I didn't want to, but Sascha said 'Yes' for us both, before I could say anything, so I had to go. The girl's name is Susan, and she didn't talk much, but seemed to be enjoying the game. It was good that she was quiet, because I didn't want to talk to her, as it feels like she has pinched Justin from me.

Sascha asked me if I was alright after we had finished, so my coolness must have shown. I told her I was just feeling tired after a busy day.

Sunday, 15th April

Ruby is keen to go and see Grandma with me, and asked when we can go. I told her I didn't know yet, but I will take her. Then Aunt Pearl asked me to go and tell Uncle Ray lunch was ready, and I found him digging a ditch, by the cow barn.

'Uncle Ray, lunch is ready.'

'Okay Gelany.' He put his spade down and we started walking back up to the farmhouse together.

'I hear you want to take Ruby to meet your Grandma in Easten.'

'Yes, I've told her about Ruby and she wants to meet her. I thought it would be nice for us to have a day out together too.'

'Yes. I'm just a bit concerned, because I don't want Ruby getting any more ideas in her head about God. She's very impressionable, and we don't want her to get into trouble. She's a bit young to keep it to herself.'

'If I write to Grandma first and tell her that we mustn't talk about God to Ruby, and I promise you, would that be alright.'

'I'm not sure. If your Grandma didn't believe in God, I wouldn't mind at all about you taking Ruby.' He stopped walking and turned to face me. 'It's not that I don't believe there is a God, Gelany. It's just that it's too risky to do anything about it. Like your mother protected you as a child, and didn't tell you why your father disappeared, I feel I must protect Ruby.'

'Yes, I understand that.

I was disappointed, but I knew if I took Ruby to see Grandma, God might get into the conversation, because they are both so enthusiastic about Him. It was nice to hear Uncle Ray say he hadn't ruled out believing in God.

After lunch Ruby and I went to the barn to see the cats, and I told her what her Daddy had said to me.

'But I want to go.'

'I know. But we have to have your Daddy's permission.'

'I'll tell him I believe in God already, so it won't make any difference.'

'I don't think he will let you go then, because he will want you to stop believing, not make you believe more, by others encouraging you.'

She pouted her lips.

'What can we do then.'

'I don't know. We could both talk to God about it and ask Him.'

'Yes, we'll do that. Let's go and see Jimmy at the tree house now. He's making a flower garden round the tree, and said I can help him.'

Wednesday, 18th April

We finished the Identity Cards today – hurrah! Sascha and I worked nearly all day on them. So it is the last full day I have to work as well, and I have some time off owing. Mrs Newsby told me I must make a poster tomorrow, telling people to come and collect them. I'm glad to get them finished, but don't like the idea of everyone having to carry identity cards, and the police requesting to see them.

I asked Mrs Newsby if I can have Friday off, so that I can work on the allotment all day, and she agreed.

Friday, 20th April

Mother keeps on talking about the new cottage, and moving, where we will put things, and what else we need. She is very enthusiastic, but I can't muster up any enthusiasm at all. The more she talks about it, the less I want to go.

I took Ruffles on the cliffs after dinner, and decided it was time to have a word with God about it. I told him I don't want to move. But I can't stay because I can't afford the land tax with just my money, and I think I would be a bit scared living here on my own anyway. As I talked about it, I found myself sobbing. I sat down on the grass, and cried and cried, until there were no tears left inside. Ruffles snuggled up to me and whined. I felt better when I had finished, but it doesn't solve anything. It's not only that I don't want to move from our cottage, I don't want to live in the one Mother is moving to either.

16

Decisions

Saturday, 21st April

I was working on the allotment this morning, with Justin and his father busy nearby, when Peter appeared, dressed in his uniform. It did give me a shock and probably everyone else on the allotments too, seeing a policeman turn up. He stood at the edge looking for me, and then came over. Ruffles growled.

I held her collar and said 'It's okay. It's only Peter.'

'Hallo Gelany, I want to talk to you. Are you going home for lunch soon?'

I looked at my watch. 'Yes.'

'Can I come back with you.'

'Yes, okay.'

I put my trowel down and brushed my hair out of my eyes. I must have looked a bit of a mess. I saw Justin, and other people looking at us as we walked away, probably wondering what I had done. We walked back to the cottage and I invited him in. I put some elderflower juice into cups and carried them into the sitting room. Before he sat down by the fire, he took his hat and jacket off. I was pleased to see that underneath he had an ordinary jumper. It made him look a bit more normal.

'I would like you to come to Wells with me this afternoon, so I can show you the houses being built for the police, to see if you'd like one. Will you come?'

'I really should be working on the allotment.'

'I can only go today. It won't take long. Please come.'

He did look like the Peter I used to know, sitting there in an ordinary jumper, so I found myself saying 'Alright. I'll get us some sandwiches first, I'm really hungry.'

As we were eating I suddenly had an idea. I'm not sure if it was a good one, but I thought it was worth asking.

'Peter, if I married you, would you come and live with me here, in this cottage. My mother's moving to Easten soon.'

'I don't think I can. They're building these houses especially for the police to live in. Come and see it, I'm sure you will like it.'

After we had eaten, I called Ruffles to come with us, but Peter said it would be better if I left her behind.

'Would I be able to take her with me if we lived there?'

'I expect so, I'll have to check. But only one house is finished, and it will be easier looking round without her.'

I reluctantly left Ruffles at home and we walked up to Wells. Peter talked about his job. I asked him if he had arrested any one yet, but he said he couldn't talk about specific things, only in general. I asked him if he had a gun. He said new policemen didn't carry them, he had to have some training in shooting first. He asked me about my work at the Information Centre and I told him about the Identity cards. He approved of that, and said it would make his job much easier. By the time we got to Wells, I was wishing I hadn't agreed to go with him.

The police houses were surrounded by a high wall, with a big gate at the entrance. Peter said there would be a guard there, in a hut, so it was going to be quite safe.

'Safe from what?' I enquired.

'Well, if the people have any grievances, and want to take it out on the police.'

We looked inside a two storey house. It was quite nice, better than the cottage Mother was going to move to. The rooms were larger, it had three bedrooms upstairs, and it would have electricity for lights and cooking. The garden was seeded for grass.

'Where are the allotments Peter?'

'There aren't any. You wouldn't need one. I'll earn enough money to buy all the food we need, even when we have a family.'

'I haven't agreed to marry you yet.' I said, blushing at the thought of having his children.

'I know. But you can see it would be nice living here, can't you. You'd be nearer the town, in a lovely house, and no hard work to do on the allotment.'

Someone else came in, so we couldn't talk anymore, and decided to leave. I walked with him to the station.

'I need to know by the end of the month, Gelany. I have to ask for a house before they all go, and ask to be transferred too.'

'Can I think about it and write to you?'

'Yes, but hurry up and make up your mind. I think we could be happy together. We've known each other for a long time, ever since you were born I suppose.'

The horn sounded.

'I must go. Goodbye Gelany.' He leaned towards me to kiss me, and I backed away. I only saw his uniform and couldn't see the Peter I once knew.

'Sorry, I can't kiss a policeman in uniform.'

He turned and ran to get on the Electra.

As I walked home I felt sick. Why can't I see Peter when he is wearing that uniform? He seems to disappear inside it. 'God, please help me,' I cried out in my mind, 'I am confused.'

I quickly had a big drink at home, collected Ruffles and went back to the allotment. When I got there Justin came over to me.

'Are you alright Gelany?'

Before I could answer Sarah came up to me too and asked 'Is everything alright love?'

'Yes. It was Peter, someone I used to know before he joined the police,' I told her. 'He just wanted to show me something. Unfortunately, he has to wear his uniform when off duty.'

'Oh, good.' She replied, ' We were really worried about you, when you went off like that with a policeman.'

I smiled at them both and we all went back to our work. As I worked there in silence, alongside all the other people, it had the comforting feeling of 'This is where I belong'.

I didn't go to the Youth Club this evening. I still felt upset and too tired really. I didn't tell Mother about Peter coming and going to see the house, but I expect she will hear about it from his mother.

Monday, 23rd April

As we were walking home from work, Sascha said 'Did you see Peter on Saturday? He called in to see us, and said he was going to show you a police house in Wells.'

'Yes, I went to see it.'

'What did you think?'

'I don't want to move from where I am.'

'But you can't stay there on your own, when your mother moves.'

'I know.'

I was glad she didn't ask me anymore.

I took Ruffles on the cliffs in the evening, and had a word with God. 'Should I or shouldn't I marry a policeman?' I asked.

I heard God say 'Do you want to?'

I realised I don't. What would I be marrying him for? I would still have to move, to somewhere I don't want to go. And I'd be married to a policeman. What was I thinking of? It all suddenly seemed clear. I would write to Peter, make an end to it, and stop him asking me anymore. I felt free. But free to do what?

'God, I don't want to move either.'

All I heard Him say was 'Trust me.'

I can't see what I can do, but I feel more peaceful.

When I got home, I wrote a note to Peter. It was quite hard to think of what to say, and I tore up a few notes before I got to the final version, which was rather short.

Dear Peter

Thank you for asking me to marry you and showing me the house. I know you need an answer, so I am writing to say no. I'm sorry, but I really don't want to be married to a policeman. Please don't ask me again.

Gelany.

Thursday, 26th April

Gordon came to see me today. He told me he had been to see Grandma again, and had taken her some fish. She was really pleased to see him.

'Thank you Gelany for introducing us. I've lost my

father, but found a new Grandma. She's lovely, isn't she.'

'Yes, I was so glad when I found her too. I wish she wasn't so far away.'

We sat down on the seat. The trees on the green were full of pink blossom and the sun felt warm through the cool air.

'Donna and I are going to get married soon. My mother said we can have her cottage. Her brother is a builder, and he is going to add two more rooms on the side, for her to live in. She gets on well with Donna, so it should be alright.'

'Oh that's good.'

It didn't seem so bad knowing that Gordon was going to marry Donna, now that I know he's my cousin.

'Next time you come to Easten, I would like you to meet each other. I've told her lots about you.'

'Okay.'

'You look a bit sad. Is anything the matter?'

'I don't want to move to Wells with Mother. I want to stay where I am, near the sea, and have the same allotment. I've got so many memories of Daddy there too. It would be like leaving him behind. I don't know what to do.'

He put his arm round me.

'I'm sorry Gelany. Why don't you stay there?'

'I can't afford the tax on my own.'

'Is there some way you could earn more money?'

'I could make more baskets, I suppose. I'd have to make them all year round.'

'What about the allotment, could you grow more produce to sell?'

'Yes, I think so. Do you know Gordon, I think you're right. I think I could do it. In fact, I'm going to. I'm not sure I'll like living there alone, but I could try it.'

'Good Gelany, but I don't like to think of you living there

alone either.'

'Well at least I've got Ruffles.'

The horn made me jump, and Gordon got up. 'Sorry I have to leave you like this.'

'I'm alright. I think you've helped me to make up my mind.' I shouted as he ran to get on the Electra.

I walked home, feeling happier, and making plans.

Friday, 27th April

This evening, after dinner, I told Mother of my decision.

'Mum, I don't want to move to Wells, I've decided to stay here. I'm going to make baskets all through the year to pay for the extra tax, and grow more of the crops that fetch a good price.'

She looked at me incredulously.

'Gelany, why would you want to do that? You'll have to work so hard, and it will be lonely down here on your own.'

'I think I'll be alright. I've got Ruffles.'

'Why do you have to be so difficult? Why can't you just marry Peter?'

'I can't marry Peter because I believe in God. And that has nothing to do with Daddy, I found Him for myself. I've found out He's real. So I can't marry a policeman can I? The police arrest people for talking about God.'

'You could keep quiet about it.'

'Don't you think he'd guess? It would be awkward between us. Anyway, I've decided I want to stay here, and Peter said he couldn't live here.'

'Well you can try it Gelany. I don't think you will like living here on your own, away from everyone else.'

'Well I'll find out, won't I.'

'What about furniture? I've been planning to take most of it. You'll only have what's left in your bedroom.'

'I'll manage. I can gradually get what I need from the second hand shop in Wells.'

'I could leave the curtains and one or two other bits. I don't like the thought of you living here on your own though.'

I've come into my room to write this. It feels right, what I've decided to do. I feel so much better and peaceful, I'm sure God will look after me.

Saturday, 28th April

I couldn't get to sleep last night. I suppose I felt so excited that I had decided to stay here, and I was thinking about how I would furnish the cottage. Then as I was staring at the ceiling, I remembered the writing I had seen on it before, and it was as if I could see it again, only more faintly. It said *'Tell Justin the truth'* and then gradually faded away. I struggled with that. I knew it was because I haven't told Justin about my prison visit yet, and that Daddy is alive. But I didn't want to tell him, now that he liked Susan more than me. Eventually I fell asleep without making a decision about it.

Justin was working with his father on their allotment again, when I arrived there. He made a remark about the sunny weather and then returned to his work. After lunch, only Justin came back, and he came over to me.

'Gelany, it's such a lovely day, why don't we down tools and go for a walk on the cliffs. I've only got to finish planting those cabbages. It seems ages since we've had a chat. You'd like it, wouldn't you Ruffles?' he said, as he stroked her silky head. Ruffles looked like she had understood the word 'walk', and wagged her tail furiously. 'See Ruffles thinks it's a great idea.'

'I've still got all these leeks to plant out, and they can't wait really.'

'I'll come and help you, when I've finished the cabbages.'
We both went back to work. I was in two minds about going for the walk with him. Part of me longed for his company, but I was still feeling hurt about his new friendship with Susan. I knew I should tell him about my prison visit, so decided I would go with him to get that over with.

When he came over to help me finish planting the leeks, it was so much quicker, having an extra pair of hands to help. As we planted them, he chatted away about the allotment and how things were doing on it, and the plans he had for it. We finished the leeks and looked at the neat rows with satisfaction.

'Are you ready to go now? You are, aren't you Ruffles.'
'Yes, let's go.'
We put all our tools away, in the wooden boxes, and headed for the cliffs. Ruffles ran round us in circles several times, until her nose got onto the scent of a rabbit.

'It's so lovely to feel the warmth of the sun, after the winter, isn't it?' Justin said.
'Yes.'
'I've been so busy lately, what with helping Grandfather and doing the allotment, that it seems ages since I've been for a walk on the cliffs. I expect there are a lot more birds about now.'

He seemed happy and chatty and I was quiet, brooding. In the end I decided to ask him about it.
'Justin, where did you meet Susan?'
'Meet her? I've known her all my life. She's my cousin.'
'Your cousin? Susan's your cousin?'
'Yes, why?'
'I thought she was your girlfriend.'
He laughed. 'No. She started coming to Youth Club, and is rather shy. So I've been keeping her company, until she

gets used to it, and makes some friends. You thought she was my girlfriend? That's funny!'

'Yes.' It felt like a weight had been lifted from my heart, and I wanted to hug him. Instead I said 'Let's sit down over there, by the bushes, I've got something to tell you.'

'What is it?' He asked, as we sat down on the grass.

'I've been to the prison.'

'Have you? When? Why didn't you tell me? What did you find out?'

'What a lot of questions!' He looked at me, eager to hear more. 'I went a few weeks ago. I haven't seen you on your own to tell you about it before. I wanted to.'

'Did you find out if your father is in there?'

'Yes. Yes, he is. I met Peter who was going into the prison, and he found out for me.'

'So he's still alive. Oh Gelany, that's great news. I'm so pleased, and relieved.'

Then I told him about the Electra breaking down and staying the night in the hay barn. I told him about Daddy coming out to see me, and talking with me, expecting him to tell me it was a dream. But he didn't.

'Gelany, that's wonderful,' He didn't say anymore, he seemed speechless.

'What, you believe me? My mother told me it must have been a dream.'

'But you saw him wave to you in the morning, and you found the feather he gave you.'

'Yes.'

'Then it wasn't a dream, was it.'

'Justin you believe me!'

I couldn't stop myself, I put my arms around him and put my head on his chest. Tears flowed down my face. He put his arms around me, and I could feel his breath on the top of my head.

After a little while he said 'Why shouldn't I believe you? You're special. I've seen the dove come down to you, as if it was tame.'

'Have you?'

'Yes, when I've been out bird spotting with my binoculars. I wasn't spying on you, just looking for birds. There's something about you Gelany, you're different. Something I like and want for myself. I love being with you.'

I sat there leaning against him, smiling, hoping that this wasn't a dream.

'Do you?'

'Yes. I was attracted to you the first time I saw you on the allotment, but I was too scared to talk to you.'

'Why? I just thought you weren't very friendly.'

'Well, I suppose I felt awkward really. I thought my Grandfather had caused your father to be killed, and I didn't think you'd want to talk to me. I thought you must hate me and my family. But I got to like you, and couldn't keep my eyes off you. I couldn't believe it when you rescued me off the cliff.'

'Then you rescued me! I'm sorry I was so horrible to you.'

'I don't blame you. Anyway, I'd rather have you shout at me, than ignore me!'

I felt tingles go through my body, feeling glad that someone I liked, liked me that much.

'So she's not your girlfriend.'

'What?'

'I'm glad Susan isn't your girlfriend. I was feeling jealous.'

He laughed, 'I'm so pleased. If you were feeling jealous, then you must like me a little bit.'

'It's growing Justin, to more than a little bit.'

He pulled me close and kissed the top of my head. 'Come on, let's walk a bit further. The wild flowers are looking lovely along the cliffs.'

He stood up and put his hand out to me. I gave him my hand and let him pull me up, and he carried on holding it as we walked along. His warm hand in mine felt good and right. I remembered holding Peter's hand awkwardly once, whilst walking along the cliff, and we met Justin. I hoped Justin didn't remember it.

The flowers do look lovely along the cliffs at the moment. There are big patches of thrift, like pink rugs lying on the green grass. Justin stopped a few times to look through his binoculars at the birds, and passed them to me sometimes, when there was something he wanted to show me. We turned round after a while and headed back towards home.

He told me where he lives. His parents cottage is on the other side of Uncle Ray's farm. There is a track going off on the left, opposite the windmill, and he said there is a small hamlet of cottages down there. His Grandfather lives nearby, but is bedridden now, so they have to do a lot for him.

As we got near my cottage, Justin said 'The evenings are much lighter now, so I'll be out walking on the cliffs again. Shall we meet up sometimes, and go together? '

'Yes. I take Ruffles down there after dinner. Usually about half past six.'

'I'll look out for you. Are you going to Youth Club this evening?'

'Yes, I think I will.'

'I'll see you there then. Goodbye Gelany.' He squeezed my hand, before he let it go and walked up the road.

I can't get over it. Justin believed me about seeing Daddy. He didn't ask for any proof, like seeing the dove's feather. He just believed me. I'll show him the feather anyway. I'm so pleased that Susan is Justin's cousin and not his girlfriend.

Mother let me go to Youth Club on my own this evening. She said after all, when I am living here on my own, I won't have her to go with me. The evenings are getting lighter too. Whilst Sascha and I sat at the table, I told her that Susan is Justin's cousin. She was quite surprised, as she had thought Susan was his girlfriend too. They came over and Justin asked us to join them for table tennis. Afterwards, I asked them if they would like to come and sit at the table with us, and they did. Susan still didn't say much, but answered any questions directed at her. Rayson came over when he had finished playing skittles. It was nice with the five of us sitting there talking. Justin grinned at me, when he didn't think anyone else was looking, and I think I blushed.

As Sascha and I walked home together, she remarked that Susan was very quiet.

Monday, 30th April

It has been raining on and off all day. I got soaked going to work, and then again when I went to the allotment. I didn't stay there for long. When it was time to take Ruffles out this evening, it was pouring down, so I didn't go out.

Mother said she has been told she will be able to move into her cottage the weekend after next. She is really looking forward to living in Wells, and not having to walk a mile and back, every time she goes to town.

Tuesday, 1st May

A nice sunny day today. I got a lot done on the allotment

and took Ruffles to the cliffs after dinner. I couldn't see Justin at first, and felt disappointed, but then I saw him walking behind me, and he caught up.

As we walked along together, I told him about Mother moving to Wells soon.

'Oh, does that mean you won't be coming to the cliffs anymore? And what about the allotment?'

'I'm not going. I'm staying at the cottage, on my own. Well not completely on my own, I've got Ruffles.'

'That's brave.' Then he said quietly, 'I'd like to live with you and keep you company.'

'What do you mean? Couples can't live together unless they're married, the law says so.'

'Well we could get married!'

'But you're not sixteen yet, are you? You're younger than me.'

'I was sixteen in January. Anyway for now, I could come and visit you.'

I liked the idea of Justin being around, when I am living in the cottage on my own. We sat down on the grass, looking out to sea, and I remembered the dove's feather in my bag. I carefully took it out and showed it to Justin.

'Look, here's the feather my father gave to me.'

He took it from me and examined it. 'This is a lovely specimen. It must be out of the dove's tail. The white really shines, just like the bird. Have you seen the dove lately?'

'No. Have you?'

'No. Perhaps it's nesting somewhere.'

When we walked back to the cottage, my mother was outside picking some flowers. She saw me with Justin and reluctantly returned his 'Hallo', before he walked up the road.

Inside the cottage, she said to me 'Are you friends with him?'

'Yes.'

'How could you be Gelany, after what happened?'

'It wasn't his fault, he had nothing to do with it.'

'Yes, but he's part of that family. The one who took your father away from us.'

'He's nice. I like him.'

'I'm surprised at you Gelany. You've always been so upset about Daddy disappearing. Surely you can see it's not a good idea to be friendly with the Ditchlings.'

'I'm only friendly with Justin.'

'I'd rather you weren't.'

'You can't stop me.'

'I know I can't. It seems like I can't stop you doing anything anymore. I just don't think it's a good idea.'

I went to my room, feeling upset. I wished he wasn't connected to the Ditchlings. But he is, and I like him. An awful thought has occurred to me. What will Justin think if I tell him I believe in God. Will he still want to be friends with me? His family wouldn't like him being friends with a God believer either. They got my father into trouble for that.

Wednesday, 2nd May

I lay awake again last night, staring at the ceiling, and the annoying writing reappeared saying - *'Tell Justin the truth.'* Not that again I thought, and turned onto my side, so I couldn't see it. If I tell him I believe in God, I risk losing him as a friend. I fell asleep, but kept waking up, worrying about it, not knowing what to do.

This evening, I went to the cliffs, but I didn't want to meet Justin yet, so I turned right and walked into Maplehurst Forest. Ruffles went ahead of me and I followed her to the cave. Sitting on a rock outside, I had a word with God. It went something like this. 'Look God, I've found a good friend, and if I tell him I know you, I'm scared of losing him. I just don't know what to do.'

I heard His voice, like a whisper in the wind, 'Tell Justin the truth. All will be well.'

I sat there struggling with it for a while, trying to believe I could trust God, and that I was prepared to give Justin up. I began to think that if I continued my friendship with Justin, he was bound to find out anyway, I couldn't hide it from him. The other alternative was to give up God.

I put my arm round Ruffles, and watched as the sun began to slip towards the horizon, the sky becoming ablaze with colour. The clouds were tinged with delicate pinks and mauves, and they moved swiftly across a turquoise sky, changing colour as they did so. When the sun sank below the horizon, the sky turned to brilliant shining gold. It was as if God had painted a moving picture, just for me. How could I pretend you don't exist, I thought. I decided to trust God, and to tell Justin the truth about me. If it means I shall lose Justin as a friend, or even be sent to prison if he tells his family, so be it.

17

Confession

Thursday, 3rd May

I waited for Justin when I got to the cliffs this evening. He arrived breathless, and said he had been running, as he was held up. He takes dinner round to his Grandfather every evening, that his mother has made, and does some chores for him.

'I think he wanted me to stay longer, but I said I was going out to meet someone. I stayed later yesterday, that's why I didn't get down here.'

'Will you tell him we're friends?'

'I don't know, I suppose I'll have to at some point, especially if we got married! I don't want to upset him though, as he's so frail. I know he's sorry for what he did. He didn't mean to get your father arrested. He thought the police would just give a warning, and that would stop him from talking about God to my father.'

'Wouldn't it help if he knew my father hadn't been shot, and that he's still alive?'

'Yes, I suppose it might. I'll think about it. I could tell my father first, and ask him if he thinks I should tell grandfather.'

'Will you tell your father that we're friends?'

'Yes, I will.'

We reached a grassy mound and sat down on it. I called Ruffles back as she had gone on ahead. She came racing back and laid down beside us. The sea was a deep blue, reflecting the sky, and the white puffy clouds looked like they were suspended on strings from above. My heart started beating fast, as I thought I must tell him, I must get it over with. But I knew I could lose him.

'Justin, there's something you ought to know about me.'

He turned his head and looked at me, smiling, 'What's that?'

'I believe in God too. It's not just my father. Daddy didn't tell me about God though, I found Him for myself. I know He's real.'

'I knew there was something different about you. How did you find out about God?'

I told him about the cliff fall, finding the tin in the cave, and the letter inside. I repeated the letter practically word for word, I know it so well, after reading it often. Then I told him what happened with the dove coming down out of the sky, when I asked God if He is real.

'That's amazing Gelany.'

'Since then lots of things have happened that are miracles. Like the person who appeared with a rope, after you fell down the cliff.'

'Yes, then he disappeared, didn't he, after he helped you to pull me up.'

We sat there in silence and I wondered what he was thinking. Was he going to tell me we couldn't be friends anymore? I felt uneasy, and thought I'd break the silence.

'Do you believe there's a God, Justin?'

'Well, when I look at all the different birds, and hear their special calls, there is such a variety. I can't believe that they all just developed from one bird. To me, they look like they've been created and designed very carefully, by someone who enjoyed doing it. They don't even mate with each other and make mongrel birds, which they probably would do if they started as one bird. So I think it's quite possible. Do you think I could get to know God like you do?'

'Yes, I'm sure everyone can, if they want to. What about your family though? They wouldn't be too pleased if they knew I had spoken to you about God. And even less pleased if you started believing in Him.'

'I don't know. I think my father believes in God anyway. He keeps it to himself mostly, for fear of the police. But I can tell from things he's said. He doesn't directly refer to God though, and I don't think he knows Him like you do either. How did you get to know Him?'

'It was when I was very upset about something Mother had told me about Daddy. I had a really strong desire to know if God was real, after reading that letter. So I pleaded with Him, asking if He is real, would He talk to me. That was when I was on the cliffs and the dove appeared out of the sky and landed on me. I felt so peaceful after that, I knew something had happened. Since then I've been able to hear Him speak to me, not out loud though, but in my thoughts. And lots of miracles have happened in my life, that only He could make happen.'

'I wish I could have an experience like that.'

'Do you Justin?'

'Yes.'

'So, we're still going to be friends then?'

'What do you mean?'

'I was afraid you wouldn't want to be friends with me,

after I told you I believed in God.'

'And you told me anyway. Why?'

'I believed God wanted me to tell you the truth.'

'Well I'm glad I know, I think it explains some things.'

'So we're still friends?'

'Yes, of course,' he said, and put his arm round me, pulling me close to him. Then he added 'Seems like we both want to be friends now, doesn't it?'

'Yes.'

'That's good.'

We walked back holding hands. When we were getting near my cottage, I told Justin I would start going to the cliffs a quarter of an hour later, as it is getting lighter in the evenings, then it would give him more time with his Grandfather.

He asked, "Shall I call for you, when I'm going past?'

'No, not until my mother has moved. She isn't keen on us being friends.'

'Oh, I'm sorry.'

'She'll have to get used to it.'

Friday, 4th May

Justin didn't come to the cliffs this evening. I hope his family haven't put him off being friends with me.

Saturday, 5th May

Justin came to the allotment today, on his own. I asked him if he'd told his parents about me or Daddy, and he said hadn't yet, but would try to tell them this weekend. He didn't get to the cliffs yesterday, because it was too late after doing things for his Grandfather.

I pulled up a row of cabbages and took them up to the Market Barn in the handcart. When I got back he had gone.

This evening, it was raining so hard, I didn't go to the Youth Club. I made a basket, whilst Mother was busy packing and sorting things, getting ready to move.

Sunday, 6th May

I went to see Uncle Ray's family today. Aunt Pearl and Ruby were in the kitchen preparing lunch when I arrived. Aunt Pearl asked me if I could peel the potatoes, as she was running late. Ruby said she would help me and got another peeler.

As she was slowly tackling a big potato, she said 'Rayson is going to leave home and live at the baker's shop. I don't want him to go.'

'Is he really?' I asked turning to Aunt Pearl.

'Well not just yet. Mr Baker has offered Rayson the baker's cottage when he wants to get married. He says it is too big for him and his wife, now that the children have left home. There is an annexe adjoining it, where his parents used to live, and they will move in there.'

'Is Rayson thinking of getting married then?'

'Well, he may be. He's old enough.'

'Do you know who he wants to marry?'

'I've got a good idea. But he hasn't said anything about it yet. Maybe Mr Baker's offer will make him do something about it.'

'Who do you think it is?'

'I'm not saying. I'm only guessing, and I could be wrong.'

I hoped it was Sascha. How awful it would be if it was someone else. I thought I must say something to Rayson. When I had finished helping in the kitchen, and Ruby had her arms in a bowl of flour, I went to find him. He was in the sitting room painting some very tall dark trees, with a moon behind their branches.

'Hallo Rayson. That's a nice picture.'

'Hallo Gelany. How are you?'

'Okay. Mother is getting ready to move, so it's a bit unsettling. I hear you might move too.'

'What to the baker's house? Yes, that's good of him to offer me that. He wants me to take over the business one day too. He said he will carry on working for as long as he can though. I get on well with him and he treats me like a son. They only had three daughters, and they're all married now. None of their husbands are interested in becoming bakers.'

What about you, do you want to get married?'

'Me? Yes, of course.'

'Do you know who to?'

He looked at me and smiled, 'You are nosey today.'

'Well I know a girl who likes you a lot.'

'Do you? Well let's hope it's the same person then!'

'Come on Rayson, tell me.'

'No, not until I've asked her.' He put his painting and brushes down, 'I think you know anyway. Let's go and see if lunch is ready.'

So I'm still not sure. I wonder if I should have told him about Sascha.

In the afternoon, Ruby and I helped Jimmy make a garden round the tree house. It's looking very nice. Ruby said perhaps Jimmy will leave home too, and go and live in the tree house!

I went back up to the house to wash the mud off my hands, before leaving. When I went into the sitting room, to say goodbye, Uncle Ray was there. He told me to tell my mother that Andy Drayling said he could borrow his ox and cart, to help her move next weekend. He said he would bring it down to our house about nine o'clock on Saturday morning.

Mother was really pleased when I told her. She said it would have taken several tiring trips with a handcart.

Monday, 7th May

Justin was waiting for me on the cliffs when I arrived this evening.

'Hallo Gelany. I told my father about you going to the prison, and finding out that your father is still alive. He was amazed, and so pleased to hear that he wasn't shot. He said he liked your father a lot, and regretted talking to him about God at work. I asked him whether I should tell Grandfather, and he said 'Yes'. He thought it might help him, as he's been feeling so guilty about it over the years. He said Grandfather felt like he had killed your father himself.'

'So, have you told him yet.'

'Yes, I told him yesterday when I took his dinner to him. I waited until he had finished eating, when he likes me to sit down and have a chat.'

'What did he say?'

'Well at first he was speechless. Then he said "I'm so glad. I'm so glad. I'm so thankful. Thank you for telling me Justin." He laid back on his pillows and smiled.'

'Have you told them we're friends yet?'

'No. One thing at a time. Let them get over that shock first.'

Tuesday, 8th May

I met Justin just passing our cottage, and we walked down to the cliffs together.

'This evening, Grandfather asked me if I talk to you, when I'm at the allotment. I told him I did and that we were becoming good friends. He asked me if I could bring you to see him, as he wants to ask for your forgiveness.'

'He said that?'

'Yes, honestly.'

'I don't know. Let me think about it.'

Unfortunately Mother saw me go off with Justin and come back with him, and had a word with me, when I got home.

'Gelany, I think you're becoming too friendly with Justin.'

'Why?'

'What would your father say? He wouldn't like it, would he? Don't you care about him anymore?'

'Of course I do. I know he doesn't mind, I asked him. He said he's forgiven Mr Ditchling, and he liked Justin and his father.'

'Not that again. I suppose it was in your dream.'

'It wasn't a dream.'

I felt annoyed and went to my bedroom. A bit later, she knocked on the door and came in.

'I'm sorry Gelany. It's just that it's very hard for me to believe your father walked out of the prison and then walked back in again.'

'Yes, I can understand that. But I know it's true.'

"I can't imagine why your father would forgive the man who caused him to be separated from his family, either.'

'Well he said he was the one who suffered, when he harboured unforgiveness. He said God helped him to forgive.'

'What if your friendship developed with Justin, and you wanted to get married. You'd be called Mrs Ditchling. I hate the Ditchlings for what they did, don't you?'

'Justin didn't do it, it was his Grandfather. I like him a lot Mum, and I don't know how I'd feel about being called

Mrs Ditchling.'

She left my room without saying anymore. I haven't really thought much about being related to the Ditchlings. I suppose Mr Ditchling could die soon anyway, and he is really the one who caused my father to be put in prison. I would rather keep the name Lantern though, I like it better, and it makes me feel connected to Daddy.

Friday, 11th May

Mother is nearly all packed up and ready to move. In the glass porch, there are boxes with crockery, dishes and pans, and a suitcase with her clothes in. Ruffles has been walking around whining, sensing something is up. I am beginning to realise how bare it will look, when she has gone and taken most of the furniture too.

'I'm sorry that I'm taking nearly everything Gelany. What are you going to do without a table, or chairs, or a cupboard?'

As a joke, I said 'I probably won't need a cupboard as I won't have anything to put in it!' That was a mistake.

'Now you're making me feel guilty. You can still come with me if you like.'

'No I'll be alright. I'll manage.'

'I'm leaving you a pan and a set of crockery and cutlery, so at least you should be able to eat.'

'And I've got the range to keep me warm and cook on.'

'I'll leave you a chair.'

I don't know how I feel about her going. In a way it's exciting, having to look after myself completely, and doing things my way. But it is also a big responsibility, and I hope I don't feel too lonely.

Saturday, 12th May

I woke up early this morning, to the sound of Mother bustling about, packing last minute items. As I was clearing up the breakfast things, I heard heavy hooves plodding on the dusty road, and a loud voice. I rushed outside and saw Jimmy and Ruby sitting on a cart, being pulled by a large hairy ox, with huge horns. Uncle Ray was on the ground in front of it, struggling to bring it to a halt, pulling on the reins and shouting.

When they stopped, he put his hands up to help Jimmy down, and then lifted Ruby off the cart.

'That was fun Gelany.' Ruby told me, 'I was a bit scared when it wouldn't stop though.'

Uncle Ray and Jimmy started loading the furniture on the cart, and Mother, Ruby and I carried out the smaller items, and put them on the ground for Uncle to load them.

'Won't it be fun, having your own house,' Ruby said.

'I hope so,' I replied, beginning to wonder if it would be fun, as I saw the cottage beginning to empty.

When the cart was piled high with Mother's belongings, Uncle Ray said he was pleased that they had managed to get everything on, and it would only take one trip. He took one of the reins and Jimmy took the other, and they pulled and pulled to get the ox moving again. They managed to turn it around and led it back up the road. Mother, Ruby and I followed behind with Ruffles, who still looked worried, and wanted to see what was going to happen next I think.

We unloaded it all at Mother's new cottage. Nothing seemed to fit properly like it did at home, so we did the best we could. Uncle Ray said he was sorry but they had to return the cart, and get back to the farm. I asked Mother if she wanted me to stay and help her sort it out, but she said she didn't, and that she would do it in her own time.

I went back riding on the cart with Ruby, until we reached the road that led to Andy Drayling's. Uncle Ray helped me down, and I said 'goodbye'. Ruffles walked beside me, wagging her tail, looking happy that we were going home. It was nearly lunchtime when I got there. Going inside, it looked really weird with hardly any furniture, not quite like home anymore. I made a drink and a sandwich and took it outside in the back garden and sat on the grass. At least it was normal out there, surrounded by the flowers. Mother hasn't taken any of the plants.

After I had eaten, I went back inside and looked around. It looked so bare, I nearly cried. But then I thought, at least I'm still here, and I can make it look nice again. I got a pencil and a piece of paper and made a list of what I needed. The garden and my bedroom, look completely normal, nothing gone from there. Mother's room is empty and can stay that way for now. But the kitchen needs a table, and I need another pan to cook in. If I have a visitor, I will need another chair. The sitting room needs two armchairs or a sofa. In the meantime I can sit on the rug. So that's not too bad. I asked God to help me find a table, chair and armchairs, and a way of getting them back to the cottage.

In the afternoon I worked on the allotment. Justin was busy on his too. We didn't talk much, as we had lots to do. I told him Mother had moved out now, and he said he hoped I would be alright and he will come to see me.

After dinner, I was tired, and didn't feel like going all the way back into town for Youth Club, but as the cottage seemed so quiet and empty, I did go. When Sascha and I were playing table tennis with Rayson, Justin and Susan came over and watched. I wished the four of us could play together, but we couldn't leave Susan out. When Rayson went to play skittles, Justin and Susan played table tennis with us, and then came and sat at our table. Susan still doesn't say much, but smiles, so I think she likes us.

Sunday, 13th May

I went to Uncle Ray's for lunch. Aunt Pearl asked if I was alright, as she had heard the cottage looks rather bare. I told her I was. She said she was sorry she didn't have any spare furniture to offer me.

Afterwards, I carried on into town, to see how Mother is getting on. I thought this is quite nice, I have someone to visit in Wells now. I was surprised to see that her cottage is still in a muddle, it didn't look like she had done anything to straighten it out.

'Do you need some help to sort things out?' I asked.

'I've tried Gelany, things just won't fit.'

'What things?'

'Everything, it seems. Like this cupboard. It won't go under the windowsill, because it's too tall. I've got nowhere to put things like the pots and pans, as there are no shelves. There are no hooks to hang things on either. It's the same in the sitting room. When we moved into the other cottage, your father sorted out all that sort of thing.' She sat down on a chair and started to cry. 'I wish he was here now. He could make this cottage into a home.' Then she cried some more, sobbing out loud.

I was embarrassed and didn't know what to say. I stood next to her and put my arm around her shoulders. 'I'm sorry Mum.'

She wiped her tears away with a hankie, and then stood up and made us a drink. At least she has some chairs and we could sit at the table. I helped her move a few bits of furniture to better positions and then walked home. It's sad really, as she has looked forward to moving to that cottage for months. I expected to see her smiling and happy for a change.

Monday, 14th May

Justin called for me on his way down to the cliffs this evening. We held hands, and I felt free not having to worry what Mother might think. Ruffles ran round us in circles and then took off in a straight line, with her nose to the ground, when she got the scent of a rabbit.

'What's it like living on your own?' Justin asked.

'Well I haven't been indoors much yet, I've been out most of the time. The cottage looks a bit bare at the moment.'

'Did your mother take a lot of the furniture?'

'Yes, well things like the table, chairs and cupboards. I went to see her yesterday afternoon, expecting her to be happy and sorted out. She's been wanting to move there for quite a while, and it's all I've been hearing about lately. But the cottage was still in quite a muddle, and she was upset because things didn't fit.'

'Oh dear. Does she have anyone to help her sort it out?'

'No, not really. Uncle Ray is too busy on the farm to spare any time, I think.'

'I could go and help her.'

'She won't let you.'

'Why not?'

'You know why. She's not keen on your family, after what happened.'

We walked further along the cliffs, and Justin let me look through his binoculars at a bird's nest. I could see the baby birds heads and their big open beaks, as their mother flew back to the nest, with some food. When we got back to the cottage, I asked him to come in for a drink.

He looked around and said, 'Oh Gelany, it is bare. Where

do you sit.'

'On that chair, or on the floor. I'll manage for now, until I can get a table, and some more chairs.'

'I could probably make you a table. At Woodalls, they let us have the offcuts of wood really cheaply, practically for nothing. Would you like me to see if I could get some wood? It may not be as good as you had, but at least it would be something to sit at.'

'Yes, if you can. That would be lovely. I don't mind what it looks like, so long as it works.'

'I'll have a look tomorrow, and see what's available in the offcut store.'

We took our drinks into the sitting room and sat down on the rug. Ruffles sat behind Justin and leaned against him, which made him laugh. He leant back on her.

'I see Ruffles knows how to improvise. What a useful dog.'

When it began to get dark, Justin said he had better go. At the door, he put his arms around me and gave me a hug. It felt very comforting, and I kissed him on the cheek. When he had gone, the cottage seemed empty again.

Tuesday, 15th May

I waited a little while for Justin to knock on the door this evening, but as he didn't come and Ruffles was getting impatient for her walk, so we went out anyway. He caught me up later on the cliffs, and said he had been doing some jobs to do for his Grandfather.

'I found some wood suitable for the table legs in the offcut store. The manager ask me what I wanted it for. I told him, and when he knew it was for you, he went into the workshop and found a piece for a table top. He remembers your father and he liked him. He said we can have it all for nothing.'

'That's very nice of him.'

'I'll bring it down on my handcart one evening. I can't come tomorrow, I've got things to do.'

It was getting dark when we got back to the cottage, so Justin didn't come in, he said he had to get home. He gave me a quick hug and a kiss on my lips. I missed him when I went back into the cottage on my own, but I told myself I would have to get used to it.

I sat on my chair and made a basket. I thought I had better make one every evening, so I can get enough money to pay all the tax. When I had finished, I got out my tin whistle and filled the empty cottage with the sound of music. Ruffles rolled on her back with her legs in the air, and looked like she approved.

Wednesday, 16th May

I missed seeing Justin this evening, and felt a bit lonely, but I've got to get used to it. I've chosen to live here on my own. Basket making and tin whistle routine again.

Thursday, 17th May

Gordon was waiting for me after work. It seemed a long time since I have seen him, although it is only three weeks.

'Mother moved out on Saturday, and I've stayed at the cottage,' I told him as we walked to the station.

'Good, I'm glad you've been able to stay there. What's it like living on your own?'

'A bit quiet, and the cottage is a bit bare, as she took most of the furniture. But I'll gradually furnish it again.'

'So you're okay there then?'

'Yes, I think so. It's all a bit new at the moment, I've got to get used to it. I'm glad I didn't move with Mother though,

I don't think I would like living there.'

'I'm getting married on 16th June. Can you come to Easten, and join us for the wedding? It's in the Central Hall, and we are having a buffet meal after.'

'Yes, I'd like to. Is Grandma going?'

'Yes. I told her last week, when I went to see her.'

'How is she?'

'She's very well, and she was excited about going to the wedding. She told me to check it's alright with my mother though, and it is. You'll be able to meet Donna. I've wanted to introduce you to each other. My two favourite women!'

'I'll look forward to it.'

'It would be nice for you to find a young man. Then you wouldn't have to be alone in that cottage.'

I blushed. 'I may have found one already,' I said, and then wondered if I should have said it.

'Who's the lucky man then?'

'I'm not telling you. He hasn't asked me to marry him yet.'

'Well I hope he does, if you're keen on him. Are you?'

'I think so. Well, I do really like him now.'

'It's not the policeman, or one of the Rulers, is it?' He joked.

'No, of course not.'

'That's good. You had me worried for a minute.'

The horn sounded. Gordon ran to get in a carriage, yelling as he left 'Goodbye cousin.' Then he waved madly until he went out of sight, as the carriages disappeared behind some bushes.

Justin was late coming to the cliffs again. He ran to catch me up and was out of breath.

'Grandfather is getting worse. He needs me to do more things and wants me to stop and talk. Sorry I'm late.'

'That's okay.'

'He keeps asking me when I'm going to bring you to see him.'

'Oh.'

'Will you come?'

'I don't know. If he wants me to forgive him, I'm struggling with that, and I don't want to say it unless I mean it.'

'I can understand that. But I don't know what to say to him. He's a dying man.'

'I'll have a word with God about it.'

'Can you talk to him like that, like you do to me?'

'Yes. I need to go somewhere quiet on my own though, so I can hear Him answer.'

'Does he talk to you like I do, out loud?'

'Not really. I hear it like a whisper. I'm not sure if it's in my head or in my heart.'

It was nearly dark when we got back, so Justin went home. He said he won't come tomorrow, and is busy on Saturday, so will see me at the Youth Club. I hope he won't stop being friends with me, just because I won't forgive his Grandfather. How do you forgive someone who has taken your father away when you were a child, and made you suffer so much with wanting him. I suppose it wasn't him who actually took Daddy, but if he hadn't told the police, then they wouldn't have taken him. But what if he dies, will I regret not forgiving him? Oh God I really need your help here.

18

Forgiveness

Friday, 18th May

This evening, I went out early as I didn't have to wait for Justin. I decided to go to the cave as it would be more private to have a word with God there. Walking through the wood, I was surprised when my tears started running down my face. By the time I got to the cave, I was really ready to have a word with God.

'Please help me God. Justin's Grandfather wants me to forgive him for causing my father to be taken away from me, when I was young. Oh God, I loved my father so much and I've missed him so much, and it made my mother unhappy. How can I forgive him?'

I didn't hear His voice, but it felt as if something was brushing against me, something soft and gentle and peaceful. I felt wrapped in love. I started sobbing out loud, and I cried and cried buckets of tears. When I had no more tears left in me to cry, I blew my nose. Then I realised all the hurt had gone from inside me. There was nothing there against Mr Ditchling. He was just a person like the rest of us, a person who made a mistake, and now he was sorry for it. I felt a strong desire to go and see him.

'Thank you God,' I whispered.

Ruffles came up and sat close to me, looking concerned. I had forgotten she was there, and wondered what she had thought of my loud sobbing.

'It's alright Ruffles. I'm okay now,' I said giving her a hug.

I walked back home, feeling light as a feather, as if a heavy weight had lifted off me. I thought I might fly away over the cliff edge, so put my feet extra firmly on the ground. It was a very strange feeling.

Saturday, 19th May

I missed Justin working on the allotment next to me, but I got a lot of weeding done. In the afternoon I took some cabbages and spinach to Mr Mars. I told him I was going to try to grow more fruit and vegetables to sell, and asked if there was anything he needed more of. He said he could sell more of most things, but he is often short of runner beans, strawberries and swede. So that's useful to know, I will grow more of those.

In the evening I went to Youth Club. Sascha wasn't there, and I missed her. She didn't tell me she wasn't going, perhaps she is ill. Rayson wasn't there either. I asked Jimmy where he was, but he didn't know. I went over to see Justin and Susan, and we played table tennis together. When Susan was talking to another girl, I told Justin I was ready to go and see his Grandfather.

He beamed at me, 'That's great, when can you come?'

'One evening next week.'

'How about Monday?'

'Alright.'

He explained to me where his Grandfather lived, and said

he would already be there. I must have looked a bit reluctant, because then he asked if I would like him to meet me, by the windmill at the end of his road. I agreed to meet him there at six thirty. I would rather go with Justin.

Sunday, 27th May

I went to see Uncle Ray's family today. Aunt Pearl and Ruby were busy in the kitchen.

Ruby said 'Rayson's going to get married.'

'Let Rayson tell Gelany, Ruby.'

'Is he really Aunt Pearl?'

'Yes.'

'Who's he marrying?'

'Go and ask him yourself. He's in the sitting room.'

Rayson was painting a picture of bluebells in a wood.

'Hallo Rayson. That's a lovely picture.'

He looked up and said 'Hallo Gelany, how are you?'

'I'm alright. I hear you're getting married.'

'Yes. I asked a lovely girl and she surprised me by agreeing to marry me.'

'Come on Rayson, tell me who it is.'

'Sascha, of course,' he laughed.

'Really?'

'Yes, who else?'

'Well no one. I'm so glad. When did you ask her?'

'Yesterday. We played truant from Youth Club and went for a walk, as it was such a lovely evening.'

'So that's where you were. When is the wedding?' I asked, hoping it wasn't going to be on the same day as Gordon's.

'Oh we haven't got as far as arranging a date yet.'

'Well don't get married on the 16th June, will you? I've got another wedding to go to on that day, in Easten.'

'Have you? Who's that? Not yours is it!'

'No. It's my cousin Gordon, he's getting married to Donna that day, and he invited me. I've been wondering what to give them for a present, but seeing your picture has given me an idea. Would you do a painting for me to give to them? I'll buy it off you.'

'My first commission. Yes of course. Is this size alright? What subject?'

'Umm, how about some boats on the sea, as he's a fisherman. Can you do that?'

'Yes, I think so. I did a sketch of the fishing boats on the sea once, when I was in Easten. I'll get it out, for reference. Actually if you could just pay me for the frame, that would be fine. I'd like to do it.'

Aunt Pearl called that dinner was ready, so we went and sat down at the table. After lunch, I said I would go and see Mother. Ruby wanted to come with me, but I told her I would take her another time, as Mother hadn't got the cottage straight yet, and I wanted to see if I could help. She was okay with that. I didn't want her to see Mother upset either.

I walked up the road reluctantly, as I would rather have stayed with Uncle Ray's family, who were happy about Rayson's news, than go to see my depressed mother. I hoped I could cheer her up somehow, determined to help her make things look better.

When I knocked on the cottage door, she answered it and I was surprised to see she was smiling.

'Come on in Gelany,' she said cheerfully. I thought that's a bit odd.

The kitchen looked tidy and spotless, it looked really nice. Everything had a place, and it fitted!

'What's happened? It looks so different from last week. Did you manage to do this yourself?'

'Well I had a little help.'

'Who from?'

'Justin!'

'What!'

'Yes. He came to see me on Wednesday evening. He said you told him that things didn't fit, and as he's a carpenter, he wondered if he could help. At first I said "No. I'll manage." But he pleaded with me, and wouldn't take 'No' for an answer. He told me he would come back on Saturday with his tools, some wood for the shelves, and some hooks. I was a bit annoyed, as I felt I had been pushed into it, but I also really needed the help he was offering. So when he came back yesterday, I let him in. As he worked, he talked to me in a friendly way, and I began to like him. I remembered you said it wasn't his fault about Daddy, and so I dropped all my prejudice against him. He's really nice Gelany. I don't mind you being friends with him anymore. I'm sorry I gave you such a hard time about it.'

I was almost speechless, but managed to say 'That's alright.' I wondered why Justin didn't tell me at Youth Club last night. Mother made us some drinks and we took them into the sitting room. It didn't look much different in there.

'Justin said he'll come back next Saturday, to make things fit in here, and put a shelf up. Also make the bedroom wardrobe fit in place. He's a real blessing Gelany.'

'Yes, he's going to make me a kitchen table, and the manager at Woodalls said we can have the wood for free. They really liked Daddy there.'

'Oh, I wish he was here Gelany.'

'I know.'

'You say you believe in God, but if He is true, why would He take your father away from us and have him put in prison? I can't help wondering that.'

'He didn't do it, the Tansas did.'

'But why would God let them?'

'God didn't make us like puppets, where He pulls the strings. He made us and gave us free will, so we can choose what we want to do. Some people choose to do good things and some people choose to do bad things.'

'How do you know all this Gelany?'

'I ask God questions and I hear Him tell me the answers.'

'I think I had better start asking Him some questions then.'

I smiled at her, she looked embarrassed, got up from the table and cleared the cups away.

As I walked home, I thanked God, that Mother now liked Justin, and that he had been able to help her. It makes life so much easier.

Monday, 28th May

I arrived at work after Sascha and she was already working at her desk. She turned round when she heard me come in, and smiled at me, a much bigger smile than usual. I whispered 'I know', which seemed to satisfy her, because I could see she was bursting to tell me.

We walked home together, and she was so excited, talking about getting married and the baker's cottage they are going to live in. She hasn't seen inside it yet, but Rayson is going to take her there soon. He has to help Mr Baker move out first, into the annexe. She said I can be her flower girl at the wedding. I don't mind the flowers, but I'm not sure about wearing a pretty pink dress, like she suggested.

When we reached her farm, she said 'Oh Gelany, we aren't going to be sisters if you won't marry Peter, but at least we will be cousins now.'

'Yes, that's really lovely.'

I'm so glad that two people I like a lot, are getting married to each other, and I'll have someone else to visit in Wells too.

As I carried on walking down the road, I remembered I had promised Justin I will visit his Grandfather this evening, and wished it hadn't come round so quickly. I worked on the allotment in the afternoon, and tried not to think about it. I'll just do it and get it over with, I thought. I know I have forgiven him, but it still seems hard to go there.

As soon as I had washed up after dinner, I called Ruffles, as this was to be her evening walk. Going up the road, I asked God to help me. I found Justin waiting by the windmill. He took hold of my hand, leading me towards his Grandfather's house.

'Justin, I went to see Mother yesterday. The kitchen looks lovely. Why didn't you tell me you were going to help her?'

'I wanted it to be a surprise.'

'Well it was. I was surprised she let you in.'

'Well, she wouldn't at first. But I knew it was the right thing to do, so I persisted. She was a bit cold at first when I started working, as if I was invading her cottage, but then she warmed to me.'

'I think you melted her! Thank you so much. She's happy for us to be friends now, in fact I think she wants us to be. Not just for what you did, but because she found she likes you.'

'That's good.' He stopped to kiss me on the cheek. 'Perhaps she will agree to us being more than just friends too.'

We had reached Mr Ditchling's cottage. I told Ruffles to wait by the door, and we went inside. Mr Ditchling was lying in bed, looking quite ill, his face being a greyish colour.

'Gelany, thank you for coming to see me. Sit down.'

I sat down on a chair, next to his bed.

'I want to tell you how sorry I am.' He paused and drew a deep breath. 'I didn't mean them to take your father away. I was worried my son would get into trouble, if he started believing in God. I told your father to stop talking to George about it, but when he didn't, I told the police. I thought they would just warn him and scare him. I didn't think they would take him away. I'm so sorry.' As he talked, he kept pausing. It seemed hard for him to get enough breath, and his voice was very faint. Tears started running down his face, and then he had a coughing fit. Justin gave him a drink. I didn't know what to say, but I knew I should say something.

'I forgive you Mr Ditchling.'

He put his hand out, trying to take hold of mine. So I gave it to him, and he squeezed it.

'You're a good girl, Gelany. God bless you.'

I was surprised he mentioned God in that way. I looked up at Justin, but he didn't say anything. When I looked back at Mr Ditchling his eyes were shut and he looked peaceful.

'We'll leave you to sleep Grandfather. Come and meet my mother and father now, Gelany.'

I got up a bit reluctantly, as I felt I should say something else, but I couldn't think what. Mr Ditchling seemed to want to sleep anyway.

Justin's parents are very nice. We sat at their kitchen table, and drank peppermint tea. His younger brother Henry, was playing with a wooden ox and cart, and was so absorbed, he didn't take much notice of me. Justin's father thanked me for coming to see Mr Ditchling, and asked me about the allotment. He said he thought I managed it very well, and perhaps I can teach Justin a thing or two.

Justin said he would walk back home with me.

When we were outside his cottage, I asked him 'Why did

your Grandfather ask God to bless me? Does he believe in Him?'

'I don't know. I'll ask him about it.'

'Does he know I believe in God?'

'Yes. I told him.'

'He didn't tell you to stay away from me then?'

'No. I think maybe he does believe in Him.'

When we reached my cottage, Justin said he had better get back and see if his Grandfather was alright. He was worried about him.

'Thank you Gelany for what you did.'

'I wish I could have said more, but I didn't know what to say.'

'It doesn't matter. Just going to see him meant a lot to him. And he was able to tell you he's sorry.'

Tuesday, 29th May

Justin didn't come down to the cliffs this evening, but I didn't mind. I had a good time walking with Ruffles, and talking to God. Even though I didn't say much to Mr Ditchling, it felt as if something has lifted. I don't hate him anymore. I stopped and took out my tin whistle. Whilst I was playing it, the dove flew overhead, and it seemed to glide about the sky in rhythm to the music. It was lovely. When it flew off I stopped playing and walked home. The cottage seemed empty. I wished Justin would come and visit.

Wednesday, 30th May

Justin called for me this evening to go for a walk.

'Sorry I didn't come to see you yesterday. I had a long chat with Grandfather, and he is looking much better. I told him I often meet you in the evenings, and we go for a walk on the cliffs with Ruffles. Today he told me to go to see you, and that I don't want to be stuck indoors with an old man every evening. So as he was looking better and more cheerful, I came.'

'I'm glad he's a bit better. He looked so ill on Monday.'

'I told him about your cottage and your mother moving out. I said she took some of the furniture and I am going to make you a table. He said you can have his sofa, as he doesn't use it. He's got two armchairs. Would you like it, it's green, and in good condition?'

'Yes, that would be very useful. I'd like that.'

'I'll bring it down on my handcart tomorrow.'

'Thank you.'

We reached the cliffs, and the wild flowers looked particularly lovely, making large patches of pink and yellow. As we walked along, we tried to name the flowers. We knew a lot between us, but there are some we still don't know the names of.

Thursday, 31st May

When Sascha and I walked home today, she asked me if I will go to the clothes hire shop with her tomorrow, after work. Her mother is going too. They have booked a date to get married at the Central Hall, on Saturday, 7th July. I was surprised it was going to be so soon, but she said they only do weddings on the first Saturday in a month, and can only marry two couples on one day. On that day they didn't have anyone, but the following months were quite busy.

'It's only just over a month away. Will you be ready for it?' I asked her.

'Yes, of course. I only have to hire the clothes, choose the rings and flowers, and write some invitations. We're going to have a buffet meal in the hall after, for everyone who comes. I can't wait, I'd marry Rayson tomorrow if I could!'

'Will the cottage be ready?'

'I think so. There's not a lot we have to do before we move in, and we can carry on making improvements after.'

This evening, Justin brought the sofa on his handcart, and also a chair, two saucepans, some dishes and cutlery. His Grandfather said he had too many, and expected I could use them. The sofa is quite comfortable, and makes the sitting room look more inviting. He said his Grandfather is much better, and told him to go and see his girl, after he had done some jobs for him. We gave Ruffles a walk on the cliffs, and then Justin came in, to try out the sofa.

'You just need a cupboard in here now. I could make you one.'

'That would be nice, but I've got nothing to put in it.'

'Alright, I'll make you a little table instead, and you can put a vase of flowers on it. It can go here, by the sofa and be useful for putting cups on.

'Yes, I'd like that.'

'It's your birthday next month, isn't it?'

'Yes, the fifth of June, it's next Tuesday.'

'Oh, I don't think I can make it by then.'

'It doesn't matter.'

'What are you doing for your birthday?'

'I don't know. Mother and I usually go to Uncle Ray's for a meal. I'll have to see if they invite me when I go on Sunday.'

'Could we do something together? Not on Tuesday, because I have to work all day. But what about the following Saturday?' He looked thoughtful and then continued 'How about going to the lake and taking a picnic?'

'That would be lovely. But what about your allotment? You didn't go last Saturday, because of helping my mother, and she said you're going again this Saturday. That will be three Saturdays in a row that you'll have neglected it.'

'My mother goes down there in the mornings, to pick what she needs. Does it look neglected?' Replied Justin, with a guilty smile.

'Yes, a bit. We could go down there one evening, instead of going for a walk on the cliffs, and sort it out together.'

'Alright. Let's go tomorrow. I'll come and call for you. Do you mind going again, after working there all afternoon?''

'No, I like it there. So does Ruffles. It probably won't take long to sort your allotment out anyway. You're using a much smaller area than I am.'

'Yes, Grandfather used to sell the produce he grew on the other half, but I don't need to sell any, I only grow what my family can use.'

'You could still do with keeping the weeds down on all of it, though. They will seed themselves everywhere, including on my patch.'

'My father said you could teach me a thing or two!' He said laughing. 'Anyway, shall we go to the lake for a picnic, if it's not raining?'

'Yes. I hope it isn't, I've been wanting to go back. I know, would you like to come back here after, and I'll cook dinner for us? Then we can have a full day together.'

'Yes, that would be lovely.'

'You haven't tasted my cooking yet!'

'I'm sure it's alright. You look healthy on it. I'll ask my father if he would take Grandfather his dinner that day.'

It's lovely to have someone making plans for my birthday. Daddy used to do that.

Friday, 1st June

Sascha's mother was waiting for us when we left work, and we walked to the Clothes Hire shop. Sascha chose a lovely white wedding dress that fitted her well. It has petal shapes for sleeves and larger petal shapes over the skirt. She picked out a frilly pink dress, and made me try it on, but it didn't look right on me. The lady who runs the shop with her husband, went and got me an alternative blue dress with no frills. I put it on and it looked alright but was very plain. Then I chose a blue dress with some lace on it and the lady said it looked just right. Sascha was reluctant to give up the pink idea, but the lady persuaded her, thank goodness. She said that I had to have something that suited me and Sascha gave in. She said she would have some pink flowers instead. We both chose shoes that went with our dresses. I don't have any fancy ones at home.

Justin and I worked on his allotment this evening until it was nearly dark. We got rid of all the weeds growing on the bit he doesn't use, and also the ones on his cultivated patch. It doesn't look so bad now. He went straight home after. I was really tired this evening and am going to bed early.

Saturday, 2nd June

My allotment and the Market Barn today. I sat down later in the afternoon, made a basket, and put my feet up on the sofa. It was really comfortable. I thought it would be good to have a rest before I walked back into town for Youth Club.

Susan has found a friend called Mandy. As there was six of us, Rayson suggested we had a game of skittles. It was fun, but I'm hopeless at it. Justin told me that he had finished helping my mother, no more jobs to do, and he will come and make my table soon.

Sunday, 3rd June
I went to have lunch with Uncle Ray's family today. Whilst we were all sitting round the table Aunt Pearl asked me if I would like to join them for dinner on Tuesday, for my birthday.

'Yes, that will be lovely, thank you.'

'I'll cook your favourite, sausages and mashed potato with onion gravy.'

'I'll make you a birthday cake for pudding, and put candles on it,' said Ruby.

'Will you ask your mother if she would like to join us?' asked Aunt Pearl. 'We don't see her so often, now she isn't walking past the farm on her way home from work.'

'Yes, I'm sure she'd like to come.'

Mother was pleased to see me, and showed me all the work Justin had done. The sitting room did look nice, now everything fitted, and he had put a shelf up. She had placed a vase of wild flowers on a small table. Ruffles laid down on the rug in front of the fire, even though it wasn't lit, making herself at home. She said she would come to Uncle Ray's on Tuesday. She even said that Justin and I must come to have dinner with her one day soon. I told her that would be nice.

Monday, 4th June
Justin called for me in the evening. His face seemed to be beaming and I wondered what had happened to him. He said he would tell me when we were sitting down on the cliffs. On the way, I chatted about what I did yesterday, and how pleased Mother is with the cottage and the work he did

for her.

'That was really nice of you Justin, to do that.' I felt so warm to him, I wanted to hug and kiss him on the spot, but he was quiet, and walking fast, seeming determined to get somewhere where we could sit down. I wondered what he wanted to tell me. We sat by some bushes in the evening sunlight, looking at the blue sea with little white ripples on the crest of the waves.

'Gelany, I've found God for myself. I know He's real,' he burst out, as soon as we sat down.

'How, what happened?'

'Yesterday, late in the afternoon, I came down to the cliffs, to have a word with God like you said, asking Him if he was real. I felt a great longing to know. I paced up and down on the grass, telling Him I wanted to know Him like you do. I must have paced for ages, back and forth, getting more and more determined, but also getting upset that nothing was happening. In the end I was just pleading and pleading with Him, and then it happened.'

'What did?'

'Well I collapsed onto my knees on the grass, and I was crying. I'm embarrassed to tell you that bit.'

'Then what?'

'Well, when I couldn't cry anymore, I sat down and looked out towards the sea, feeling exhausted. The sun was low in the sky and the clouds became full of rainbow colours. It was beautiful. Suddenly there was a loud sound, like the roaring of really strong wind, and I felt a breeze against my back. It had been calm before that. Then I was aware of a glow of light above me, very briefly. It felt as if a very hot hand was touching my head.'

'That sounds amazing! No dove then?"

'No, but I just knew God was real, and I felt absolutely

peaceful. I said to God, please talk to me like you do to Gelany. And a thought came to me, like a voice speaking to me. It said "I love you Justin" and that was it. And when I went home, I felt so happy.'

'I'm so glad Justin.' We hugged each other.

'Is that a dove in the distance, over there?' He pointed out to sea and I looked.

'Yes, I think it is.'

The bird came nearer and started flying round in circles above us. We laid down on our backs and watched it gliding on the wind. Then it flew off over the island.

'Wasn't that great,' said Justin.

We laid there a bit longer, looking up at the sky, but it began to get cooler, so we walked home. When we got to my cottage, Justin handed me a card.

'Have a nice day tomorrow. I'll probably see you on Wednesday.' Then he pulled me close and kissed me on the lips.

'I love you Gelany,' he said. He turned back to wave as he walked up the road.

I didn't say that I love him, but I do. Perhaps I'll tell him when we go to the lake. I'm so happy that Justin has found God for himself. I feel overwhelmed that now I have a friend who believes in Him like I do.

19

Surprises

Tuesday, 5th June

My seventeenth birthday. I opened the card from Justin before I went to work. It's very pretty with a bird amongst some blossom on a tree. Sascha gave me a card after work, with pressed pansies on it. We walked home together.

'Come and have some lunch with us,' she said when we reached her farm. 'I don't like to think of you spending your birthday alone.'

'I'm going to Uncle Ray's this evening for dinner.'

'I know, but come here for lunch.'

'Alright then. But I have to get home to Ruffles soon.'

We had a sandwich for lunch with her mother. She told us that she had got a letter from Peter today, and he says he has a girlfriend, who he met at a Policeman's Social Event. He has decided to stay in Easten now. Sascha was disappointed about that, but her mother said maybe it is for the best, as he may have had to arrest people he knows, if he worked in Wells. Then they talked about the wedding. I left just as her father and brother Jack were coming in for their lunch.

In the afternoon, I worked on the allotment. Ruffles laid in the shade of a tree, as it was quite sunny. I took her with me when I went to the farm.

It was a lovely time round the table. Everyone was cheerful, talking about the coming wedding, and also about Mother's new cottage. Ruby had made a sponge cake with strawberry jam inside, and on the top she had drawn a dog in the icing, which she said was supposed to be Ruffles. Rayson had painted bluebells on a card for me, and all the family signed it. He also gave me the painting of a bird in flight, above the trees on the farm. You couldn't tell which sort of bird it was, as it was too far away, but I knew it was meant to be the dove. My mother gave me a blue knitted hat and some soap that smells like lavender, and Aunt Pearl gave me a jigsaw with farm animals on it. Ruby said she wanted to come and help me do it.

Wednesday, 6th June

Justin didn't come this evening, and I missed him. I took Ruffles on the cliffs, then made a basket and am going to bed early. I don't fancy the long winter evenings on my own, but perhaps I will have got used to it by then.

Thursday, 7th June

Gordon was waiting for me after work. As we walked to the station, he talked about the wedding. It seems everyone is talking about weddings!

'Would you like to bring anyone with you Gelany? It's a long journey, and it would be good for you to have company.'

'Yes, that would be nice. Can I ask Justin?'

'Who's Justin?'

'My friend.'

'He's not the one related to the family who had your father put in prison, is he?

'Yes, but it was nothing to do with him, and I like him.'

'Alright, bring him, then I can see if I approve!'

As I walked home, I hoped Justin would come this evening. If he doesn't, I thought I would walk to his cottage and go and see him. But he did come, and knocked on the door. When I opened it, I was surprised to see him looking upset.

'What's happened Justin? Is anything wrong?'

'Grandfather died last night, in his sleep.'

'Oh dear. I'm so sorry. That must have been a shock, as you thought he was getting better, didn't you? Come in and sit down.' We went into the sitting room.

'Yes it was a shock. But the good thing is that I had a talk with him on Tuesday evening. I told him all about my experience of finding that God is real. He listened very carefully and believed me. He told me to be very careful of speaking out in public about it though, and to keep it to myself. He didn't want the police to take me away.'

'So do you think he believes in God now?'

'Well, yesterday evening, he told me he wanted to know God himself. I held his hand and asked God to show Grandfather that He is real. Then I left him and told him to have a word with God.

When I went back later to say 'Goodnight' and to make sure he was alright, he told me that he had fallen asleep and had a dream. He said he had seen a person in the room who was shining brightly, and his face was so bright he could hardly look at it. Grandfather felt scared, but he told him not to be afraid, and that he was from God. Grandfather told him that he was sorry for causing your father to be put in prison and for all the other wrong things he'd done in his life. The man said God loves those he has created, and forgives those who are truly sorry for what they have done wrong. He said he would take Grandfather to be washed clean. He put on some clothes and they went to the lake in the middle of the Island. The man held Grandfather and dipped him under the water. When he came up he felt clean on the inside as well as on the outside. Then he was back in his room. He took the wet clothes off and got into bed. Then he said he was awake. Grandfather said it was a wonderful dream, and he was still basking in the glow.

The strange thing is, Gelany, I saw a pile of his clothes on the floor, and when I went to pick them up, I found they were soaking wet!'

'Did you tell him?'

'No. He was lying there with a smile on his face, but didn't seem aware of me anymore. I thought I would tell him in the morning. So I just tucked his covers in and left him.'

'When did he die?'

'My mother found him this morning. She said he was looking very peaceful, and he must have died in his sleep.'

We went for a walk along the cliffs, holding hands. I could sense Justin's loss, but was also full of wonder that Mr Ditchling had found God before he died, and only just in time. Justin went home after our walk. He said he wouldn't come tomorrow, but would see me on Saturday, and that would cheer him up, having a day out with me.

Saturday, 9th June

I met Justin by the windmill at 10 o'clock. His mother had given him some cakes she had made. We stopped in Wells to buy chicken pies, and then climbed over the Electra track, when it stopped moving at 10.30am. The walk along the path to the lake was much nicer than it had been in January. The trees and bushes were covered in leaves, and there were so many flowers out. Also it was much warmer. Ruffles ran along, looking as if she was really enjoying all the scents.

When we reached the lake, we sat down straight away, as we both felt hungry. The pies were still slightly warm and had smelt good all the way. Justin produced two welcome bottles of elderflower water. We ate, looking at the still blue water of the lake, shimmering in the sun. The picnic tasted really good, and when I had finished eating, I started to lie back on the grass, but Justin grabbed my hands and stopped me.

'Stay up, I want to ask you something.'

I looked at him, 'What?'

'I want to ask you if you'll marry me.' I wondered if he was serious.

'Is that a proposal?'

'Yes, of course it is. I've wanted to ask you before, but it was difficult whilst I was looking after Grandfather, I wasn't really free.'

'Yes, I'd love to.'

'Really?'

'Yes, of course.'

He kissed me on the lips and then said 'Thank you Gelany.'

Then a thought came to me, 'Will you come and live in my cottage with me?'

'Yes, or there's Grandfather's cottage, but I prefer yours. Is that what you want?'

'I'd like you to come and live with me.'

He pulled me close to him, and we kissed again.

'When shall we get married?' He asked.

'I don't mind. We'll have to find out what dates are available at the Central Hall.'

'Oh dear.' Justin was looking past me, along the lake.

'What?'

'I think I can see policemen over there.' I looked to where he was pointing and could see people in the distance. Some were dressed in black.

'It looks like there are some other people with them,' I said.

'Yes, I think they're supervising work, perhaps on the Tansas' water supply. They take it from this lake. I don't think they've seen us, but let's start walking back. I don't want them to spoil our day.'

We picked up our things, and started walking back up the track, hidden from the lake by the bushes.

It was a shame that our romantic moment had come to a sudden end, but we held hands on the way back, and chatted happily planning the wedding, and what we will do with the cottage.

He came home with me and we collapsed on the sofa, as we had walked back rather fast. I don't know what the police would do, I'm not sure if the lake is out of bounds.

I cooked fish pie for dinner, and Justin said he was impressed with my cooking. It was nice thinking that soon we would be sharing dinner every evening. We didn't go to the Youth Club. I got out my tin whistle and Justin sang some folk songs to it, and we had a game of cards. He went home when it was beginning to get dark. He said he didn't like leaving me all on my own, and I didn't like it either, especially now I enjoy his company.

As he left, he hugged and kissed me and said 'Let's get married as soon as possible,' and I agreed.

Well, I didn't expect that on my birthday day out. What a present! Oh yes, he did give me a necklace as well. It's a chain, with a lovely blue stone on it, set in a heart shape.

Sunday, 10th June

I called at Uncle Ray's this morning, and found Aunt Pearl and Ruby picking strawberries in the garden.

'Is it alright if I go to see Mother this morning, and call

in for tea with you on the way back?'

'Yes, is anything up?' asked Aunt Pearl, looking concerned at my change in routine.

'I want to talk to her about something. I'll tell you when I get back. Come here Ruffles,' I called, as she was running off to join the other dogs.

'Can I come with you?' asked Ruby, looking expectant.

'Not this time. I'll take you with me next Sunday afternoon. I expect you're needed here, to help get the lunch ready.'

'Yes, I couldn't manage without her,' said Aunt Pearl winking at me.

'We'll save you some strawberry cake,' said Ruby.

Mother was surprised to see me.

'Would you like some lunch? I've put two chicken legs in the oven. I was going to have the other one tomorrow, but I can have something else.'

'Yes please.'

'Here, help me with the vegetables, and then I'll get us a drink.'

She handed me a peeler and I peeled some potatoes and carrots, whilst she washed a cabbage, and made a drink. It was nice and bright in the kitchen, as the sun was shining in the window.

'Let's go and sit in the garden,' she said carrying out mugs of mint tea. 'I don't see much sun when I'm at work.'

I carried two chairs out and put them in the shade of the cottage.

'I've got something to tell you,' I said.

'What's that?'

'Justin proposed to me yesterday, when we were at the lake.'

'Did he, goodness that's quick.'

'I said 'Yes.' Are you alright with that?'

'Of course I am, if that's what you want. He seems a really nice boy. I think you're well suited.'

'Do you?'

'Yes. I do.'

'You don't mind about his family connections?'

'Well I do mind about that, but I see he can't help it. It may be awkward meeting them at the wedding though.'

'Mr Ditchling has died, he won't be there.'

She looked shocked. 'When did that happen?'

'Last week, on Wednesday night.'

'Oh.'

I told her he had asked to see me the week before, and when I went, he told me he was sorry.

'It was a bit late for that. But I won't speak ill of the dead,' she said.

I didn't like the way the conversation was going. This was supposed to be good news.

'Anyway we've got a wedding to plan now.'

'Yes, that will be nice. I'm so glad you won't be alone in the cottage anymore Gelany.'

It was good to have lunch together and talk about my own wedding this time!

I called in at the farm on the way back and told them the news. Ruby jumped up and down, asking if she could be a flower girl. Uncle Ray said they would like to meet Justin, and Aunt Pearl suggested I brought him with me to Sunday lunch. Jimmy said not another wedding, he was fed up with hearing about Rayson's, but I think he was joking. Rayson said he was pleased and that he liked Justin.

Monday, 11th June

I couldn't wait to tell Sascha my news, but I had to wait until we left work. We walked home together.

'I've got something to tell you.'

'What's that?'

'I'm getting married too.'

'What? Who to?'

'Justin asked me on Saturday and I accepted.'

'Justin? But you don't like him!' She stopped walking and stared at me, her eyes demanding an explanation. 'Are you teasing me Gelany?'

'No. I didn't like him at first because of what happened to Daddy. But then I realised he had nothing to do with it, and we became friends. Now we love each other.'

'That's amazing. I never guessed. Are you sure?'

'Yes, it's what I really want.'

'Then I'm pleased for you. Come here.' She gave me a hug and kissed me on the cheek. 'When do you want to get married?'

'As soon as we can. We're going to the Central Hall to ask when they've got a date.'

"It's not the Central Hall where you book it. You go to the Clothes Hire and Wedding Shop. They do everything there, they even sell the rings.'

'Oh do they? I'll tell Justin.'

'Well I am surprised, but I'm also pleased for you. I didn't like the thought of you living alone in that isolated cottage.'

Justin came in the evening and we walked on the cliffs holding hands. I really love him now, and Ruffles always gives him a big welcome too. I told him we have to go to the Wedding Shop to book the Central Hall date, and we decided to go at lunchtime tomorrow.

Tuesday, 12th June

Sascha came with me to the Wedding Shop. She said she wanted to order the flowers for her day. Justin was already waiting outside. She congratulated him on his choice of bride, and told him he had chosen well. He replied 'I know', and I blushed.

The lady in the shop said the 7th July still had a space, otherwise it would be November. She said summer weddings were the most popular dates. November seemed ages away, and I think Sascha saw the look of disappointment on our faces.

'I know,' she said 'Let's have a double wedding. We could get married on the same day.'

'But I'm supposed to be your flower girl, we've chosen my dress and everything.'

'I can have another flower girl. It would be much more fun having you as another bride.'

'Really? What do you think Justin?'

'It's fine with me. The sooner the better.'

I turned to the lady, 'Can I change the dress?'

'Of course you can love. How lovely to change from a flower girl to a bride.'

Justin had to get back to work, but Sascha stayed with me whilst I tried some dresses on and she gave me her opinion. I would have liked to have the same one as Sascha with the petal shapes on, but there isn't another one, each dress is unique. We chose a white one with daises embroidered over the bodice, lacy sleeves with daises on, and a long slightly gathered skirt. It fitted well and felt comfortable. I hate getting dressed up, but when I looked in the mirror, I was quite surprised at how nice I looked.

So that's settled. Sascha and I are getting married together. I think it's a lovely idea, I hope our mother's do. Oh I've just thought, they were both hoping I was going to marry Peter all the time we were growing up. Sascha and Peter's weddings together would have been nice for their parents, but it's not going to happen now. Oh gosh, I've only got three and a half weeks to get ready for it, I hope I can!

Justin came in the evening for a walk, and when we were talking about the wedding, I suddenly remembered it's Gordon's on Saturday, and I hadn't asked Justin if he would come with me. He said he will, if I thought it would be alright to leave his allotment for another Saturday. We decided to go there tomorrow evening and do some work on it together. It seems like I am taking on another allotment already, but he said he will help me with mine when I need it, especially now he will be sharing the food with me.

Wednesday, 13th June

Sarah saw us working together this evening on the allotments, and came over to chat. We told her we are going to get married, and she said it was lovely news.

Thursday, 14th June

Justin met me at the Wedding Shop again, at lunchtime. He chose a suit to hire, and we chose the rings and flowers.

Friday, 15th June

A news sheet arrived at work today, saying that Emerald Tansa has had her baby and it is a girl! The Tansa family has only had boy babies born to them, for the last hundred years. It is a custom on this island, for fathers to name their sons and mother's to name their daughters (although my parents didn't stick to that, as my father named me). She has called her Phoebe.

Saturday, 16th June

As I walked up the road to meet Justin at the windmill, I felt so excited. I was going to have a day out with Justin and see Gordon too, even if he was getting married to someone else. It doesn't bother me anymore though. It's lovely to have Gordon as a cousin, and know that I can carry on seeing him. He's changed roles with Justin and become a friend instead.

I left Ruffles at the farm, and we got on the Electra at 8am and reached Easten at 10.15am. We found the Central Hall and waited outside, as we were a bit early. Grandma came along, and she was so pleased to see me, and asked if we could sit together. I introduced her to Justin and told her our news.

'Hallo Justin, pleased to meet you. You kept that quiet Gelany, I had no idea you were planning to get married.'

'I'm sorry Grandma, I haven't written, but we only decided to get married a week ago.'

'Well it's lovely news.'

'Would you be able to come to our wedding too, Grandma?'

'Yes, I'll try to come. I'd really love to.'

People had started going into the Hall, so we went inside and sat down. Donna looked very pretty, with her long black hair piled up on top of her head. I wondered if I could do that with mine.

Gordon smiled at everyone as he, and Donna, walked to the front of the room together, and he gave me a wink.

After the ceremony, we went into another room, where food was laid out on plates, for us to help ourselves. Gordon came over to us and introduced Donna. She seemed very nice and said I must go to see them. Gordon shook Justin's hand and seemed to approve, he was very friendly to him. We told them when we are getting married, and asked if they could come to our wedding. Gordon looked amazed, and then said of course they would.

Donna and Gordon opened the pile of presents that had been left on a table. He was very pleased with the sea picture that Rayson had painted. It had two boats in the distance.

I saw Grandma talking to Gordon's mother, which was quite a step forward for them. Justin told me he liked Grandma. We had a lovely time, and the time soon went. We had to leave at 3.15pm in order to get home on the Electra, before it stopped for the night.

Sunday, 17th June

I met Justin at the windmill, and we went to Uncle Ray's for lunch. Everyone was very nice to him, and it helped that Rayson knew him already. He fitted in very well. Ruby was very quiet and kept staring at him. When we were alone in the kitchen, she whispered 'Does he know God?' and I assured her that he did. After that she seemed happier. She asked him if he would like to go to the barn and see her cat, so we went down there. She reminded me I had said that I would take her to see my Mother, this afternoon. I had forgotten, but we took her with us. She skipped happily up the road at my side, and then started playing with Ruffles and throwing sticks for her.

Mother was pleased to see us all, and is much happier. The cottage looks really nice now, and the sun was shining in the windows. We had tea together, sitting on the lawn in the garden.

Monday, 18th June

Justin called for me after dinner and we took Ruffles on the cliffs. He said he would bring the wood for the table to the cottage, and come and make it next Saturday. So I offered to look after his allotment this week. There is not so much to do on mine at the moment. Things are growing nicely, and I just have to keep the weeds down.

Saturday, 23rd June

Justin turned up early this morning, before I had even finished my breakfast. In his handcart was one large piece of wood, four long pieces, and his toolbox. He laid it all out on the grass in the front garden, and started sawing away. I took him out a drink mid-morning and we sat on the grass, whilst he had a break. It already looked like a table, and he said he was going to sand it down next.

'I saw some wood stacked by the side of the cottage. What's that for?' he asked.

'Oh, Daddy was going to build a veranda on the front of the cottage. He was collecting offcuts from work, but then he was taken away before he could start it. I saw a veranda on a cottage in Wells, and liked it so much, that he said he would build one for us.'

Justin looked thoughtful, and then said 'I'll build you one if you like. I think that's a lovely idea. We could sit on it together and look out towards the sea. It's a sunny spot at the front too. I'll have another look at the wood later and see if any can still be used, if it hasn't gone rotten.'

He got up to carry on with the table, and I went indoors to clean the house. I had started preparing the lunch, when Justin came in.

'You might need to make a bit more lunch, we have a visitor!' He said.

'Who? Who's that? Where?'

'Come outside.'

I followed him out of the door, and there on the path stood a man.

'Daddy!' I flung my arms round him and hugged him. He put his arms around me and kissed me on my cheek. 'Have they let you out?' I asked.

'No, unfortunately not, I'm just here on a visit. I have to go back after.'

'Come inside and sit down, you've had a long journey,' said Justin. 'I'll get you a drink.'

I held Daddy's hand, led him into the sitting room, and we sat on the down on the sofa. I needed to sit down, my legs had gone weak, it had been such a shock. Ruffles came up, sniffed Daddy and wagged her tail. He stroked her head, as I stared at him in wonder. Justin brought in some drinks, and then sat down on the rug.

I asked 'What happened? Why have they let you out to visit us?'

'Do you remember that I told you I was making nursery furniture for Emerald and Charles, and I wanted to decorate it, but wasn't sure how? You suggested blue ducks, yellow chicks, and black lambs. Well I have plenty of time in there, so I did that, painting the furniture white, with borders of coloured animals. I really enjoyed doing it, and it did look rather nice when I had finished.'

'Did it? What happened next?'

'Well last week when the baby was born, I went with the men to deliver the furniture, and help fit it. We went to the Tansas' estate and inside Charles's house, which is like a palace. We put the furniture in the nursery, and then Charles and Emerald came to see it. Charles was so pleased with it, he asked who made it, and the men told him that I did. He realised I was a prisoner, and said he hadn't expected the furniture to be made with such care and attention to detail. He asked if there was anything I would like in return. I knew straight away what I wanted, but I didn't think it would be allowed.

Then he said "Come on there must be something. It can't be that wonderful in the prison."

So I told him the thing I wanted the most was to go home and see my family. I said "I have a wife and a young daughter, too." He looked a bit downcast and then said he'd see what he could do. Anyway, yesterday a guard came to see me and told me that my wish was granted. So here I am.'

'Oh Daddy that's wonderful. I'm so pleased to see you.'

'Where's your Mother?'

'She's moved to Wells. Justin and I are getting married in two weeks' time, and we're going to live here together.'

Daddy smiled at Justin. 'I'm pleased to hear it. You take good care of her for me, won't you.'

'Yes, I will,' replied Justin.

'I'm glad you're staying here Gelany. I love this cottage, and often picture you here and wonder what you are doing. The allotment too, I'm glad you've still got that.'

'I'll take you to see Mother this afternoon. I don't know how she'll react. She's been quite cross about it. She can't understand why you don't just tell them that you don't believe in God anymore, so that they would let you out.'

'Well, we'll go and find out. I've got to see her.'

'I'll go and get the lunch, we can have it in here, or outside in the garden. Unfortunately, the table isn't quite finished, is it Justin?'

'No not quite.'

We went out in the garden and sat on the grass. It was lovely having Daddy with us, I could hardly believe it was happening. For nine long years, I've been waiting for him to come home.

'Daddy, can't you stay out? We could hide you somewhere.'

'No, they'd come and find me, and things would be worse for me. I can stay until Monday, so let's make the most of it.'

After lunch, we took Daddy to see the allotment. He was very impressed and said he couldn't have made a better job of it himself. Justin told him that I had been helping him with his too. I told Daddy that he had been a good teacher, when I was young.

Then we walked into Wells. I said to Daddy that if Mother didn't want him to stay, he should come back to the cottage, and he promised he would. He said if he stayed, I was to come and see him tomorrow. I knocked on Mother's door. She opened it, looked at me and started to say 'Hallo Gelany'. Then she looked past me and her mouth fell open.

'Timothy!'

Justin grabbed my hand and pulled me away. I looked back, wanting to make sure she was going to be friendly to Daddy. I saw her let him into the cottage, then I burst out crying. Justin put his arm around me, as we walked back to our cottage. It was so hard leaving them, but I suppose Justin was right.

Justin finished varnishing the table, whilst I tidied up the cottage garden. Then we to the allotments. All the time I just wanted to go to Wells and see Daddy, it was hard staying away, whilst he was so near. If I hadn't had Justin stopping me, I expect I would have gone. He told me to let my parents have some time together, and I hoped Mother was being nice to him. Justin said I could go tomorrow morning.

In the evening, I couldn't sit still, so Justin suggested we go to see his parents, and that is what we did. Justin's father said he wanted to see Daddy, and apologise for being the one who caused him to go to prison. We decided they would come to Mother's cottage tomorrow afternoon. Justin walked me home later, and said he hoped I would be able to get to sleep tonight.

When I was alone, I spent some time thanking God for the wonderful gift of Daddy being allowed home to visit, and I begged Him to make things alright between my parents. Daddy hasn't come back, so I suppose that's a good sign.

Sunday, 24th June

I was up early this morning, feeling impatient to go and see Daddy, but waited until I thought they would have had breakfast. Then I set off up the road to Wells, Ruffles running by my side, probably wondering why I was walking so fast. I called in at Uncle Ray's farm, told them the news, and that I probably wouldn't be coming to lunch. Uncle Ray asked if they could call in and see Daddy in the afternoon, and Aunt Pearl suggested they only stay half an hour, so they don't intrude on our precious time together.

I got to Mother's cottage about 9am, and knocked on the door not knowing what to expect. Mother came to the door.

'Come on in Gelany,' she said in a pleasant tone.

Daddy was sitting at the kitchen table, and he got up and came and gave me a big hug. Mother got me a drink and I sat down and joined them. I could sense things were alright between them straight away, and I was so pleased. We talked for ages catching up with each other's lives, and it was so lovely, the three of us being together again.

'Daddy, please stay, don't go back, we can hide you somewhere, I'm sure we can.' I begged.

'Yes, Timothy.'

'No, you don't understand. The guards said if I didn't go back, they would go and get my wife and daughter, and they threatened me. They were very reluctant to let me go, and said it was unheard of, a prisoner going out to visit his family. But they had their orders from Reginald Tansa, so they had to let me go. I don't want to put you two in danger, or be a fugitive for the rest of my life. I'm sorry. I believe I will be free one day, though. God has told me I will, and I have dreams about it. We must be patient and do things God's way. Let's make the most of the time we have today, and not think about tomorrow.'

'What do you want to see whilst you're here Daddy?'

'Well apart from my lovely wife and daughter, let's go for a walk round Wells together. It would be nice to experience that sense of freedom.'

So that's what we did this morning, just went for a walk around the town, and stopped to look at Woodalls, which was closed. It was good to hear my parents remembering things that happened in the past, before he was taken.

In the afternoon, Uncle Ray and all his family called in and stayed for about an hour. Soon after Justin and his father came. Justin's father asked if he could speak to Daddy alone and they went down to the field where the allotments are going to be. When they came back, they hugged each other before Justin and his father left. Daddy shook Justin's hand, and said he was sorry he wouldn't be here to give his daughter away on our wedding day, and to take care of me.

After tea, I felt I should leave, to give my parents a bit more time together on their own. I said I would come and see Daddy off tomorrow. It was awful leaving, and I called in at Uncle Ray's to spend the evening with them, I didn't want to be at home on my own. When I arrived, I burst into tears and couldn't speak, and Aunt Pearl hugged me until I had stopped.

'I wish Daddy had come in two weeks' time, then he would have been here for my wedding,' I said.

'No, I think it is better this way,' said Aunt Pearl. 'If he had come the weekend you're getting married, you wouldn't have been able to spend so much time with him.'

Ruby looked concerned, and suggested we all played a card game together. So we did, and it was fun. Then we ended up laughing when Jimmy started joking about what could go wrong at Rayson's and my weddings. Aunt Pearl told Rayson and Jimmy to walk home with me.

I'm alright now, but trying not to think too much about tomorrow.

Monday, 25th June

Ruffles and I got to Mother's cottage at 7am. Daddy had to report to the police station first, and two policemen went with him, to escort him back to the prison. We all walked to the station in silence, Mother and I on each side of Daddy, holding his hands, and the two policemen walking behind us. There were hugs and kisses, and Daddy whispered that maybe, if they know he can be trusted and he behaves well, they might let him visit again. He said he was very sorry he wouldn't be there for my wedding day, but he would be thinking of me. Then they got in the carriages.

After the Electra started moving, Mother and I watched until he became a speck in the distance, then she started sobbing quietly. I held her hand and walked back to her cottage with her.

When we got indoors, she sat down on a chair, looked up at me with tears running down her face, and said 'I still love him Gelany.' Then she started sobbing out loud, and added, 'I don't think I'll ever stop crying.'

I put my arm round her shoulder and said 'Yes you will, when there's no tears left.'

I was so concerned for her, I forgot my own grief. I made some drinks, and sat down beside her.

When she managed to stop crying she said 'Daddy told me they don't just let them go, if they say they don't believe in God anymore. They have to go on a brainwashing programme, where they are made to deny God three times and say things against Him. Also, the guards threaten that if they speak of God again, after they come out of prison, not only will they be shot, but also their family as well.'

'Oh, I didn't know that. Why are they so bothered about God, if they don't think He exists?'

'Daddy said they want people to bow down and worship Ferdinand Tansa and his family instead.'

'Well I don't want to do that.'

'He believes he will get out one day. I hope he's right. I don't know how though.'

She seemed to have calmed down, so I left her and went to work. I was late, but told Mrs Newsby what had happened and that I would do extra time to make up for it. She said, it was only half an hour, and not to worry about it, under the circumstances.

Sascha looked at me with questioning eyes, but I had to wait to tell her about it, when we walked home together. She wondered why Daddy didn't just say he didn't believe in God anymore and stay out of prison. When I told her why, she was shocked and said she hoped Peter didn't have to shoot people and their families, for talking about God.

As I walked home the rest of the way on my own, I wondered what I would do, if I was arrested for talking about God, and taken away from Justin, Ruffles and the cottage. It was just too awful to think about, and I hoped it would never happen to me.

Thursday, 28th June

Gordon was waiting for me after work. As we walked to the station he joked, 'We'll have to stop meeting like this. I'm a married man now!'

'Well I'll be a married woman soon.'

'It's a good thing we're cousins. I can keep meeting you with a clear conscience.'

'Yes.'

When we sat down on the seat, I told him about my father being allowed to visit. He thought that was most unusual, and I suppose it is. Daddy must have made a great job of decorating the furniture. But I'm sure God made it possible too. Gordon could hardly believe that Daddy went back to prison voluntarily, until I told him the guards had threatened our family.

When Gordon went off he said 'See you at your wedding next week.' Then he kissed me on the cheek and added 'That's the last kiss you will get from me, whilst you're an unmarried woman.' Then he ran off, waving. I'm glad I'll still be able to see him when I'm married. It would have been awkward had we not been cousins. But I'm also so glad I'm marrying Justin, and not Gordon now. I think I was infatuated with Gordon, but I really love Justin.

Friday, 29th June

After Justin and I took Ruffles for a walk on the cliffs this evening, and he had gone home, I picked up a basket to work on as usual. I haven't been spending much time on them lately, as I usually see Justin in the evenings. He goes home at dusk, and at this time of year it gets dark late. When I said to Justin that I haven't been making many baskets lately because I keep going out walking with him, he pointed out that I won't need to make them when we're married, as he will help to pay the taxes on the land. So soon I shall just go back to making them in the winter, like I used to, when I'm not working on the allotment. Instead of sitting here making baskets on my own, I won't have to make them, and I'll have Justin's company. I'm really looking forward to that.

Justin told me that his parents have decided to keep Grandfather's cottage for Henry, to live in when he is older. In the meantime they are going to let it out to someone.

Thursday, 5th July

This afternoon two new mattresses were delivered, and some new sheets, pillows, pillow cases, and blankets. It was all paid for by Justin's parents, as a wedding present, with some money that Mr Ditchling had left. The men brought them all on a large handcart, and put them in Mother's old room on the floor. Justin told me they were coming. He said that we can sleep on the mattresses on the floor at first, until he makes a wooden bed frame for them. Mother's room is larger than mine, so we decided to use that one. I'm pleased that I can keep my old room as it is, for now.

Friday, 6th July

Justin and I decided not to see each other today. I spent the afternoon cleaning and tidying the cottage. In the evening, I took Ruffles on the cliffs and talked to God, thinking about all the things that have happened in the past year, and thanking Him for them.

Since I started writing a year ago, I've found out why my father disappeared, where he is now, and I've even seen him. Now I'm almost on the last page of my journal book, and it seems a good place to finish, with my wedding. Shall I start a new journal? I don't know. Maybe, if I have the time.

Saturday, 7th July

My Wedding Day! Well, not just mine, it was Justin's, Sascha's and Rayson's too. What a great day it was. Instead of doing one wedding after the other, like they usually would have done, we were asked if we would like to be married at the same time, as we knew each other. So we took it in turns to say our vows, it was lovely.

Ruby was a flower girl for both of us, and also another young girl, Katy, who is a cousin of Sascha's. We had a buffet meal in the Central Hall, and all the families mingled together.

Grandma had travelled on the Electra, with Gordon and Donna, so that was nice.

She kissed me on the cheek and whispered 'God is good, He has given me back my two grandchildren. You look beautiful my dear.' I was able to introduce her to Ruby at last, and they got on really well together, as I thought they would. Even Mother and Grandma talked to each other, although I think they still felt a bit awkward.

At dusk, Justin and I left with Uncle Ray's family, and collected Ruffles from their barn. Ruby took the pink bow out of her hair and tied it to Ruffles' collar 'to make her look more wedding like', she said.

Then, alone at last, Justin and I walked happily along holding hands, with Ruffles trotting by my side. Ahead of us a full moon, shone down on the sea. A beam of light fell onto our cottage, and on the roof were two doves.

About the Author

L J Osborne lives in East Sussex. The setting for this novel has been inspired by the tall straight cliffs on the south coast of England.